Awakening

Psi War Book 1

I have seen the dark universe yawning,
Where the black planets roll without aim;
Where they roll in their horror unheeded,
without knowledge or lustre or name.
(Extract from Nemesis by H.P. Lovecraft)

For Lynn, Winifred & Savannah
From Hamish!
Enjoy

Copyright

Author: Tony Warner
Title: Awakening - Psi War Book 1
© 2022, Tony Warner
Self-published
(Contact: psiwarbook@gmail.com)

All rights reserved.
No part of this publication may be reproduced, stored in a retrieval system, stored in a database and / or published in any form or by any means, electronic, mechanical, photocopying, recording or otherwise, without the prior written permission of the author.

Acknowledgements

This book has taken a long time to write. I can't say for sure, but I think that it must have been at least 20 years ago when I first started it. For some reason long since forgotten, I stopped writing, and it sat on a hard disk gathering digital dust.

Fast forward to 2021. And after many conversations with a friend, who reads books like I eat chocolate, I started thinking. Where was the book I had started all of those years ago? Did the story make sense? And was it worth finishing?

Sarah, you are that friend. Without you, this book would have been forgotten forever. Thank you for your encouragement, reading and ideas in the early days.

I'd also like to thank all my family and friends for their support and help, and in particular, all the 'book club' members for the many afternoons reading and editing. Without their help and support this book would never have been published.

The following people deserve special mention:

My wife, Sue, for her help with editing, proofreading, and providing the meals at 'book club.'
My daughter, Jennie, for her superb spelling and grammar skills and for encouraging me to add 'more description.' Jennie, this book would not be the book it is without you. My son, Jonathan for coming up with the title. My granddaughter, Ruby, for consenting to pose for the front cover photograph. Sorry Ruby, you ended up on the book spine. My granddaughter, Ella, for her punctuation skills.

Hopefully the second book won't take 20 years!

Prologue

In a remote star system, on the opposite side of our galaxy, a planet orbited its star at just the right distance to support life. While it was not life as we know it, it was life nonetheless. It had started on this planet almost ten billion earth years ago, which made it the most ancient life in the Milky Way.

At first the inhabitants evolved normally. They progressed through the Stone Age, the Bronze Age and the Iron Age. Later, they harnessed the power of steam and went through their own version of an Industrial Revolution. Once they had developed the technology to replace fossil fuels with nuclear fusion power, they expanded into their solar system, colonising nearby planets. After many hundreds of years of expansion, they solved their ever-increasing requirement for energy by harnessing the entire output of their sun. Once they did so, they became a type two civilisation as measured using the Kardashev scale which is a simple method of measuring and categorising the technological advancement of any civilisation. Type one utilises the entire energy of their planet, type two of their sun, and type three, their entire galaxy.

It was at this point that their evolution took a new turn. Now that their immediate energy needs were met, they applied their prodigious intellects to harnessing the power of the mind.

At first, they utilised machines to help interface with the energy fields required enabling them to direct and control their thought derived actions. Latterly, their mental faculties had grown so much that they were able to discard their machinery. The scope and power of their mental abilities increased exponentially as they adopted the use of their mental powers as the main instrument for all physical work. Now tapping into the energy that pervaded the whole of the universe, their abilities eventually became practically unlimited.

They became the most powerful race in the galaxy, and it was fortunate for all of the other sentient races that this oldest and most powerful of all of them all was largely benevolent.

They called themselves the Non'anan.

On the Non'anan home world, atop a 500 foot tower in a small room, sat an entity. The room was circular in shape with no openings for doors or windows. It was dark and damp as per the entity's requirements.

The sound of tinkling water could be heard as it trickled down the walls to be collected and recycled back to small openings at the top. Hissing mists of water vapour pervaded the entire room emanating from outlets in the ceiling. In the centre of the room, dim lighting revealed the entity as it sat in a cup-shaped pedestal which contained its pseudopod form. It had no fixed shape, having no skeleton - it simply exuded manipulating flesh when needed. However, there was little requirement for such physical actions as most of its work was achieved through the use of its highly evolved and powerful mind. Sustenance was simply teleported directly into its digestive system and waste was teleported out. The mist condensed onto the entity's pale greasy flesh and ran as rivulets around and over its pulsating form to be filtered and collected at the bottom of the pedestal.

It had spent most of its long life within this very room. There was no need for it to change location, as all contact was conducted through telepathic means. Its designation was a mind pattern that could not be understood by a human. To less intelligent species, it referred to itself as E984F.

Currently E984F was engaged in exploration. Its mind stretched across thousands of light years: probing, discovering, and cataloguing. Storing all of the minutiae of information within its prodigious memory, it moved from system to system, not looking for anything in particular. Its task was to map the entire galaxy, noting all systems containing life-sustaining planets and any life forms. The galaxy was a big place. This was E984F's one thousandth cycle working on this task.

This time period was the same as all of the others. The next star was catalogued, its position, magnitude and number of planets recorded as usual. But almost immediately, it was apparent that this system was different from all the others that had been mapped. While investigating the fourth planet from its sun, E984F detected energies that were very unusual. Its interest piqued, it projected downwards to the planet surface and was not surprised to see a small-scale battle. It was known that lesser intelligent species often fought over things that they deemed important such as resources or even their primitive ideologies. This was nothing new. What was new were the weapons and energies being deployed in the battle.

E984F was amazed to see an obviously primitive life form wielding energies that could only be accessed with a highly evolved mind such as its own. This should not be possible. Investigating further, it moved undetected amongst the primitive bi-pedal forms as they fought and killed each other. It soon saw the truth. These beings were tapping into high order energies with the help of machines. The battle taking place between two different species. One had devices fitted to their bodies, the other had modified their entire bodies.

For obviously primitive life forms to be accessing and directing such high order energies was so unusual that E984F did something that it had never done before. It chose the leader of one army and teleported it to a holding cell. The opposite army had no leader. It was clear that they were being remotely directed from some, as yet, unmapped world. That would be investigated later. Meanwhile it studied the teleported life form in its holding cell and called for specialist help.

Alien thoughts flashed back and forth instantaneously between Non'anan inhabiting many worlds.

The Non'anan were fascinated, and some were alarmed. Their examination of the life form was swift and thorough. Conclusions were made, actions were taken.

The Non'anan collective had never seen such a young species be so developed. They seemed to have made some kind of evolutionary leap. Such a species was potentially dangerous. They were so young yet wielding such power. They could easily wipe themselves out or worse, others, and it looked as though this was already happening. The collective debated removing this species from the galaxy, but this was dismissed in short order. A wait and see approach was adopted. The life form would be returned to its home world with all memory of this examination removed.

Meanwhile the Non'anan would watch. And if necessary, they would intervene.

Chapter 1 - The Stranger

In the streets of Oxford, a figure shuffled along the pavement. Dressed in a dirty black coat and jeans with its head covered in a filthy hood, it moved slowly and purposefully through the crowds and through the shopping district along High Street. People did their best to avoid any possibility of contact, considering it to be a dirty homeless tramp, some even crossing the street to keep as far away from it as they could. No one offered any help, most forgetting it as soon as they had passed it.

Although its face was obscured by the hood, it was obvious that the figure was a man, the broad shoulders and long, sometimes stumbling strides giving it away.

Ploughing forward, the stranger continued its journey through the evening rush of people, crossing Magdalen bridge and into East Central. After an hour, as the sun moved lower in the sky, he turned right onto Shelley Road continuing his progress towards St Frideswide Primary School.

As he approached the abandoned and derelict school the stranger suddenly stopped. He staggered slightly and leaned against a nearby lamp post. There did not seem to be any reason for the sudden cessation of its motion.

The figure leaned there, still as a statue, as it grew dark, the sun slowly setting below the buildings. The lamp above the stranger's head flickered into life, bathing him in an eerie orange glow. The other streetlamps were dark, possibly faulty, the single light providing the only illumination in the road.

From the footpath on the stranger's right, shouting could be heard slowly becoming louder and louder. Suddenly a dark figure flashed out of the unlit footpath, running hard. It ran straight past the stranger turning towards the fenced off school car park where it crashed into the steel fencing. It gave a grunt of pain as it fell backwards, bouncing off the mesh of the barrier to land onto its side. In the sodium glow of the light, a girl's frightened upturned face framed with black hair looked back over her shoulder towards the footpath, as a gang of five youths came racing out, clearly chasing her. None of them noticed the stranger, all five ran straight past him.

The five dressed in hoodies and baseball caps surrounded the girl on the floor.

"Come on darlin," shouted one.

"Give us your money," stated another as he bent down and started to pull at her clothes.

"Get off me!" screamed the girl, beating at the hands gripping her clothes.

"Give it now or I'll cut you," shouted the tallest of the youths as he brandished a knife.

The girl went still and allowed her pockets to be emptied. In short order, her money was taken from her, and the young man brandished it in the air.

The gang cheered and laughed. Four of them withdrew into a huddle rifling through the cash, laughing and joking together. The remaining youth stepped up to the defenceless girl still on the floor and kicked her savagely in the side.

The girl screamed in pain and rolled into a ball.

"Bitch!" he shouted and kicked her again.

The others noticed and moved to join in, grins plastered over their faces.

One turned and looked over his shoulder and noticed the stranger.

"Hey!" he shouted. "We got company."

The gang turned as one to the stranger, they all went quiet as they studied him. Clearly, he was in a position to have seen everything.

The girl on the floor uncurled herself and looked around to see what was happening.

"What are you looking at, dickhead?" shouted one at the stranger.

When there was no answer, the gang looked at each other and came to an abrupt decision. They all sauntered and swaggered over to the stranger.

"I asked you a question, dumbass." One gang member taller than the others stabbed his forefinger into the stranger's chest.

The stranger ignored the finger, instead he moved a hand up to pull back his hood, revealing dirty long blond hair and startling bright blue eyes.

All five gang members involuntarily stepped back as the almost luminous blue eyes looked at each one of them in turn.

For a moment there was silence which was broken by the tallest youth, clearly the leader.

"You saw nothin. You understand me?" The leader raised his knife which glinted in the lamp light.

The stranger raised his right hand pushing it towards the leader, spreading his fingers wide.

One of the gang started to laugh. "Look, he's wearing rings like a girl!"

The others saw the rings and chains adorning the stranger's hand. Greed lit up in their faces. Jewellery could be sold for cash.

"Give us your rings now, or I'll cut you," the leader brandished his knife.

The stranger said nothing.

The leader shrugged and raised the knife higher making ready to move in.

There was a bright blue flash, and all five youths were thrown backwards to land on their backs. There were four grunts of pain and one scream. They all quickly got back to their feet except the leader.

"My wrist!" he shouted. "It's fucking broken!" He lay on the floor cradling his bent wrist with his other hand.

One of the youths helped the leader to his feet, who was moaning with the pain. They all looked back at the stranger, fear and pain now in their eyes. Then, as one they turned and shuffled off back down the footpath.

The stranger watched them as they passed him. One shouted at him as they passed.

"Remember what we said. You saw nothin!"

It started to rain. A light drizzle came down from the night sky, soaking both the stranger and the girl as they looked across the road at each other. Neither moved, the girl staring in incredulous disbelief. What had she just seen?

Chapter 2 - Prisha

3 years ago

Prisha Pathak was having a bad day. And today was the worst day to have a bad day. Of all the days in her short life of 18 years, it had to happen on this day.

The morning had started as normal - she had left home making her way to school exactly as she did every weekday. Today was different of course; this was the first day of her exams. She was nervous and anxious, but she knew she had done everything she could do to prepare.

It was important to her. She wanted to be a lawyer and that meant hours of study and revision. This was the first step. She needed to pass these exams. Not just pass them, she needed to ace them. She needed very good grades to get into the university of her choice. There, she would study law for three more years, and after that, a job in a law firm where she intended to work her way up the ladder.

She was ambitious. She always had been. When she was 12, she had decided that she would be the fastest runner in her class. It took her 3 months to get into shape. At her school's sports day, she had won all the short distance races.

But today was not about fitness and strength. Today was about knowledge and recall, and just like at her sports day, she was going to be the best.

But as she sat down at her small table in the school hall, surrounded by other students in uniform rows, it had all gone wrong.

The voices started shouting.

"No!" she whispered to herself, "Not now."

Holding her head in her hands she looked down at the exam paper, her black curly hair covering her face.

It had started when she hit puberty. She had never told anyone, not even her parents. At first, she thought it was because she was turning into a woman. Her mother had explained what was happening and helped her, but she never said anything about the voices. After a while and since talking with her friends, she realised that it was just her. No one else heard voices in their head.

Searching the internet hadn't helped either. It was nothing to do with puberty. All of those articles talked about underage sex and period cramps. No, it wasn't that. But what she did find scared her. The internet told her she was going mad.

Conditions like psychosis, PTSD, schizoaffective disorder, and bipolar disorder kept coming up. Her voracious mind read them all. She didn't know what to do. She felt ashamed and angry at the same time. But she decided that she would not let it get in the way of her ambition to become a lawyer. So, she learned to live with the voices and told no one.

Over the years, she experienced good days and bad days, as the voices waxed and waned. Some days they almost disappeared completely, so much so that she felt what she imagined was how normal people felt. Other days were truly awful. On these days the voices overwhelmed her, so that she could hardly separate them from her own thoughts. On these days, she told her mother that she had a migraine and took to her bed, waiting for them to subside.

But most of the time the voices were an annoying buzz in the background that she had learned to ignore. The good days and the bad days became less and less frequent. She had not had either for 8 months. So the sudden increase in volume surprised her.

She knew that completing her exam with the voices screaming in her head was going to be impossible, but she tried her best. She sat through the entire two hours of the exam, writing and writing, but she knew that her answers were not good. She could not always control it, sometimes writing words being voiced in her head that were not her own. Again and again, she crossed out the wrong words and re-wrote whole sections. In the end, it was a mess. She knew that she would fail.

Afterwards, she ran out of school and headed home. Fortunately, her parents were both at work, so she would not have to explain why she was no longer in school. She let herself in, climbed the stairs and threw herself on her bed, where she could no longer stop the tears.

She cried in frustration and anger, the voices screaming in her head, seemingly joining in, howling between her ears, drowning her in a crescendo of sound that no one else could hear.

Presently, she calmed a little and the volume of the voices dropped slightly. She knew from bitter experience that it would be morning before they settled down to their normal background buzzing. She rolled over onto her back and screamed when she saw a figure sitting in her chair at her desk.

"It's Prisha, right?" asked the young man, who sat calmly watching, his arms folded and legs crossed.

He was wearing a long black coat with a hood that covered his head, casting a shadow over his face, but she could see long blond hair and a pair of bright blue eyes.

She sat up and moved up the bed to put as much distance between herself and the stranger. "Who are you? What are you doing here?" She asked in a quavering voice.

"I'm not here to hurt you," he replied. "Please don't be frightened."

Prisha was not so sure. How had he got in? She hadn't heard anything, but then the voices were so loud. But she had also locked the front door of the house. So had he picked the lock, or even battered it down and she had not heard that either?

Her dark eyes were wide in fright as she spoke in a tremulous voice, "Please go away, I haven't got any money."

The stranger smiled and looked a little sad. "I only want to talk. I won't hurt you."

Prisha pulled her legs up beneath her. She tried to think, but the voices clamoured for her attention, making it difficult to concentrate.

"Talk about what?" she whispered.

She figured the best thing to do was to keep him talking and while he was doing so, call the police. She tried to remember something about her mobile phone. Didn't it have some sort of SOS feature? Her brow furrowed as she tried to shut out the voices to remember.

The stranger continued. "My name is Joe. I've been wanting to meet you for some time. Are the voices bothering you?"

Her eyes grew even wider. No one knew about the voices.

"How do you know about them?" she asked in a timid voice.

Joe's smile widened. "Because I used to hear them too," he replied.

"You did?" Her interest piqued.

He nodded sagely. "They can be very loud, can't they?"

She nodded back. It had never occurred to her that someone else might hear the voices as well as her.

"But now they don't bother me at all," he continued. "I've learned to control them. Do you know what they are?"

She shook her head.

Joe brushed at some imaginary dirt on his leg. "They are the thoughts of people around you."

Prisha's mouth opened wide in surprise. That couldn't be true, could it? No one could hear other peoples' thoughts. It was much more likely that she had some form of mental disorder, one of those that she had read about on the internet.

Joe nodded. "It's true," he said. "You're probably not aware that you have a talent. With it you are able to 'hear' thoughts other than your own. It is quite a rare ability."

She was speechless. She closed and opened her mouth and closed it again.

"That's not possible," she managed to say.

"Sure it is," replied Joe, "I can do it and so can the rest of the people I work with."

This took Prisha by surprise. There were more than just him? How many were there? Why was he telling her this? Why was he here? The volume of the voices rose until she could hardly think, causing her to wince. She didn't know what to do.

"I can see that the voices are causing issues for you. Let me help."

He raised his right hand and spread his fingers wide. She watched through slitted eyelids as he briefly closed his bright blue eyes. Suddenly the voices were gone. It was so sudden that the release toppled her forward. It was fortunate that she was on her bed as her face mushed down into the duvet.

She turned her head sideways to look at Joe from her prone position.

"How did you do that?" she gasped.

Joe was smiling. "It's easy enough," he said, "Not only can I control the voices, the thoughts of others, I can also do lots of other things."

She sat up against the bed's headboard. "How?"

"With the help of this." He held up his right hand and she saw rings on each finger, connected with tiny chains.

"What's that?"

"I call it an Assist. It helps me focus and direct forces with my mind."

She considered this for a moment. Her mind was incredibly clear. It hadn't felt like this for many years. It felt wonderful.

"Can I have one?" she asked.

"Yes, but there are conditions." Was the reply.

"Conditions?"

He nodded. "You can have one and my people will train you how to use it, but you have to come and work for me."

"Work for you? What do you do?"

He grinned. "Ah, that would be telling." He grew serious. "Look, it's simple. You can't go on as you are. Eventually you will become overwhelmed with these external thoughts. You can't control them, and it will drive you mad. But there is an alternative." He uncrossed his legs and leaned forwards. She pressed her back into the headboard. "Come work with me. I can promise that you will be with other people like you, that you will not have to fight with the 'voices' again, and you will find the work interesting and fulfilling."

She considered what he was saying. Was she ready to give up her dream of becoming a lawyer? But she had just had a setback. She had surely failed her exams. She could probably re-take them later, but who's to say that the same thing wouldn't happen again?

"I'm not sure," she replied. "I had other plans, and I'm only 18."

"I understand," said Joe. He rose from the chair suddenly. He produced a business card from a pocket inside his long black coat and held it out to her. "When you change your mind, come and see me."

Her eyes flitted from the outstretched hand with the card, to his face and back again. She snatched the card quickly.

He turned and walked to the door, waving back at her.

"See you later," he said as he stepped through her bedroom door and closed it behind him.

She could hear his footsteps as he walked down the stairs. As he walked further away, the voices came back. Softly at first and then louder and louder.

She moaned to herself. It had been such a blessed relief when they were gone. Now they were back once more, clamouring and shouting. Looking down at the card in her hand, she saw that the only thing printed on it was an address, somewhere in Oxford. As the volume of the voices reached a crescendo, she knew that she had no choice really. No choice at all. She couldn't go on like this, and if the voices continued, then her dream was in tatters anyway.

She looked at the closed door to her bedroom. How was she going to tell her parents that she was giving up on her dreams of becoming a lawyer and was going to live somewhere in Oxford?

There was going to be a huge argument.

Chapter 3 - Connection

The girl used the mesh barrier to pull herself up. She was not sure what had just happened. Somehow a stranger had appeared and had fought with the gang and had driven them off. There had been a strange bright blue light, but that was gone now. Looking up at the streetlight above the stranger's head, she wondered if it was faulty. Maybe it had been an electrical discharge.

Lowering her gaze, she noted that the stranger stood unmoving, his head down facing the floor. She held her hand to her left side and grimaced in pain. Looking down to her hand to see if she was covered in blood and seeing nothing, she pulled her filthy jacket to one side and lifted her top, exposing her flesh. There was a large bruise, but no broken skin. She sighed in relief. She did not want to go to A&E. They would ask questions.

All of these thoughts raced through her mind but were soon replaced by a single, crystal-clear realisation - the gang had taken everything. She had no cash, and her stash of drugs was gone. What was she going to do? There were only three ways to get cash to buy drugs. One was to steal it.

In her current condition, that was not going to be possible. Another was to beg on the street, but that would take too long. And finally, she didn't want to think about the last option.

She hesitated, maybe there was a way. She gazed across the street again, and then shuffled her way towards the stranger, clutching at her side.

Shortly, she was looking up at him into his bright blue eyes as he stared back.

"Thanks for chasing them off," she said.

The stranger did not reply, he just stared at her.

"Are you alright? she asked.

He nodded his reply, his gaze sliding from her to look up into the sky. "Is there somewhere we can go to get out of the rain?" His voice was weak.

The girl hesitated. She had been on her way to a nearby squat when she had been accosted by the gang. It wasn't far away, but did she want to take him there? She had discovered it a week ago and it had become her place of sanctuary, where she was safe. But if her plan was to work, she would have to risk it.

She nodded. "I have a place."

The stranger slowly lifted his hood back over his head, although it was too late to keep his hair dry, the rain had started to come down heavily. He stepped one pace forward and waited for her to lead on.

She hesitated again. This was risky, very risky, she thought to herself. But she wasn't sure what else she could do. Turning around, she walked back to the barrier surrounding the school. Turning left when she reached it, she led the way along its length through long wet grass.

Shortly, she reached a section that had two pallets leaning up against the steel fence. Looking over her shoulder to check the stranger was following, she stepped up onto the first pallet. Pain flared in her side as she did so, but she did her best to ignore it and stepped up again onto the second pallet.

"We have to jump over," she explained to the stranger who was looking up at her.

Normally, this would present no problem for her, but with her injured side, she knew that it was going to hurt when she dropped to the ground on the other side. Gritting her teeth, she held onto the fence with one hand and threw her legs over. When she hit the ground, she cried out in pain and fell to the wet grass, clutching at her side.

Lying there gasping in pain, she heard the stranger land next to her. He reached down and helped her to her feet, concern on his face.

When the pain subsided, she continued to lead the way. Skirting around the building, she located a low window that had cardboard covering its broken panes. She deftly moved it to one side and gestured for the stranger to enter, which he did. She followed, wincing with pain as she struggled to get through the small space. Placing the cardboard back into position, she walked into the blackness. Inside there was very little light, but she knew where to go. There were many rooms with doors that were missing or broken. Graffiti was everywhere, as was the filth.

The discarded rubbish from years of neglect lay scattered around. Smashed bottles, paper, and black bags full of rubbish.

She led him through a corridor, towards the back of the building into a small room. The room was as dirty as the rest of the building, but in the corner was an old mattress.

She sat down upon it with a sigh, wincing once again with the pain. The stranger followed. He lay down on the mattress and closed his eyes.

In the darkness, she waited, all the while her side throbbing with pain. Her joints ached and her hands shook. She knew why. It was the onset of withdrawal. She needed her drugs. And to get them she needed money. There was only one place she could get the money from.

She waited until she thought he was asleep and then crouching down over the man, she started to go through his pockets.

She was unaware that her spleen had been ruptured and that she was bleeding internally. In a few hours, she would be dead.

Chapter 4 - The soldier

Prisha was scared. More scared than she had ever been in her life. Her stomach churned with fear as she waited at her assigned position in the dark. She was not too cold or too warm. She was alone, but not, because she was in constant mental contact with the rest of her company. And although it was dark, she could see.

All of this was made possible thanks to her HAZPRO suit. The HAZPRO kept her comfortable and allowed her to function in any number of hazardous environments. Without it, she would be dead already, for the atmosphere outside the suit contained no oxygen. It was also packed with a multitude of offensive and defensive equipment and it was semi-automated. It looked after her and protected her - it would take action to maintain her life functions. Part of its role was to keep her alive, but it would also continue fighting any opponent if she became injured. It was a marvel of engineering, designed and built by the clever Alliance scientists and engineers.

She remembered seeing it for the first time.

"I'll never be able to work that!" she had said as she looked up at its giant 2 meter red bulk.

The engineers had just smiled. It used power assist technology, they had said. When you move, it moves with you, amplifying your strength. It would feel as light as a feather, they said, she would hardly notice it.

Looking up at its impressive bulk, she was not convinced.

"And it will protect me?"

The engineers had waxed lyrical about its multiple shells of protection and that the outer shell of dull, rust red, metal and ceramic material was tougher than any other known substance. They had also explained about the multiplexed force screens, designed to block any known energy and projectile weapon.

"But what about when I need to pee?" she had asked.

It would take care of all of her needs, the engineers had told her. It had a complete, built in, waste management system and even carried food supplements as well as water that she could draw from tubes within reach of her mouth inside its massive helmet.

"So I just pee?"

Yes, they told her, the suit would take care of it.

"How do I drive it?" she had asked.

She would interface to it via her Assist, she was told. Once connected, it would feel like a second skin and would carry out all of her commands - there were no switches or manual controls.

She should not have been surprised to discover that they had been right. Its soft padded interior cuddled her body, leaving no gaps, like wearing lycra. And when she moved, sure enough, it moved with her. She could not feel its weight. Connecting to the suit through her Assist was easy and straight forward - it responded to her commands instantly. It was like an extension to her body.

That had been 6 months ago. Now she was on the planet Arcadia, holding her position as instructed and scanning for contacts. She lifted her head once more and peered over the sand bank of ground she was crouched behind.

"I.R." she told her suit, which dutifully switched from normal vision to Infra-Red, enabling her to see any heat sources through her suits visor. Nothing. The landscape was dark and flat, nothing was moving. Over to her right, she could clearly see a single infra-red signature of one of her company. She knew it was Erica. She could identify her through her mental pattern. And over to her left was Mohammed, Mo to his friends.

"U.V." he said. The suit switched vision receptors. She looked around again. Still nothing.

"Scan all." And she waited the five seconds her suit took to scan the surrounding area for any contacts that were not friendly.

"No contacts." The suit reported. It had a friendly, melodic, but slightly mechanical, female voice.

She slid back down the bank, propped up her triple barrelled rifle against the bank, and settled in to wait. How much longer? Maybe nothing would happen, and they would be recalled.

How had she got herself into this position? She was no soldier. And yet, here she was on an alien planet, wearing an advanced armour suit with advanced weaponry. She shook her head inside her helmet as much as it would allow, cushioning the sides of her face with soft foam. You never knew where things would end up. But she wouldn't have it any other way. Three years ago she had made a huge decision, and she had no regrets. She had made friends. She belonged to a family - the Alliance, and she had learned how to control her own mind and was able to manipulate forces she never knew existed with the aid of her Assist.

And best of all, she met Abeko.

Lovely Abeko, she thought as she recalled the smooth, black skin of his body and the rough stubble on his face. No, she decided, she had made the right decision, even if she had ended up on this inhospitable planet.

She looked at the distant horizon and watched two moons slowly rise.

Chapter Five - Jim

Jim was in his workshop. On the bench, in front of him, was his latest creation. A suit of webbing material overlaid with metal strips. Wires and circuits sprouted everywhere and were connected in a bewildering spaghetti all over the suit. It looked cheap and it looked like a mess. But Jim smiled down upon it with pride. This was his baby that had taken 3 months to build. He knew it would work; his initial small-scale tests had shown him that there would be no problem scaling up into a full sized protective webbing suit. And he had finally done it. It was finished. All he needed to do was a bit of a tidy up with some of the connections to make sure that everything was robust enough and that it didn't break the first time he tried it on, and to fit the power supply in a backpack. After that, he would be ready to go.

He was excited to put his suit to the test. This time it would be different. This time he would show them. He seethed with anger as he recalled his last encounter with his twin brother, Joe. He had finally plucked up the courage to confront him. Striding into the building, where he knew

Joe worked, he had walked up to the receptionist and demanded to see him.

He got nowhere; instead, he was humiliated. The receptionist had smiled condescendingly and had told him that Joe was not available and if he were, he wouldn't want to meet with the likes of him. As she did so, she pushed back a strand of hair with her right hand. He could not help but notice the rings and chains adorning her fingers. It was only when he saw the same rings on the two security guards that he realised what they were.

Joe and his gang had been busy. He had built a Psionic booster.

As the two security guards frog-marched him out, he was thinking furiously. If Joe's bunch of freaks had Psionic boosters, then it was going to be much more difficult to kill Joe.

Ever since they were fifteen, Jim hated his twin brother. Once they had been close, as close as only twins could be, but then on their fifteenth birthday, everything had changed.

They had been walking along a busy road on their way home from school when they had witnessed an accident. Two cars had collided. It wasn't a high-speed collision - one had braked too late and had hit the other in the rear. Despite the low-speed impact, the consequences of the crash were serious. The car that had been rear-ended, burst into flames. After a few short seconds, the driver of the car got out and ran round to the opposite side of the car and struggled to open the passenger door. The crash must have dislodged something in the door locking mechanism because the door would not open.

"Help!" she screamed. "My baby is in the car."

Jim had been frozen in fear and indecision. Not so Joe - he had leaped into action. Without hesitation, he had run up to the car and had dived through the driver's door, which had been left open. Even as the flames grew higher and higher, Joe threw himself over the driver's seat to reach the baby. He quickly unbuckled the baby seat harness and lifted the baby out. Shuffling backwards, he exited the car handing the crying baby to the weeping mother. He had then moved them quickly away from the burning car.

Throughout it all, Jim had stood rooted to the spot unable to move.

Later, when the police and the fire brigade arrived, Joe was hailed as a hero. He had saved the life of a six-week-old baby girl.

Jim, on the other hand, was a coward. While his brother had risked his life, Jim had done nothing. He had not even helped. Things had never been the same since that day. Jim and Joe had grown further and further apart.

Although they did their best to not to show it, Jim knew that their parents favoured their hero son. Over time, Jim grew more and more angry at the unfairness and the blatant favouritism. As soon as he could, he left home and struck out on his own, forging a path away from Joe. Their parents were not short of money and had given him enough to enable him to buy his own place, where he started his research. It was the one thing, he thought bitterly, that they had helped him with.

He buried himself in his research and eventually discovered Psionics. He did not realise it at the time, but Joe had made a similar discovery five years earlier. But now, grudgingly, he admitted to himself that Joe must be ahead of him. Once again, Joe was in the lead. The favoured twin.

Well, this time he would show them. This time he would make them pay. They wouldn't laugh him out of the building this time. He would demonstrate the full power of his talent. They would not be able to ignore him as he strode into the building with this suit on. They would not be able to stop him either. Projectile or beam weapons couldn't touch him while he was wearing it. He would show them. He would blast the whole building until there was nothing left but rubble. The whole building and everything in it, including Joe.

He seethed with anger at the thought of his twin. He stroked his hand lovingly across the suit as he thought of what he would do. Joe hadn't been there last time. Well, that's what they had told him.

Joe was the eldest by 5 minutes, and he thought that made him wiser and better than him. Joe was going to find out just what his younger brother was capable of. Joe was not going to survive - he would make sure of that.

Chapter 6 - Cure

A bright, full moon had risen, its light shining through the broken panes of glass in the single window. The angle was just right to cast enough light onto the dirty mattress in the corner, allowing the girl to see just enough.

As she went through the stranger's pockets, she did not notice that he was awake, his bright blue eyes glittered in the moonlight, watching her as she lifted his coat feeling for inside pockets. Her movements becoming more and more urgent as she found nothing. She paused as the pain in her side became worse. She bit back a moan. She had no time for this. She needed to find some money and to get out, now.

Suddenly the stranger's hand shot out to grab her wrist. She cried out in fright and pain.

"Hey!" she shouted, fear gripping her.

She tried to pull away.

"What are you looking for?" he asked in his weak voice.

She froze. She stopped trying to free herself. It was useless anyway, he had a grip like iron.

"Nothing," she lied.

"Who are you and how do I know you?" he asked.

The girl was at a loss, she had no idea what he was talking about. She realised dejectedly that her plan was not going to work. She wasn't going to be able to steal any money from this stranger even if he had any.

"Why was I drawn to you?" he asked, another unanswerable question.

She frowned at him.

"I can't call for help. I'm too weak," he stated.

Help? What help? What on earth was he talking about?

She looked deep into his penetrating eyes. There was something about them that she did not like. It was as if they could see deep into her soul.

As though he could see what she was thinking. She whimpered under his scrutiny. Another pulse of pain from her side washed over her like a wave crashing onto a shore.

The blue gaze travelled down the length of her body and then back up again. His eyes locked with hers again. They stayed like that for a time. Then, slowly, the man raised his other hand. She watched with fear. Was he going to hit her? She wished she had never bothered helping him. She should have left him on the footpath. This could was going to be bad. He was going to smack her around until she was barely alive. He might even kill her. She shuddered in pain and fear, small animal sounds coming from her throat.

He raised his hand and moved it slowly to her injured side. She noticed in a distracted way that each finger had a ring on it. The rings flashed in what little light there was coming from the broken window. There were tiny chains and other rings that had marks on them. She could not see well enough in the light and through the fear and the pain. His hand hovered over her side. There was a blue glow and the pain suddenly disappeared. She gasped at the suddenness of it. One moment it was there, the next it had gone.

His hand moved up to her cheek. He touched her briefly. Her eyes flicked wildly between his hand and his eyes. She whimpered again. Then his hand moved up to her temple and the blue glow appeared again. There was a flash behind her eyes; she could not identify where it had come from. There was a sudden piercing pain in her temple. She screamed and fell to the mattress, half on top of the man. The world went black.

As she lost consciousness, she saw dancing images of sparkling rings and chains in her head.

Chapter 7 - Mike & Sammy

3 years ago

Sammy was blindfolded, sitting on a chair in the centre of the stage at the Strat Hotel, Las Vegas. It was deathly quiet as she concentrated. Her partner, Mike, was in the audience and was holding up an item volunteered by an audience member, high in the air. A moment earlier, after taking the item and holding it aloft he had asked, speaking into a microphone, "Sammy, can you tell me what I am holding in my hand?"

Most people who came to see their act assumed that it was all a trick, that Mike was somehow signalling her so that she could correctly identify various items given up by random members of the audience. It being a trick did not detract from the audience loving the show. The mind reading was just a part of their two-hour show, the rest being the standard illusions like sawing a woman in half, and disappearing from a box and reappearing in the audience.

But what the audience did not know, could not know, was that the mind reading was not a trick. It was real.

When they had first met, Mike and Sammy knew that they had something special. In a single day, they had coincidentally bumped into each other four times. Each time they had met in a different location; in a coffee shop, at the mall, in the car park and finally at the local Walmart. Sammy was convinced that she was being stalked by Mike, which was creepy as hell. Mike thought that Sammy had been following him, which he found flattering as hell. Six months later, they were on the stage.

Sammy concentrated hard. It usually took a little while for her to get into the zone. Once in it, if she tried really hard, she could see images sent to her from Mike. Sometimes they were clear, sometimes they were not. When they were not clear, it was like looking through misted glass and it was very difficult to figure out what the object was. When this happened, she sometimes got it wrong and it always left her with a really bad headache. Today was a bad day - it was so misty she could not tell what the object was that Mike was holding in the air.

"It's a pen," she guessed.

She could see that it was small and long. She knew that she had guessed wrong when she heard a loud collective groan from the audience. She winced inwardly.

"That is very nearly correct," replied Mike. "Can you narrow it down for us?" He stared at the item and projected the image as hard as he could.

Sammy concentrated, but she knew it wasn't going to work. The image was not clear, and she knew from experience that it would not become clearer. She desperately tried to figure out what it could be. It was long and slim, but not a pen. What else would someone have in their pocket? It made no sense.

"*It's a tablet stylus,*" she heard the voice in her head with startling clarity.

"What the fuck!" she thought.

"*Just say it,*" said the voice.

With the image becoming no clearer and the audience stirring and murmuring, she blurted, "It's a tablet stylus!"

The audience cheered and clapped. Sammy sighed with relief, but she was also confused. Who had spoken to her?

In the audience, Mike moved through the rows of seats, beaming.

"You had us all going there, Sammy," he said into the microphone.

Continuing his path through the audience he talked as he walked. "Ladies and gentlemen, for our finale we will perform one more astounding mind reading for you."

He stopped beside a couple. They were typical of about half of the audience, being middle aged, and American, holidaying in Las Vegas for the shows and the gambling. The other half were tourists, mainly from Europe.

"Sir, what's your name?"

The man looked surprised. Pushing his glasses up his nose with a finger, he coughed and then said, "Theo."

"Nice to meet you Theo."

He held out his hand and shook Theo's hand.

"And you madam?" asked Mike turning to the woman next to Theo.

She was a large, overweight woman wearing horn rimmed glasses with bright pink curly hair.

"Candice," she spoke with a squeaky, high-pitched voice.

Smiling all the while, Mike shook her hand, "Nice to meet you, Candice."

He moved around to face both and, speaking into the microphone, asked, "Would the two of you be willing to take part in our finale?"

Theo and Candice beamed and nodded enthusiastically.

"Before we start, can you confirm, for the rest of the audience, that we have never met before?" Mike gestured to the audience.

"Oh no," squeaked Candice. "We have definitely never met before. I would remember someone as handsome as you!" Her head bobbed as she licked her lips, her pink curls bouncing.

A few of the audience smirked and some laughed out loud.

"Very well," continued Mike ignoring her lascivious smile. Instead, he reached into the inside pocket of his jacket. "I have here a note pad and pen." He held it up for everyone to see. "In a moment, I am going to hand both to you Candice, and I want you to write a single word on it. It can be any word you like." He turned to the audience, "Just make sure it's clean, no rude words please!"

The audience laughed.

"Once you have written the word, I want you to hand it to Theo." Looking at Theo he continued, "Theo, once Candice hands you the note, I will hand this microphone to you. Then I want you to hold the note so that I can see it, but

Sammy on the stage can't." He waved his arm to Sammy, who remained on the stage, still sat on the chair, and still blindfolded.

"Theo. To prove that I am not giving any clues to Sammy, I want you to ask Sammy what is written on the note. Is that okay?"

Theo appeared to consider what he had been asked to do. Then said "Yeah, I got it."

Standing tall and turning around to face the audience, Mike rotated around and spoke into the microphone.

"So, you can see that I have chosen these fine folks completely at random and that we have never met before. Candice will come up with a completely random word, and I will not communicate in any way with Sammy, who is all alone on the stage." He paused for dramatic effect. "There is only one way that Sammy will be able to know what the word is. And that's by reading my mind."

A murmur rippled through the audience as once again Mike paused. After a while he turned to Theo and Candice. "Candice, would you please write down your word on the notepad? As you do so I will pass the microphone to Theo."

Candice bobbed her head and studiously bent to the notepad and began to write.

"Ladies and gentlemen, I will now pass the microphone to Theo, who will hold up Candice's note for me to see and who will ask my beautiful partner, Sammy, to read my mind. Once again, ladies and gentlemen, at no point will I be able to communicate with Sammy. I will not be able to give her any clues or indicate in any way what is written on the note." With a flourish he handed the microphone to Theo. "There you go, Theo. The show is yours!" The audience gave a small laugh.

After relinquishing the microphone, Mike stepped back until he was a couple of paces away. He turned to look at Sammy who was sitting still on the stage as before. He hoped that this was going to work. They had practiced it many times. Normally he would be confident, but Sammy's mistake earlier on made him worry.

Candice finished her writing and passed the note to Theo. Holding the note in one hand and the microphone in the other, Theo stood. He coughed into the microphone making everyone wince at the sudden blast of noise.

"Sorry," he croaked. He held up the note high in the air so that Mike could see it. He cleared his throat. "Er. The note is in my hand and I'm holding it up," he said nervously.

Mike could see the word on the note clearly. He closed his eyes and concentrated. With all his might, he pushed the word towards Sammy.

Meanwhile on the stage, the lone figure of Sammy tried hard to see the word. Seconds passed as she tried harder and harder, willing the image to become clear. It did not. Pain blossomed behind her eyes as she kept trying. More seconds passed and the audience started to grumble. Try as she might, the word would not become clear. As the seconds passed, she knew that she would never be able to get the word no matter what she did. The grumbling in the audience grew louder. She couldn't think what to do. Should she guess, or just say that she didn't know? Either way would be a disaster. They would lose their top billing at the Strat as well as their reputation. They might never work again. She was about to shout out a guess when she heard the voice in her head again.

"*Poodle.*"

She shouted out, "Poodle! The word is Poodle!"

The audience erupted with deafening applause and cheers, and she sighed in relief. She pulled off her blindfold and stood. Mike ran to the stage, leaped up and took her hand. Together they bowed and raised their hands in the air soaking in the applause.

Much later, in their dressing room, Mike collapsed into his chair.

"Wow, that was close. I thought you weren't going to get it."

Sammy walked to her chair and flopped into it in much the same way as Mike had. She rubbed at her forehead, trying to ease the pain.

"I didn't," she said. "Someone told me."

Mike looked up, puzzled. "What?" he asked.

"Someone told me," she replied, pulling open a drawer of the dressing table and rifling through the contents.

Mike looked on, not sure what to say.

"Do you know where the pain killers are?" she asked.

Mike stood, walked over to a jacket on a hanger, fished out a box of Advil and threw it towards Sammy. She tried to catch it, missed, and winced at the pain in her head as she leaned down to pick up the packet.

"What do you mean?" he asked. "There was no one else around. If someone shouted it, everyone would have heard it."

"They didn't shout it," she replied as she swallowed two capsules with water from a bottle. "I heard it in my head."

Mike snorted, "impossible," he scoffed. "No one can do that."

Sammy shrugged. "It's what happened."

Mike considered. "Well, who was it?" he asked.

At that moment the dressing room door opened, and a man walked in.

"That would be me," he said.

Both Mike and Sammy watched as the man entered and closed the door behind him. He was tall and slim, wearing a long black coat. Bright blue eyes could be seen peering through long blond hair that fell across his face.

"Who the hell are you?" blurted Mike.

The stranger smiled. "I'm Joe," he replied, "And I am Sammy's mystery voice."

There was a moment of quiet as all three stared at each other. Sammy was the first to recover.

"Thank you," she said. "You just saved our careers."

Joe nodded his head. "My pleasure," he said. "I thought you might get it on your own, but I could see that it wasn't going to happen, so I helped out."

Mike looked at Joe warily. "How did you do it?"

"Simple telepathy," came the quick reply.

"I've not heard of anyone else who can do that. I thought me and Sammy were the only ones. Why should I believe you?"

Joes voice appeared in both Sammy's and Mike's head. *"Because I am the real article and I do it all the time."*

Sammy and Mike were stunned into silence.

Joe continued. *"The two of you have talent. I'd like to recruit both of you."*

"Recruit?" asked Sammy aloud.

Joe nodded and also spoke aloud. "I'm putting a group of talented people together and I'd like you to join me."

"What's in it for us?" asked Mike, "We're doing pretty well as we are. And we don't know you."

Joe's smile was infectious. "Of course you don't know me, we just met! Seriously though. There is everything in it for you. You would be joining a group of like-minded people, all of whom have similar talents to yourselves. And best of all," he held up his right hand, "I can boost your faculties with this."

Mike saw rings on Joes fingers. "I don't wear jewellery," he scoffed.

Joe gazed at his hand and moved his fingers, Mike caught sight of chains as well as the rings. "Yes, it's pretty, isn't it? But this is more than jewellery. This is a device. Its sole purpose is to boost your talents."

He waved his upheld hand and the entire contents of Sammy's dressing table moved in time with the hand and crashed to the floor.

Sammy jumped. She looked at the mess on the floor and then across at Joe. "You did that?"

Joe nodded.

Sammy turned to Mike and said, "I want one."

Mike looked into her eyes. "Me too." he replied.

Chapter 8 - Contact

"Contact at 11 o'clock from your position. Coordinates available," the HAZPRO suit reported in its mechanical female voice.

Prisha sat up alarmed. She had been daydreaming, thinking about her lovely Abeko. That was stupid. What was she thinking? She must remain alert. What was it the suit had reported? A contact? There was a blinking red dot in the bottom left corner of her HUD display. She stared at it dumbly.

"All patrol members. Alert. We have possible incoming," came a thought from her commander.

This announcement galvanised her into action. She scrambled up the bank and looked over the top. The blinking red light in her HUD remained at her 11 o'clock position.

It was dark, but the twin moons cast a surprisingly large amount of light over the alien landscape. Her suit's audio receptors picked up a moaning wind that blew across the plain in front of her, which stirred up the occasional tiny dust devil. The plain was featureless and barren; no vegetation grew anywhere in sight, it was rocky and sandy. Picking up the rifle from beside her, she hefted it over the bank and sighted down the barrels.

The rifle was large and bulky, but at the same time it had a sleek length to it. It had three barrels and a huge magazine. Underneath the stock, a wire as thick as a man's thumb snaked down and connected to the rear of her suit. Although she had tried it out, taking pot shots at rocks here on Arcadia and targets at the practice centre, she was not fully familiar with it. The engineers had told her that it was multi-functional, and she should switch functions if one had no effect upon the enemy.

The enemy.

No one knew yet who the enemy was. Ever since they had set up and built the staging post here on Arcadia, there had been encounters with something. Something that they called the enemy, for lack of a better word. It had started with just one Alliance member disappearing. Initially it had been assumed that they had fallen off a cliff or into a sink hole. But then that would not kill the wearer, not while wearing a HAZPRO. The suits were practically indestructible. A fall from almost any height could not kill the wearer - the suit's automatic systems would see to that. And in any case, the suit had emergency beacons should the worst happen. So, they knew it had to be something else. Whatever had happened, it had been quick. So quick that the unfortunate Alliance member had not managed to send a single thought of warning.

A team was sent to investigate, but they found nothing. Not a single trace. In response, all HAZPRO suits were retrofitted with a GPS tracking system so that they could be tracked at all times. Such a system had not been used before because the wearer was always in contact via mind link.

Just two weeks later an Alliance patrol of three members disappeared in exactly the same manner. This time, the investigative team could track the exact route of the patrol. After losing contact yet again, when they arrived at the terminus of the route, they found three piles of melted metal and ceramic.

The conclusion was obvious. They were being attacked, and who or what, was behind the attacks was staying hidden, perhaps using guerrilla tactics and booby traps.

Strategically, Arcadia was important. They all knew that. So, they dug in, reinforced the staging post, stopped the patrols, and concentrated on defence by guarding the perimeter. Over time, the perimeter was pushed outwards, slowly, but carefully. The Alliance was determined it was not going to lose any more members.

And so, on the furthest perimeter, Prisha manned her station, watching for movement, crouching behind a sand bank.

The contact did not move. She wondered what it was and why there was only one. Maybe it was an armoured vehicle and not a person. If it was, she wondered if her rifle would be able to knock it out. No one had told her anything about armoured vehicles. Her pulse began to race, adrenalin flowed in her veins and the rifle she sighted down began to shake. Was she going to make it out of here alive? Little training, an unknown enemy, and a briefing that did not give away much information. It all added up to bad news and gave her an uneasy feeling about the whole mission.

"Contact moving. Speed estimate - 12km per hour. Direction - 12 degrees from magnetic North." her suit told her.

She tightened her grip on the rifle. Where was North anyway? But she could see in her HUD that the red dot was moving in a diagonal path from her right across to her left, getting closer all the time.

"Distance?" she asked her suit.

"10 kilometres. Speed increasing to 15km per hour." her suit replied. "Auto shielding engaged."

Shit! What a rookie! She had forgotten to switch on her screens! What else had she forgotten?

"Set shield to reflective mode, Power on XO-assist. Set visor to auto, power up counter measures." she ordered.

Although she still had a bad feeling about the mission, she had absolute faith in her suit. She had yet to encounter anything that could touch her when she was wearing a HAZPRO.

"Confirmed. Power envelope now at 230 minutes." her suit informed her.

It was telling her that it could only sustain her for 230 minutes at these new power levels. After that, she would be on reserve power. At that point, all of her armaments would be inoperative, and her suit would focus on keeping her life support systems running for as long as possible. She wasn't worried. If there was a battle ahead it would be over very quickly and one contact, whatever it was, shouldn't be too much of a problem. In the worst case scenario, she could always get away or even power down and lie low with her suit's camouflage screen on. Even so, she was still scared, more scared than she had ever been in her life. She figured it was the unknown.

Chapter 9 - Escape

She fought her way to the surface of consciousness from a deep sleep. She realised that she was no longer in pain; not just from her side where she had been kicked, but also the whole-body buzz was gone. That buzzing all over pain that she felt when she needed her drugs was gone. She puzzled about this for a while, all the time keeping her eyes closed and trying to doze.

Then, with a shocking suddenness, she remembered, and the blackness enveloped her soul with a crushing terror and sadness. It was a familiar feeling and was not a surprise to her. She had been fighting it unsuccessfully for the last three years. She hadn't won in all that time, and she wasn't going to win now. Her only respite was the drugs. They helped her forget, if only briefly. They numbed the pain and held the blackness away. Wailing softly to herself, she succumbed, and wallowed in the darkness, as the waves of pain swept over her again and again.

When the anguish subsided a little, she rolled over onto her front and dry retched. She could not remember when she had last eaten or drunk. She dry heaved again and then lay panting, drool dripping from her open mouth, her eyes closed tight shut.

    After a little while, she wiped her mouth and tears on the cuff of her sleeve and opened her eyes. She sat back on her haunches and looked around. It was no longer dark - she must have been asleep all night. A pale light came through the broken window. Partially blocking the light stood the blond man. It looked as though he was gazing through the broken panes. He had pulled his hood back revealing his dirty and greasy hair that reached his shoulders. He did not move, even when she shuffled to a seated position. She could not help looking down at her legs and body to check if she was okay Her clothes were as she remembered. She silently breathed a sigh of relief. What the hell was going on? She remembered the intensity of his eyes, the flash, and sparkling rings.

    She mustered up the courage to ask, "Hello?"

    She cleared her throat to attract his attention. He stood motionless and did not make any sign of acknowledgment. He made no movement at all. She was mildly annoyed.

She thought about what had happened last night. She had been trying to rob him, but then he had stopped her. She remembered the flash of pain in her head. Had he hit her? Bringing her hands up, she rubbed her face. There was no soreness, no bruising that she could tell. And there was the puzzling fact that the jangling need for drugs was gone. What had happened? What had he done?

And then a sudden realisation came over her. The bastard had knocked her out and drugged her! Fuck, how long had she been out? Hurriedly, she pulled up her sleeves and desperately searched her arms for new needle punctures. But although her arms were covered in old punctures, collapsed veins and scars, she could not find anything new. She was baffled.

Still, that did not mean anything. He could have injected her in her leg for all she knew. She gazed up at him, much more warily now. She suddenly saw him as a threat, as an enemy. She needed to get out. Now.

She eyed the dark doorway across the room. Could she make it if she ran? Looking back at him at the window, she slowly and quietly got to her feet. Once fully upright, she started to move to the doorway as silently as she could, which was difficult given all of the debris on the floor. She winced every time she crunched on a piece of glass, looking back at the man at the window. He still made no movement.

As she crossed the threshold of the doorway, she began to feel much better. She was free, she was going to make it! She felt massive relief as she suddenly broke into a run and ran as fast as she could, down the corridor and out into the morning sun. As she did so, the blackness of her memories threatened to overwhelm her once more.

"No," she panted, "Not now."

She pushed them back once again, but she knew that she could not resist it for long. Soon it would take over and she would fall down into the familiar black well of despair. She needed drugs now, anything to stop her from remembering.

Chapter 10 - Attack

The building in front of him was a large grey edifice that stood about 10 storeys tall. To Jim it looked menacing and evil. To anyone else it looked ordinary, but then Jim knew what went on behind those dark windows. He knew that this building was full of evil freaks. Men and women that performed evil tasks every single day. Oh yes, it was evil all right, and he was about to put an end to it.

It had taken two months of persistent and dogged research to discover where Joe and his freaks were working. In the end he had been surprised to find that it was in the centre of town, hiding in plain sight. At first, he couldn't believe it. He walked past this building every week when he visited the grocery store. He imagined that every time he walked past, the freaks would be watching him.

He was wearing his suit, and it functioned perfectly. It still looked jerry-rigged and incomplete. Wires were everywhere, metal strips were bonded to the suit's material, crystals glowed softly. On his back he wore a rucksack, from which, large, finger thick wires fed power into a small control panel mounted on a belt that went around his waist. The panel was angled upwards so that he could easily read the displays, and the many small lights blinking and glowing. In the centre there was a small 4 inch display, and off to one side a big red square button. In his right hand he held what was obviously a weapon, although it looked like a simple metal tube. Another thick wire ran from the tube to the control panel.

The suit was perfect, he thought to himself. Right now, it was in invisible mode. No one could see him. It rendered him completely undetectable, allowing him to walk straight to the building without anyone knowing he was there. He intended to surprise the freaks and kill as many as he could before they had a chance to act. Strangely, dogs knew where he was, and he could not disguise the noise he made as he had walked from his parked car to the front of the building. The rustling and squeaking made more than one person look around in an effort to locate the source of the noise. When that happened, he simply stood still and waited. The pedestrian usually shrugged or scowled and then walked on. He would have to work on some sort of sound dampening field. Numbers, equations, and ideas flowed through his mind as he approached the building entrance.

Now.

Now was the moment he was going to make it right. He stood and looked upwards. Joe was in there. He smiled. Joe and all of his freaks were going to suffer today. Still smiling, he walked through the revolving door.

But as soon as Jim had stepped through the door he had been spotted. Impossible as it seemed, two guards standing on either side of a reception desk looked up and approached him. They both wore a black uniform with shiny buttons and caps. Jim could not believe it. They should not be able to see him. They should have looked up puzzled as the door rotated and no one came through. How could they see him? As they walked up to him, he noticed that they were both wearing dark glasses. Could they have some sort of detector built into the glasses? Well, no matter, he would soon take care of them. He raised his right hand and pointed the metal tube at the nearest of the guards.

Both guards stopped about 4 metres in front of him, one held up a hand in a stop gesture.

"Hold on there mate," he said in a calm voice. "There's need for that."

Jim smiled and flicked one of the switches on the panel at his waist. He pointed his tube-like weapon at one of the guards. When he pressed his thumb on a button on the tube, a semi-transparent beam of pure silver shot out and splashed against the guards chest for one second. The guard cried out and fell instantly onto his back, his uniform smoking. He was beating at his chest, writhing in agony, pain etched on his face.

Jim was pleased. The invisible mode might not be working as well as he had planned but the weapon was. What should he call it? He thought. Silver Shot? Silver Beam? No. How about Silver Force? Yes, that was it. Silver Force it was. He moved the tube around to fire at the other guard as he stepped forwards towards the writhing man he had just shot. But the guard was no longer there. Jim frowned. That was fast.

He looked around the reception area. It was completely clear. Everyone had disappeared.

There was no one to shoot at. No one to try out Silver Force on. Never mind. There would be more people deeper into the building.

He shrugged and continued forward. As he did, he heard two distinct thumps behind him, as though something heavy had fallen to the floor. Something heavy and large. And judging by the shaking of the ground, very large indeed. He spun around, and gasped.

In front of the doorway, blocking any escape, was a huge, dull red suited figure. It towered two metres tall, its arms and legs bulging with thick metal joints. Its red armoured surface glinted under the building lights. Its large head was equipped with a jet-black visor which moved back and forth as it scanned the area. Its musculature whined as it raised an arm with remarkable speed.

"Stay where you are," its mechanised voice boomed.

Jim peered up at it trying to see through the visor to see if there was a person inside, but it was too dark. Of course, there might be no one inside.

The whole thing could be a mechanism, some sort of robot or remote-controlled device.

As he was studying it and trying to figure out what it was, a faint blue halo suddenly materialised around it. Jim knew what that was. A force field! His stomach lurched, and he realised that he was in trouble. Big trouble.

Chapter 11 - The Girl

He didn't know where he was. He stood looking through the window. There was nothing out there to help him figure out the location; just a steel barrier, overgrown grass and weeds and rubbish scattered around.

When he had awoken, he was surprised to see a girl lying next to him. It had taken a little while to remember what had happened. She was a drug addict. But she had led him here to this derelict building out of the rain. And then he had caught her going through his pockets. Looking for cash he surmised. He had perceived that she had been injured. It took all of his remaining strength to save her and then cure her addiction. After that, he had blacked out.

What was the connection with this girl? Why was she here? He turned to look at her sleeping form on the mattress, his eyes lingering on the jet-black matted hair falling across her face.

He was annoyed. His thoughts kept coming back to the same questions - what had happened and why was he here? He had no answers, and he couldn't reach out for help. Not yet. He needed to recover a little more, build up his reserves of energy. Curing the girl had taken everything he had left.

He heard her stir and then retch. He was undecided what to do next. He could either stay here for a while; build up his strength and then call for help - although he wasn't sure how long that would take. Or he could walk out of here and try and make his way to the flat or maybe the Complex. He wondered if he would be able to find them as there were no landmarks around. Maybe once he left this place, he would recognise a building or a street and then be able to figure it out.

The girl behind him rose and crept across the room. He let her leave. Maybe that was for the best, he thought. He was in no state to help her anymore.

———

The girl ran until she could run no more, given her poor physical shape and the years of alcohol and drug abuse it wasn't far. She was almost back at the town centre when she stopped and collapsed on all fours, in a shop doorway. She lowered her forehead to the ground as she panted, drawing in deep breaths, struggling to get enough air into her lungs. She heard a roaring in her ears and closed her eyes as spots of colour danced in her vision.

Most pedestrians ignored her and walked past without a second glance, but one woman stopped and looked on with some concern. She hesitated, looking around, but no one else seemed to be bothered, not wanting to get involved. She opened her mouth to say something, but then closed it suddenly, turned, and walked on.

Meanwhile the girl slowly recovered, and she sat up, leaning her back against the shop door. She raised her head upwards with closed eyes and breathed deeply. After a while she was able to look around and think clearly. She had escaped! Now that she had recovered physically, she could think more clearly. It was a lucky escape, she thought as she gazed around, watching the people troop past, studiously ignoring her. She didn't mind, she was used to it.

It was a while before she realised two things. The first was that she had no money. She had intended to steal whatever the strange man had, but somehow it had not happened. That was a missed opportunity, because without money how was she going to buy the drugs she needed?

Secondly, she felt different. She couldn't tell exactly what was different, but she knew that she didn't feel the same. The pain in her side was completely gone. She remembered how much it had hurt when one of the gang had kicked her. Now there was nothing. There was also something else. The withdrawal symptoms were gone.

But before she could identify what it was, the blackness welled upwards again, saturating her mind with the old despair and terror. There was nothing to hold it back, nothing to stop her from remembering. She dropped her head to her chest, moaning as it overwhelmed her, and she could think of nothing else.

It was some minutes later that the blackness retreated a little, letting her think normally again. She had no idea what was happening to her. She began to understand that nothing was the same anymore, since meeting the stranger. She needed her drugs. She had to have them. It was the only thing that made her forget. And to get them she needed money. It always came back to money.

She puzzled once again over the fact that she wasn't feeling any withdrawal symptoms. Usually, her whole body would be jangling with the need by now. But she felt nothing. Her thoughts came back to the idea that maybe the stranger had given her something. That was the only thing that could explain how she felt. But she didn't feel drugged. Instead, she felt alert. What kind of drug could do that? Maybe it was a new kind of designer drug? She shivered and closed her eyes. What was she going to do?

She sat for a while, debating with herself, trying to figure out the best course of action. In the end it came down to two choices. Either she could forget it and carry on hoping that she would be okay. Or she could go back and ask the stranger what he had done and maybe try and take his money, if he had any. If he was asleep, she could try again. Not much of a choice really. In fact, no choice at all. She would have to go back.

But this time she would be prepared. This time she would not be tricked or fooled. She had no one to take with her as backup. She was on her own. She had no friends. All of them had long since given up on her as she had steadily declined into a drug and alcohol induced lifestyle. Living on the streets and associating with the drug addicts, the homeless and life's dropouts had driven all of her remaining friends away. She had no idea and did not care where her family was. There was no solace or help there. She shuddered.

Quickly blanking the black memories that reared up again out of the dark corners of her mind, she found herself wishing and longing for the mind-numbing haze that the drugs gave her. Again, she was puzzled. Why was she not overcome with the shakes? Where was the bone aching need? The cramps? The nausea?

Her mind made up, she got up and slowly retraced her steps. She was completely unaware of the watcher across the street that followed at a discreet distance.

As she stepped back into the building, a sinking feeling grew in her stomach. She was afraid. Although her body was not craving, she wished she had something to take the edge off. Something to dull the fear and make her stronger. She was about to confront the stranger. He could be violent as last night had shown. And he was tall, and physically much bigger than her. She would have to keep her distance so that she could make a quick getaway if things went south.

In no time she was at the doorway to the room where she had left him. She half expected to find it empty. Instead, he was still there.

He was still standing at the window. He turned as she entered the room. She was again struck by his bright blue eyes. They seemed to be almost luminous as he stared at her through his long blond hair. Like a cat's eyes in the dark reflecting light from a torch. Impossible, she thought.

Gathering her courage she spoke, "What have you given me?"

The stranger's brow furrowed.

"Given you?" he asked," his voice was much stronger than the night before.

"A drug. You've given me a drug."

The stranger smiled a thin smile.

"Ah, I see. No, I have not given you a drug."

She was taken aback. "Well, if it's not a drug then what have you done? I feel different."

"Who are you?" he asked.

"Never mind who I am, I asked you a question." She kept her distance and stayed in the doorway so that she could make a quick exit.

"I cured you," he replied.

"Cured me of what?"

"You were injured."

Her hand went involuntarily to her side. There was still no pain. Could he really have cured her? No, that was impossible.

"I don't think so mister," she replied. "Stop lying."

He stared at her.

"I'm not lying. I cured you. You were dying."

She could not help herself, she laughed. "Yeah, sure."

"You were dying, so I fixed you."

Anger flared inside her. What a total bullshitter, she thought. Who did he think he was? Talking as though he was a doctor, and they were in some hospital instead of this dirty squat. It was a total fabrication, he was obviously a liar.

As if reading her thoughts, he said, "Have you noticed that you aren't in pain anymore?"

Well, that was true, she thought. But there was no way he was responsible. She had just slept if off, that was all. She pressed her side where she had been kicked. Nothing. It felt completely normal.

"Who are you?" he asked again. "Do I know you? Have we met before?"

This was getting more and more bizarre, she thought.

"No, you don't know me, and I don't know you," she replied.

There was silence between them, his bright blue eyes never leaving hers. She stared back defiantly.

"We should leave," he suddenly spoke up. "Come with me." He stepped towards her and held out his hand. "I can help you."

She stared at his hand incredulously. What was she going to do now?

Chapter 12 - Simon

3 years ago

Simon had struggled with dark moods and depression all his life, although he had successfully hidden it from everyone around him, including his wife and his work colleagues.

He had been a successful career soldier and had risen through the ranks to Sergeant Major before being thrown out of the army. He had disobeyed orders, struck an officer and gone AWOL, and not for the first time. This time, he had no defence. After all, how could he defend himself when all he had was a feeling?

They had been out on exercises, on Salisbury Plain, when it had happened. He had one of his premonitions. It was something that he had no control over and had been plaguing him all of his life. He would sometimes just know that something was going to happen; and it was almost always something bad.

Often, he would just let it happen and pretend that he knew nothing about it, which was true really. Most of the time, he never knew exactly what was going to happen, he just knew something would. But this time, he had decided to do something about it.

He had disobeyed his commanding officer, and to top it all, when the officer had refused to listen Simon had lost his temper and punched him full in the face. He had then walked out of the camp.

He was found by military police two days later. When asked, he could not tell them why he had done what he had done. They would not have believed him. At his hearing he had no defence. His superiors had no other option - he was dishonourably discharged.

Simon found out later that his foreboding premonition was right. During the exercise a soldier had been killed in a live fire incident.

Two weeks later, his wife walked out too. Fortunately, they had no children that particular joy being denied because of his low sperm count. Yet another thing he had failed at. His depression surged forward, and he descended into the darkness and self-loathing that it brought with it.

The next few weeks were a blur of self-destruction, hatred and black moods.

Eventually, he found himself in hospital. He had been admitted after trying to commit suicide. It was fortunate for him that this particular hospital had a mental health wing and even more fortunate that they had a spare bed.

He lay in his hospital bed, feeling miserable. He had failed yet again. He couldn't even successfully kill himself. He had lost everything but couldn't lose his own life. He smiled bitterly at the thought. Well, he would just have to try again. This time he wouldn't fail, he would make sure of it. He raised his arms and looked at the bandages on his wrists. Slashing at them hadn't worked. What he needed was something that he could not be rescued from. Maybe jumping from a bridge, a high bridge. He briefly thought of the Clifton Suspension bridge near Bristol. He had driven over it once. Now there was a bridge to jump from. There was no coming back from that jump.

He was startled out of his suicidal thoughts by a stranger who stood by his bed. He had never seen him before - a tall, young man dressed in a long black coat, with long blond hair falling across his face.

"Who are you?" he asked, knowing that it could not be a doctor or a nurse.

The stranger smiled down at him. "I'm here to help you," he said.

Simon was puzzled. If he wasn't a doctor, how could he help him? Then it came to him - he must be a psychiatrist. Of course, they had sent someone to "make him better", as if any form of therapy could help him. He laughed.

"Sorry, no. I don't need anyone to tell me to snap out of it."

The stranger's eyebrows raised. "Of course not. That would never work. I'm here to get rid of your parasite and maybe offer you a job."

Simon was dumbfounded. Parasite? What the hell was he talking about?

"Sorry, mate, you've got the wrong guy."

"Nope, I have the right guy alright. If you would just stay still for a bit, I'll remove it for you."

The stranger raised his hand towards Simon's head. Simon shrank back.

"Hey, what do you think you are doing? Nurse!" he shouted.

The stranger stopped, his hand still outstretched. "No one will hear you, I've seen to that. Just hold still and it will soon be over."

Fear hit him, like a punch in the solar plexus. He pressed himself as far back as he could into the bed and raised his arms to ward off an attack. Was this stranger going to kill him? Was he a murderer who had somehow got into the hospital, and was going round killing patients?

But then the fear left him as he suddenly realised that it didn't matter. If this guy was going to kill him, then let him. He wanted out anyway. He would be doing the job for him. He dropped his arms and relaxed.

"Just make it quick," he said, as he watched the hand approach his head.

He's probably going to strangle me, he thought, as he closed his eyes. As he did so, he was a bit puzzled by the rings and chains on the stranger's fingers.

He felt a hand on his forehead, not his throat. He frowned, confused. Then there was a flash that he could see even with his eyes closed.

Something changed. Something undefinable. A weight lifting. A blackness fading. A light brightening. He opened his eyes.

The stranger had gone. He looked around, up and down the ward. Nothing, just patients, nurses and doctors going about their business. None of them looked his way. It was as if it had never happened. There was nothing out of the ordinary.

Then he noticed a card leaning against a glass of water on his bedside table. It had not been there before. He reached over and grabbed it.

Printed in neat, black lettering was an address. He turned it over, on the reverse there was something written with a ball point pen. It said:

'Come and see me when you are recovered. A job is waiting for you.'

What the hell? he thought. What just happened? Who was that guy? What sort of job?

He lay there puzzling over the events for the rest of the day, the card clutched in his hand. The next day, he was discharged from the hospital with multiple appointments with the local mental health team.

He never attended a single one. He had never felt better in all of his life, and he came to realise that the stranger was responsible. He had to find out what he had done.

Later, at the Complex, the stranger had introduced himself as Joe. He had described how he had removed a parasite. A mind sucker, he had called it. An insubstantial thing that lived in our world but could not be seen with ordinary eyes. It had been feeding on him for years, clinging on to him with its Psi enabled tendrils sucking him dry, causing his depression and black moods.

He had been outfitted with an Assist and joined the Alliance without hesitation. And of course, his skills had proven invaluable. Soon he was put in charge of the military arm of the Alliance.

Chapter 13 - The Escape

Jim was fighting for his life. At first, he had thought that he would be able to beat the armoured figure, but now he was rapidly concluding that there was no way. He had no idea how, but the armoured figure was clearly technologically superior to his suit. Its screens were very strong, and he had not been able to penetrate them. Worse, its weapon, some sort of beam similar to his, was stressing his own screens to their limits.

His screens squealed in protest as he was hit again. They held, but he could tell it wouldn't be long before they failed. Flashing streamers of force rebounded off his screens, splashing into the walls. The air was hot, making it difficult for him to breathe. But it wasn't just the heat; it was the acrid smoke, soot and debris that choked him. He noted absently that this was why his opponent was inside a sealed suit. On top of that, the noise was deafening. Another reason for a sealed suit, he thought. The air screamed and howled as it was super-heated by energies from both adversaries. The reflected beams crossed each other, hitting walls and the ceiling, melting through plaster and brickwork, causing great cracks and holes to appear, and raining down rubble to crash onto the marble floor.

The glass frontage of the building had long gone, it being shattered and melted. People outside were screaming and running away, as clouds of smoke billowed outwards into the street. Some were taking pictures and videos with their smart phones, hiding behind cars and lamp posts.

Jim dived for what remaining cover there was, rolling behind an upturned and burning desk. He crashed into a wall. He winced. Not in pain, but for his suit. The reality was that it was fragile and could easily fail. If a wire popped out or a component fell off, he was as good as dead. A loose or disconnected wire could mean his screens failing. He needed to get out of here and fast. But before he made his exit, he had one more trick to try.

He quickly pushed a button on the control panel at his waist and popped his head above the desk. The armoured figure blocked the exit. There was no escape that way. Briefly, he wondered why it was not pressing its advantage, but he did not hesitate. He raised his weapon and depressed the fire switch. The beam that erupted from the tube in his right hand was no longer silver. Instead, it was a deep azure blue, and it followed a straight line to smash into the armoured figure's screen. There was a loud crash and a whoosh. The whole room became a light display as beams and streamers reflected everywhere, bouncing around the room. Whatever the reflected beams touched was instantly vapourised in an explosion of molten material and steam that sprayed the whole area with white hot debris. Jim smiled to himself as globs of liquid gold dropped downwards onto his own screens, which howled in protest.

The armoured figure staggered back from the force of the beam, clearly taken by surprise. Grinning madly, Jim fired again, hitting the figure dead centre. It staggered back again and fell through what was once the glass entrance. Scintillating beams and flashes of force rebounded everywhere, the remaining glass windows shattered, and plaster boiled from the walls. The smoke filled the room completely, making it impossible for Jim to see his target. He jumped up, keeping his finger pressed down on the firing stud as he walked forwards, a manic grin plastered all over his face. His own screens continued to flash and scream from the reflected force of his own beam weapon, as he walked forwards, even the reflected force was stressing them hard. But no matter, this was it. This was the best that they could throw at him, and he was winning! At last! Justice would be his.

Back to his plan. He would level the building, killing everyone in it. Then they would know who was the boss. They would know who had the best technology. All those brain enhancing freaks would die.

He approached the figure, which was now lying on the floor. It raised an arm as though to fend off the attack, but it was not firing back. It seemed unable. It was then that Jim noticed that although the figure was down and appeared to be losing, his new beam weapon was not penetrating its screens. Also, a large red flashing light on his control panel was signalling for his attention. His screens continued their flashing and screaming, as beams continued to shoot around the room. The walls were disintegrating, the noise was deafening, the light was blinding. Then the figure started to push itself up off the floor.

The flashing red light on his control panel meant that he was out of power, he could no longer continue the fight. It was over. And in any case, his secondary weapon was proving to be ineffective. He could not penetrate the red armoured figure's screens. He was out of options. There was only one thing left to do. Resignedly, he smashed his thumb down hard on a large black button on his control belt.

In a flash of light and a crack of sound, Jim disappeared.

The armoured figure rose and scanned the room. When the scans revealed that the danger was over, it sent a mental thought, *"Threat neutralised for now, but the building is no longer safe. I advise complete evacuation."*

The reply was instantaneous, *"Good work, Mike. We have already withdrawn everyone to the Complex. Could you identify the assailant?"*

"Yeah." replied Mike, *"It was Joe's brother again, this time he came packing. I couldn't capture him. He teleported out."*

"You did your best. If only we knew why he hates his brother so much. I'm at a total loss to understand his motives."

Mike nodded in the confines of his HAZPRO suit. *"I wish Joe was here to help, but...."* His thought trailed off.

"He's gone. We have to manage things without him."

"I know," replied Mike, *"I still wish he was here."*

"Okay. We have already removed all trace of our activities. Come straight back to the Complex for a debrief."

Mike took one more look around the destruction and then initiated his teleport jump.

The red armoured suit disappeared with a snap of wind, the smoke roiling around with the movement of the air.

Chapter 14 - First Skirmish

"*Hold your position. Open fire when the target is within range, and you have a clear shot!*" the urgent thought pierced her rambling mind and fear.

Prisha shuffled inside her suit as much as she was able within its cushioning inner shell, and concentrated hard on the contact. There was still only one, its speed and direction were constant. At this rate it should be within range in the next few minutes. She continued to sight along the barrel and waited. The shaking had stopped after her suit had administered a calming drug into her system. As well as keeping her alive, the suit's primary purpose was to maintain her fighting ability and to do that it could pump her full of all manner of drugs if it deemed it necessary. She had no control over the fight and life maintenance functions of the suit.

Some soldiers called it "Fuck and Luck" on account that if the systems kicked in then you would be fucked and lucky to survive. Fucked because the chemical soup it pumped into you could leave you unable to function for days afterward, and lucky to survive after being super accelerated with drugs. Not to mention that if it ever happened, you would have to be in a serious fire fight. She fervently hoped that it would never come to that.

She watched the red dot in her HUD track slowly across her field of view. Any moment now it would be in range. She noted that whatever it was, the object would appear from behind a low hill some 5 kilometres away. She moved the barrel to where she thought it would appear and watched the dot get closer and closer.

"Magnify," she told the suit, which dutifully complied. Her vision zoomed in on the object as it appeared from behind the hill.

"Incredible" was her first thought. "I don't believe it!"

The object turned out to be a human shaped figure. Totally naked and devoid of any genitalia, but with two arms and two legs which pistoned up and down carrying it forward with incredible speed. How did it cope without a suit? she thought to herself. It wasn't even wearing a mask, so how could it breathe? Maybe it was a robot? This thought was reinforced when she noticed that it had no nose or mouth, but glowing red eyes. As it ran, it kicked up a dust cloud behind it and around it legs, some of the dust coating its matte white body. Behind its shoulders, she saw what she assumed were barrels, one on each side of its head, both pointing skywards.

She pulled the trigger. There was a "thunk" sound, accompanied by little or no recoil. She watched a blue pulse of light leave the end of the barrel and flash towards the figure striking it in the chest. The blue light enveloped it completely for a few seconds and then it died away. The figure tumbled forward end over end, until it finally came to rest on its face and lay still.

"Good shot," the thought of her commander was loud and clear.

That was easy, she thought. Maybe too easy.

"Scan all" she instructed her suit.

She kept her gaze on the fallen figure, humanoid, or robot, or whatever the hell it was, as she waited for the suit to report back.

"No contacts," was the eventual report.

Hmmm, maybe that was it. Maybe it was easy after all. She started to relax. Nothing happened. She waited for further instructions. Should she go and investigate? Or should she wait?

"Hold position until further notice." was the commander's thought.

Well, at least that cleared that up.

"Vision normal, set mode to normal," she instructed her suit.

As one of the two moons started to fall below the horizon, she sat back down and settled in to wait.

Chapter 15 - The Parasite

"Just where the hell are we going?" asked the girl.

She had been following the stranger for a while. They had long since moved from the less desirable part of town to a much better, up and coming area. People moved along the streets, involved in their own worlds. Shopping, running errands or visiting friends. Without exception, they all ignored the dishevelled and filthy couple. The man led the way, the girl followed. Occasionally he would stop at a junction and look around as though trying to figure out which way to go. Then he would purposefully stride onwards. The girl followed grudgingly. Then stopped suddenly.

"Tell me where we are going or I am not going any further, you freak." she shouted at his back.

She had followed him long enough. She had no idea where she was being led or why. And she still knew nothing about this guy. He was a total stranger and here she was following him. What was she thinking? She had had enough. This was it. She was going no further. She felt as though she had finally come to her senses. She was doing this no more. For all she knew she was being led to her death. This guy had been acting totally weird since they had first met. She had no idea what his intentions were, nor was he saying anything.

The only reason she was going along with this was because of his promise. She thought back to their conversation at the squat.

"I'm not going anywhere with you." she had said.

He had looked sorrowful. "I can help you."

"I don't need any help."

"I think that you do."

"Like what?" she asked scornfully.

"Well...." his voice had trailed off.

"That's what I thought." she said. "Now, what did you give me? I feel different."

The man was quiet for a while. "I cured your addiction."

She gaped. "Rubbish. And in any case, I don't want to be cured. You're talking bullshit."

"I understand," he replied. "But you know it would have killed you in the end."

"That has nothing to do with you. It's my life. I need the drugs."

"Why?"

And there it was. Such a simple question, but one she could not answer. She could not afford to. No one must know, and that included her. And now the question he had asked triggered her. She felt the ground move as she struggled to think of something else and keep the memories away to no avail. The blackness overwhelmed her once more as she sat suddenly on the floor. She did not see the stranger approach her, a look of concern on his face. Nor did she notice that he sat next to her, putting his arm across her shoulders. She moaned quietly to herself, rocking back and forth in quick jerky movements as she descended into the black hole of her despair.

She wasn't sure how long it was before she surfaced back into the world around her. When she did, she felt his arm on her shoulders and his closeness to her.

"Get off me!" she screamed at him as she shuffled away.

The stranger looked hurt. "I was only...." He started to say.

"I know what you were trying to do. Keep away from me."

The stranger nodded slowly. He hesitated and then said, "I can get you what you want."

She looked at him suspiciously. "You're just saying that." she replied. "You just want to get me alone somewhere."

The stranger smiled. "Aren't we alone already?" he asked.

The girl looked around. "Okay, smart arse. How are you going to get drugs?"

His smile widened. "It won't be a problem. If you come with me, I'll show you."

She thought furiously. Was this a trick? She wasn't sure. One thing was for certain, she couldn't trust him. What was he doing cuddling up to her? But at the same time how else was she going to get money or drugs? Clearly, she couldn't steal from him now that he was alert.

"Okay, I'll go with you, and you give me what I need. But no funny stuff, alright?"

He nodded. "Of course not, I wouldn't think of hurting you."

Back in the street, she stood waiting for him to answer.

He turned and looked at her with those strange bright, blue eyes. He stood for a minute, staring at her. People brushed past them, busy with the things they had to do.

"You must come with me." he said.

"I'm not going any further with you. We've walked far enough. Do you even know where we're going?"

He stood there and looking at her. Then he looked around at the people striding by. He walked back to her. Standing in front of her he looked down and said, "do you want to see?"

She looked back up at him, surprised.

"What? See what?" she asked.

He held out his right hand. Immediately she noticed the rings once again. This close she could see delicate scrolls and swirls on each one as well as the tiny chains linking each one to the other in one continuous loop. She had never seen anything like it before and definitely not on a man.

Without thinking she took his hand in hers. It was warm and she felt a small tingle travelling up her arm as he gripped her hand tightly.

"Look," he said, and he gestured around him.

She did as he said. At first, she saw nothing out of the ordinary. There were buildings and shops and cars. People dashing around purposefully, sitting in cafes and restaurants, eating, drinking and talking. Nothing different or unusual.

Then she noticed the colours. There were rainbow colours flowing outwards from the people. Or more accurately, from their heads. Upwards and outwards they flowed. Fanning out as they soared skywards. Coloured streamers of light that spread outwards with slow flowing movement. She gasped, it was so beautiful she thought. She had never seen anything like it. What on earth was it? She opened her mouth to ask him what she was seeing when she saw something else.

A dark brown shadow appeared at the end of the street. It seeped around building corners and, flowed along the street as though it were alive. As it oozed along, it touched people. None of them seemed to notice a thing. They were blind to it, she realised. They could not see it. As she watched it closely, she saw that it was not just touching people; it was forming into tentacles which it was wrapping around peoples' heads.

The tentacle stayed there for a second and then unwrapped itself and moved on to another head. In this way it seemed to be tasting everyone it came to.

"What is it?" she whispered in dread. "What is it doing?"

She watched as it continued to flow down the street, sampling heads as it went. He pulled her back as it flowed past.

"It's a parasite." he said, "It's looking for a victim. Watch."

They both watched, as it weaved along, touching, squirming, and seeping as it crossed the street. A semi-opaque miasma, behaving like a living thing, searching for something along the street. She shuddered. There was something about it that she did not like, something that sickened her.

In a cafe across the street, a man sat nursing a coffee, staring into his cup. He sat alone and was clearly not happy about something. Maybe he had just had an argument with his girlfriend or wife. Or maybe he had just lost his job. In any case, he did not notice the brown tentacle wrapping around his head. This time, instead of moving on, the tentacle stayed where it was. Other tentacles joined in and soon the entire thing was surrounding him. The coloured light flowing outwards from the man's head flickered and disappeared. The cloud shrank and contracted until it was a dark shadow coating the man's forehead, the top of his skull, and down the back of his neck. It seemed to settle in, like a sucker fish latching on to a passing shark. The man slumped his shoulders forward and lowered his head.

"What is it doing?" she whispered again.

"Feeding," he replied. "It feeds on psychic energy. That man will be depressed until it's had its fill."

She felt a moment of sympathy for the man in the cafe. How horrible. She did not have time to ask any more questions or watch the thing feeding on the man. She was pulled down the street by her wrist. This time she did not object and went willingly.

Chapter 16 - Battle

Prisha awoke with a start. She remembered that she had just taken out the enemy and had been told to hold position. Somehow, she had fallen asleep. That was stupid. What was she thinking? Falling asleep while on patrol. That could be fatal.

She looked around. What was happening? What had woken her? It was quite dark. The two moons had long since set. The darkness did not pose a problem because the suit automatically compensated for the available light and boosted what she could see in her visor. And although everything had an eerie green cast, she could see perfectly well.

"*Prisha!*" her commander barked a thought at her.

Before she had a chance to reply, the thought continued "*Get up now! You have incoming!*"

It took two full seconds to register what was happening, before she acted.

"Fuck!" She exclaimed, as she jumped to her feet, being careful not to jump too hard because that would send her sailing into the air, making her an easy target.

Bringing up her rifle, she vocalised instructions to her suit.

"Power on full counter measures, set screens to reflect and power on XO Assist now!" she shouted.

In her HUD, she saw a red dot closing fast.

"Launch counter measures now," she said.

She heard two "thunks" and felt two small pushes from her back as her suit fired two counter measure devices into the air to her left and right.

She sighted down barrel of her rifle. As she did, something hit her screens with a loud clang and a flash of light. Her visor went dark, automatically protecting her eyes from the glare. She cursed. She could not see a damn thing. Fortunately, her HUD display still worked. She could see the red dot denoting the enemy moving towards her position. She could also see Mo and Erica closing, but they were too far away to help immediately. For now, she was on her own. As her visor cleared, she pulled the trigger and held it down for 5 seconds.

There was another crash as something landed next to her. Reflexes kicked in, and she jumped away from the object, which promptly exploded throwing her sideways. Whilst flying through the air, she whipped her weapon up and around to face the enemy. She pulled the trigger again as she fell to the ground.

She hit, but her suit protected her. Her heart raced and her breathing turned to gasps as pain lanced through her shoulder. Automatically, the suit looked after her. She felt it inject her with pain killers and stimulants. It also boosted the protective shielding around her injury to better protect that area. Although she had landed on her left shoulder, she managed to roll up into a crouch. All the time, her weapon was still pointing in the direction of the enemy. She noticed that the red dot was still moving towards her and was closer than ever. She stood from her crouch and ran for cover.

The suit's exo-muscles boosted her speed. enabling her to reach cover faster than a diving kestrel. She dived forward and rolled. As she did so, she saw a beam flash, and heard crackling as the air above her was ionised. In her HUD, she noticed that the red dot was still closing fast.

"Counter measures deploying," the suit informed her.

High above her, each of the counter measure missiles had reached apogee, whereupon each one separated into 20 tiny pieces. 10 of them were conventional counter measures and flared into bright, white hot heat sources, designed to attract any heat or light seeking projectiles.

The second set of 10 components were homing missiles. Each had a micro warhead consisting of a core of Psi energy, held in stasis within a small forcefield, and encapsulated inside a casing of enriched uranium. Equipped with a minute rocket motor and a guidance computer, its job was to home in on any target not designated as friendly and crash into it. When it hit its target at terminal velocity, the psi energy warhead would deliver the equivalent of 5Kg of

TNT. Multiply that by 10 and you had one large explosion.

In less than a second, all 20 of the homing missiles from both counter measures, had locked onto the enemy target making 20 projectiles of death, streaking downwards, while the conventional counter measures spread apart like an umbrella, drifting slowly to the ground below.

As she looked around to reacquire the target, she saw streamers of light pierce the sky as something shot upwards into the air, plainly going for the counter measures. She smiled grimly to herself. That should keep it occupied for a while. Hefting up her rifle, she brought it around to face the target. Her HUD magnified her view, what she saw, shocked her.

The same humanoid figure that she had shot and killed a while ago was still running towards her, arms and legs pumping as it shrank the distance between them. On its back she saw what must have been two muzzles pointing upwards towards the sky. As she watched, she saw a small flash from one of them and something rocketed upwards.

Aiming at the figure, she pulled the trigger again and saw the pulse of light from her weapon strike the running figure full on its chest. This time the figure did not even pause. It just kept coming. Something was different. She had been able to knock it out before, but now her weapon had no effect. It must have adapted.

"Shit!" she exclaimed.

She quickly selected the third function on the rifle, sighted again and pulled the trigger.

Everything happened all at once.

The humanoid figure raised one arm and fired something from a tube that emerged from its palm. Clearly it had located her position from her previous shot. Then the homing missiles struck from above. All 20 of them impacted upon the humanoid's screens with a huge crash and a blinding flash of light. Her visor blanked her vision again as well as turning off the external microphones, as the pulse of energy from her rifle also hit the humanoid.

She was suddenly thrown backwards into the air as the enemy's beam hit her. Her screens screeched and screamed and then failed. She flew through the air for a third time. The beam played along her suit for 0.75 seconds before it died.

The outer armour of the suit could not withstand the assault. It burned and boiled off rapidly, exposing its inner workings and mechanisms as well as Prisha's flesh. The integrity of the left arm was compromised, allowing the noxious atmosphere to enter the suit, while the left leg of the suit was entirely vaporised as it met the full brunt of the attack. In the last moments before she hit the ground, the suit took emergency action. It injected her with multiple pain killers and other drugs to prevent shock, and then shut off the left arm and leg from the rest of the suit with a micro laser and an emergency sealing mechanism, allowing what was left of the arm to fall away to the ground. It also filled what was left of the suit with a shock resistant foam to prevent further injury when she hit the ground.

She crashed into the ground hard, what limbs she had left flailing. This time, she did not roll, she bounced and came back down to the ground with a crunch on solid rock. The suit had saved her life. She did not lose consciousness because of the stimulants it had given her, and the protection it had deployed before she hit the ground. She lay there, on her back, in no pain, listening to the suit, fully aware of what it was doing to her. She could feel yet more drugs being pumped into her and could feel the shock foam dissolving away. She heard two thunks as it deployed two more counter measures, as well as a hissing as it stabilised her air supply. She could feel it testing various functions. Her right arm and right leg twitched as the exo-muscles contracted and relaxed. Red warning lights were all over her HUD reporting the function and damage she had sustained.

There was a whirring noise, and she felt the suit lift her torso from the ground by contracting various exo-muscles until she was sitting up, facing toward where her HUD was reporting the enemy to be.

"Target is stationary, 32 meters away, 41 degrees from magnetic North," her suit reported.

Her weapon was gone. But her arm wrist holster automatically deployed a small hand weapon into her right hand. The suit raised her arm for her, allowing her to sight down its short barrel in the direction of where she knew the enemy was.

She was absolutely calm and in no pain despite having lost both her left arm and leg. The suit performed its function perfectly as it was designed to do; keeping her alive and able to continue fighting.

"Shields," she said to the suit.

"Secondary function only," reported the suit. "Counter measures deploying."

She knew that once again, high up in the air, the counter measures were separating, and would be homing in on anything that they could not identify as friendly.

"Deploy drone," she told the suit.

She might not be able to move, but she could still find out what was going on. With a bang and a slap on her back, the drone was fired into the air. It whooshed upwards and moved towards the humanoid's location, which she could see in her HUD was still not moving. A window flickered into life in the bottom left corner of her vision. It was the live video feed from the drone. She also noticed that Mo and Erica were still closing in. They would be here in 65 seconds.

Unable to move, she sat there with her arm held straight out and her hand weapon steady, watching the video feed from the drone. The homing missiles circled high overhead unable to acquire a target. 20 burning, impossibly bright balls slowly fell from the sky in concentric circles around her, lighting up the barren alien landscape. There was no fear, no pain. She just waited.

Chapter 17 - The Flat

The stranger and the girl continued their slow walk through the town, where eventually they entered a residential area. The girl trailed behind the stranger, following at a distance.

As they walked, the stranger finally felt that he had recovered enough strength. He sent out a faint thought, *"Mol, are you there?"*

There was an immediate response, *"Joe!"* It was practically a scream. *"You're alive!"*

He felt the warmth, relief, and surprise of her thoughts.

"Where are you? I'll send someone to get you straight away. Your contact is a bit weak. I assume you can't teleport?"

Joe smiled inwardly as he let the feelings from his closest friend and fellow founder of the Alliance, wash over him. He was not surprised at the feelings of concern from Molly, after all they had been working together for the last 5 years. But he was surprised how good it felt to hear her thoughts. He could feel the power of her mind through their contact as it pushed at his so that she could integrate further into his senses. He was too weak to resist and let her mind insinuate into his.

"*Who's this?*" she asked, raising images of the girl inside his thoughts.

"*I don't know yet,*" he replied. "*But I intend to find out.*"

Molly reeled through his memories quickly and saw everything that had happened. "*You have no memory of where you've been all this time?*"

He frowned. "*No. How long has it been?*"

"*Two weeks,*" came her quick reply. "*I can see you have a few superficial injuries. I'll sort that for you now, but you should visit Sally.*"

He sensed her power surge and felt tendrils of her thoughts snake into his consciousness, connecting and soothing as they went. He felt the benefit immediately.

"Two weeks?" He was shocked. "I'll visit Sally later. I need to sort something out first."

"The girl?"

"Yes. The connection with her can't be a coincidence, and I can sense that she has talent."

"More recruiting?" she asked. He could feel her smiling. "I thought you had given that up for now."

"She has talent, so she is definitely a candidate. But she is a feisty one, and she clearly has some baggage."

There was a brief pause in the conversation. "You like her." It was a statement.

"I don't know her," protested Joe.

"You can't fool me. Remember, I'm in your mind." She was practically laughing.

"Well, okay. Maybe a little," he grudgingly admitted. "I'm at the flat now, so I'll call you later.

"You don't want me to come and get you then?"

"Not yet, let's see how this pans out."

"Okay. It's so good to hear from you Joe. We all thought you were dead."

"I'm still here," he replied. "Maybe I'm harder to kill than you think."

As her mind left his, he could hear her laughing, until the contact was severed.

"So, just who the hell are you and what is going on?" the girl demanded of the stranger.

They were in the entrance hall of the flat, which was plain without any decoration. No photographs or pictures adorned the walls, and no furniture cluttered the small corridor. The walls were painted a neutral grey, as was the floor and the ceiling. The effect was mildly disorientating, and she did not like it.

The stranger held out his hand, "I'm Joe. Who are you?"

Automatically, without thinking, she took his hand. She felt rings and chains and the warmth of his skin against hers. She was about to speak when she suddenly felt her hand tingling.

"What the fuck!" she exclaimed when she saw the hallway walls change.

They flicked from the plain grey to a dull yellow interspaced with bright metallic stripes running up the walls, over the ceiling down the next wall and across the floor. These regular stripes ran along the entire length of the hallway. She looked around wildly, trying to make sense of what was happening. Why had the walls changed? What did it mean? And perhaps more importantly, was it real? Maybe it was all some kind of illusion, after all, why would there be metal in the walls? It didn't make any sense.

"What can you see?" asked Joe, concerned. He gripped her hand tightly.

She struggled for words. "Some sort of metallic stripes in the walls," she stammered.

Joe looked thoughtful, but not worried. "That's interesting," he said. "Is that all?"

She stared up at him incredulous. "Is that all?" she shouted. "For fuck's sake, what the hell is going on?" she demanded.

Joe smiled. "Don't be frightened," he said calmly. "There's nothing to worry about. I'll explain later. But first things first. What's your name?"

"Kate," she replied. "And don't fob me off with that bullshit. Tell me what's going on now, or I am out of here."

She was incensed. The arrogant prick. Who did he think he was? Joe let go of her hand. The walls flickered and changed back to plain, dull grey. She shuddered. There was definitely some sort of weird shit going on here. And she didn't like it. Not at all.

"Look," replied Joe. "I'm not trying to be funny. It's just that I've been out of it for a while and I'm not back to myself yet."

Kate stared into his bright blue eyes. He seemed genuine. But how could she really know? She frowned. She did not know what to do. Should she leave? Or should she stay? Was she really safe? Could she trust this strange young man? Then she remembered the menacing brown tentacle flowing down the street touching people as it went along and frowned harder. Maybe she should stay, even if it was only for a little while.

"Okay Joe," she replied. "I'll stay for the time being. But you had better start explaining soon and then I want my drugs."

Joe smiled again. She could not help but notice that it was a nice smile.

"Fair enough," he said. "Come through."

He led the way down the hall.

Chapter 18 - Molly

5 years ago

Entering her office, Molly read the sign on the door. It said in bold gold letters Professor Molly Taylor. It always made her smile and feel good inside every time she walked through the door, entering her very own office. She had worked hard all her life for this and finally it had happened. She was Molly Taylor, Professor of Psychology and Philosophy at the department of Experimental Psychology, Oxford University.

As she entered, she asked "Morning Edna, any messages today?"

Her personal assistant looked up from behind her desk. She was an older woman, a paragon of efficiency with meticulous attention to detail.

"Good morning professor." was the reply. She pushed her glasses firmly back up her nose. "You have several messages from some of your students asking for one-on-one sessions. I have referred them to our website meeting request system. You also have one message from a pharmaceutical company requesting your presence at one of their evening events. They would like you to give a talk, but I put them off as per your instructions."

Molly sighed as she walked across the room towards the inner office.

"Well done, Edna, good job as always. Hold my calls for the next hour, will you? I have some important work to do."

She reached the office door, opened it, and stepped through.

"Of course, professor," came Edna's reply.

Molly closed the door and removed her coat. She hung it on the back of the door and stepped across the small room to her desk. She slipped into her chair and looked at her reflection in the powered off monitor. A 31 year old woman with auburn hair looked back at her, brown eyes framed by fashionable glasses and a petite nose. Not bad, she thought as she leaned forward to power on her desktop computer. Once the computer booted up, she set to work and was oblivious to the world around her.

"You can't go in there!" Edna's voice broke through her concentration.

Molly cocked her head to one side, listening, but could only hear murmurings from the other side of the door. She thought that she could hear a male voice. She stood and as she did, her office door opened. A man was framed within the doorway.

"What's going on?" she asked. "Who are you?"

She glimpsed Edna behind the man, stepping from foot to foot as she anxiously looked on.

"I am very sorry professor." she shouted past the man in the doorway. "This man would not listen to me and barged his way in."

Molly's gaze flicked back to the stranger. He was wearing a long dark coat that was open at the front. Underneath were jeans and a dark top that was possibly a T-shirt. He had long blond hair that fell across his face, but Molly could see that he was grinning.

"I need to see you professor," he said.

"But I don't need to see you," replied Molly. "Please leave before I call security."

The stranger's grin widened, and she glimpsed a very blue eye behind the hair.

"No need for that." he replied. "I just want to talk. I need your help. It's about your hobby."

Molly was taken aback. No one knew anything about her hobby - she was very careful to make sure of that. Was he guessing or did he know something? She decided that she needed to find out. She moved her focus back to Edna.

"It's okay Edna, I will handle this. Call me on the intercom in 10 minutes. If I don't reply, call security." She moved her gaze back to the man. "Come in and take a seat."

She waved a hand towards a chair across from her desk and sat back down into her own.

Edna did not look happy. She scowled at the stranger's back.

"Very well professor."

Edna turned and moved back to her desk. The man stepped through the doorway, closing the door behind him. He strode across the room and sat in the indicated chair.

He gathered his coat around his knees and looked around the room. Molly sat patiently. When his eyes returned to Molly, he sighed.

"Thank you for seeing me." he said.

Molly nodded and did not respond. She folded her arms across her chest and waited.

"I'll get straight to it then." he said after a little while, "My name is Joe and as I have already said, I need your help."

"Help with what?" asked Molly.

Joe shuffled in his seat. He seemed unsure of himself, thought Molly.

"I've been tinkering and have come up with something that I think will interest you." He paused waiting for a response. When none came, he continued. "I need your help to develop it further." He paused again. Molly still did not respond. "I believe that you have degrees in psychology and electronics?" he asked.

"What of it?" replied Molly.

"An unusual combination." commented Joe.

"My academic qualifications have nothing to do with you." she replied.

Joe brushed at imaginary dirt on his knee. "True", he replied. He waited for her to reply. When she did not, he sighed again. "Maybe the best thing would be for me to show you."

He reached into his coat pocket with his right hand. Molly stiffened, but Joe held up his left hand. "It's okay," he said. "It's just a small gadget, nothing more."

He pulled out his hand from his pocket clutching a small black box, placing it on the desk.

Molly leaned forward and peered down at it. She observed that it was a small, rectangular black box, about 10 centimetres on the long edge and about half that on the shorter edge. It was also about 4 centimetres deep and it had three gold circles on its upper surface.

"What is it?" she asked.

Joe shrugged. "It doesn't have a name yet," he said.

Molly's curiosity was piqued. "What does it do?" she asked.

"Ah well, that's the thing."

He reached forwards with his right hand and placed three of his fingers on the gold disks. Molly realised that they weren't disks at all; they were electrical contacts.

Joe looked over at a desk lamp. It turned on. Molly jumped in her seat.

"When I am in contact with this device, I can affect things nearby." explained Joe.

Molly looked doubtful. Joe noticed and brought up his left hand. He waved his fingers, the lamp switched on and off several times. Molly stared at the lamp.

"It could just be a faulty connection." she said. Joe moved his fingers again.

The desktop PC turned off, its fans whining down. Then a heavy textbook slid sideways across the desk and fell onto the floor with a loud thump.

Molly's jaw dropped as she gasped. Joe removed his fingers from the device.

"When I'm not touching the contacts, I can't do it."

Molly looked at Joe. "Are you telling me that you can affect the physical world with your mind with the aid of this device?"

"Just so." smiled Joe.

Molly sat back in her chair. She stared at Joe. She said nothing for a long while. Then she said, "how does it work?"

"Well, I think I have the basics nailed down." replied Joe. "It's something that I've been messing with for a while." He drew a quick breath. "I'm ready to move to the next stage, but I need your help."

Molly understood. She now knew why Joe had referred to her hobby. It was a perfect fit. The thing that she had kept hidden, had been investigating and researching for years, had just been proven by Joe's demonstration. She had always been fascinated by the paranormal. But it was seen as un-scientific and was touted by scammers, charlatans and conspiracists. But Molly believed that there was some truth behind some of the stories and claims. This was something she realised that she had to keep quiet. If it became known that she was a believer in things like telepathy, telekinesis or ghosts, she would lose her job. And that was something that must not happen.

"How exactly do you need my help?" she asked.

Joe leaned forward. "This device," he picked it up and held it out to her, "interfaces with the mind and gives the user abilities. Abilities such as communicating mind to mind, the movement of objects and the projection of energies. There is nothing like it. It is unique. I want to modify this box." He dropped it into Molly's outstretched hand. "I want to make it into a wearable device so it can interface permanently with the wearer."

Molly turned the box around in her hands. She laid it on the desk. Hesitantly, she touched three fingers to the three contacts.

"Will it work for me?" she asked.

"Go ahead, try." replied Joe, "I've tried it out on others without any success."

Molly pressed her fingers to the contacts, looked at the lamp and concentrated. Nothing happened.

"Told you." said Joe.

As soon as he said those two, slightly gloating words, the lamp exploded, and the desk phone rang.

Both Joe and Molly were startled. They both sat staring at the lamp, the phone continued to ring. Molly reached and picked up the handset without looking away from the lamp.

"Yes?" she asked mechanically. Continuing to look at the lamp, she listened to Edna speaking into the phone. After a short while she said, "No, everything is fine. Don't call security. Clear all of my appointments for the rest of the week. I'm going away for a few days. Yes, that's right."

She replaced the handset and looked over at Joe.

"I'm in." she said.

She never returned to her office or the university again.

Chapter 19 - Good News

The watcher observed the two of them as they walked through the town. He saw them stop and talk for a while and then move on. They made a strange couple, he thought. Both filthy, dressed in thick, largely black clothes, the girl with matted, long black hair and the man with long blond hair.

There was a strange dynamic between them. The girl often trailed behind, sometimes as much as 6 metres. They both occasionally weaved a little, as though they were drunk.

Soon, he was following them into a residential area. It became more difficult to follow without being noticed because there were fewer people around. But it was not a problem for the watcher. He was a professional, and well experienced in this sort of work. It was easy anyway; neither of them looked around. They were both oblivious to their surroundings. Hiding behind cars, he continued to watch.

Then something happened that was very strange. He noticed that the man suddenly started to walk with more purpose, and adjusted his posture, walking taller and straighter. Shortly afterwards, they both entered one of the flat doors.

How odd, he thought. He waited until they had entered, then removed his cell phone from his pocket and dialled a number.

Jim was distraught. His plan had failed. He had achieved nothing and worse, he had barely escaped with his life. He slumped over his work bench, his head in his hands. What a disaster! He had planned on levelling the building, on killing everyone in sight, including his hated brother, Joe. Instead, he had discovered that he was not the only one with talent. That damned brother of his had been busy. That red armoured suit was no ordinary suit. It was like his, only better, much better. He hated to admit it, but he had been out gunned and out classed. What was he going to do next?

He was startled when his phone rang. He ignored it for a while, wallowing in his self-pity. After a while he picked it up.

"Yes?" he answered with a sigh.

He listened as the person on the other end of the line identified themselves, then he spoke, "I hope you have good news for me, Mr Thompson. It has not been a good day today. What have you found out?"

As Jim listened to the reply, he suddenly sat up excitedly. "Yes, of course I want the address you idiot! Give it to me now."

He scribbled down the address on a scrap of paper. "You have done very well, Mr Thompson. This is excellent news. I will transfer your final payment today. I no longer need your services." He put down the phone.

He smiled to himself. Joe! He had found him at last! Forget the building. Joe was never in there in the first place; he was downtown all the time! And even better, Joe was on his own! Well, with some girl, but she didn't count. What fantastic news! He stood up. Time to recharge and get his suit in order for another trip. Joe was about to receive a visitor.

Chapter 20 - The Flat

Joe had walked into the flat and left her in the lounge. Kate walked around the room. It was clearly masculine. Simple furniture, all plain and neutral colours. No floral prints or ornaments. She found herself strangely pleased that there was no hint of a feminine influence of any kind. She stopped and frowned. What was she thinking? She had been virtually kidnapped by this stranger. She definitely had no thoughts of a romantic nature. She just needed to get some drugs and then she was out of here, she told herself.

A large flat panel TV dominated one wall with the usual electronic equipment underneath it with two comfortable chairs facing it. Another wall was completely covered in books. A phone stood to attention in a sound system dock. A large window on another wall viewed the street.

She wandered around the room and explored. A door off the disorientating corridor opened into a bedroom. She peered in and saw a large double bed, a wardrobe and bedside table with an electronic clock flashing. There was a kitchen in another room, full of the usual kitchen stuff. Her eyes momentarily held on a knife block, and she had to fight the memories from surging. Closing her eyes, she concentrated on not thinking and this time she was successful. The blackness receded and she breathed a sigh of relief.

Other rooms included a guest bedroom and an office. The office was the only room that was cluttered. A large desk held two of the largest computer monitors she had ever seen, along with the usual keyboard and mouse. Another wall was filled floor to ceiling with yet more books, and a coffee machine sat on a small table in a corner.

As she explored, she heard running water. The one room she had not yet seen was occupied by Joe. He was clearly taking a shower.

Joe. It was a nice name, she decided, he suited it.

Wait! There she was again! What was she thinking? She knew nothing about this man called Joe. She must remain objective. The memories flooded through her mind again. Memories that she did her utmost to forget but could not. Pain and misery ripped through her heart. Shaking, she once again banished them.

Only one thing helped her when this happened. Drugs! Where was his money? Maybe things would turn out not to be so bad after all. If she could find some money, she could steal it and do a runner. Frantically, she started to look around the desk and in the drawers. Money would buy her drugs and alcohol. She found herself longing for the blackness and forgetfulness that the drugs gave her.

It was at that moment that it all crystalised in her mind. She had had enough. She was tired and was too clear minded. The memories kept coming back and she could not stop them. She had been dragged across town by a complete stranger and seen things she did not understand. There was no telling what was going to happen next. She decided that she was not going to be around to find out. After she found his money she would leave, visit her dealer on the way back to the squat and would be back in that drug induced haze where she belonged.

Maybe Joe was a good guy, maybe not. Either way, it didn't matter. Joe could go fuck himself, she decided as she pulled open a drawer and saw a very, very, fat wallet.

She smiled. At last, something was going right.

The wallet was stuffed with notes. There was no way of knowing how much there was, but Kate knew there was a hell of a lot. She closed the wallet and held it against her chest. She would have to be very careful. If anyone found out that she had this much cash, it would be taken from her. She was not strong enough to keep hold of it if anyone decided to take it. She would need to make sure that no one saw it. The dealers were the worst. If they thought you had more money, they would first try to sell you more drugs. If that failed, they would give a mate the nod and she would find herself face to face with another gang.

"That feels so much better," said Joe.

Startled, Kate spun around. As she did, the wallet slipped from her hand and flew across the room. It fell at Joe's feet with a slap sound. Joe looked down. He sighed.

"You don't need this," he said quietly.

"What the hell do you know? You don't know me, you don't know a single thing about me and my life," she spat.

There was a moment of silence as they stared at each other. She with defiant sparkling eyes, and her chin up in the air, he with his bright, almost luminous blue eyes looking sad.

"I know more than you think," he replied. "I know that you were addicted to drugs and that you have been hiding. And that you have a dark secret in your past that you don't want anyone to know about."

She was speechless once again. This was getting to be a habit. He was always surprising her. She flushed and looked down at her feet.

"It's none of your business," she paused. "I want to leave."

He looked at her in his strange, piercing way.

"Running away again?" he asked. "It's not the answer. And in any case, you should stay here for a while. You'll be safe here."

She bristled with anger. "I am not running away!" she retorted. "I don't want to stay anymore. I need to leave. You promised."

There was silence once again, until Joe broke it, "Kate, you don't have anywhere to go. You need to stay here, at least for a little while." He paused. "Look, I know I promised to get you drugs and I will keep my promise. I'll try and keep the 'funny' stuff to a minimum. I won't mess you about and I won't ask any difficult questions. But I really, really need you to stay here for a little while at least."

She calmed down somewhat at his speech. What did he want? What was all this about? Why did he need her to stay? Just what the hell was going on? She thought about it. The memories flooded up again. Memories she wanted to forget. Inside, she wailed. Where was the comforting blackness? Where was the mind-numbing blankness that kept the memories away? With an effort she pushed them away and held herself together once more.

"I'll stay if you can get me some smack right now."

She looked at him defiantly. She was getting desperate, she needed the comforting forgetfulness that only drugs could give her.

"You don't need drugs anymore," he replied softly.

"You haven't got the first fucking clue,." she spat at him again. "I need them now. If you don't get them for me, I'm leaving."

Their eyes locked again.

"Okay," he said resignedly. "I'll sort something out. Can I get dressed first?"

She suddenly noticed that he was standing in the doorway clad in a single towel around his waist. Her eyes lingered over his chest as they travelled down to his feet. He had some sort of jewellery on his left foot. She frowned. She had never seen jewellery on a foot before. Her gaze lifted to the towel. She couldn't help noticing his naked chest, not to mention the bulge at the front of the towel. She flushed again and looked away.

"Sure," she stammered a reply. "Get dressed but make it snappy."

He turned away and entered the bedroom. Her gaze flicked to the wallet he had left on the floor. What was the matter with this man? Did he want her to steal his money? She walked over and picked it up. Looking through it again, she pulled out a few notes and stuffed them into her bra over her left breast. Then she walked back over to the desk and returned the wallet where she had found it. She left the office and walked into the lounge and sat in an extremely comfortable easy chair and waited.

As she waited, she thought that she could hear voices. She cocked her head to one side and listened intently. She had not seen anyone else. Maybe it was the radio? She got up and approached the bedroom doorway. The door was pushed to but not closed. She crept up to it and placed her ear close to the door jam.

"I'm fine, stop worrying. I'll be back soon," there was a pause.

"It's good to feel you again too Sammy. I had forgotten how good it felt." There was another pause. "No, I'm fine now. Not back up to full strength yet but getting there. How are things?"

He must be speaking on the phone, she realised. The bastard was calling the police, or friends or someone. He was going to turn her in! She swore under her breath and put her hand to her left breast, feeling the cash hidden there. What was it he had said? 'It was good to feel you?' What the fuck? She crept forward and put her eye to the crack between the door and the door frame.

"Yes, I'll be coming in soon. Give me some time. I've found someone." Pause. "Well, I think that she is a natural. She seems to be able to tune in using my Assist." Pause. "Yes, I'll take it easy on her. No, I won't frighten her." Pause. "Look, I'll talk later. I have a situation right now that I need to sort out." Pause. "Yes, it is to do with her, nothing I can't handle." Pause. "No, I don't need any help. Let me talk to you later and I'll tell you all about her."

She could not believe what she saw. He was lying on the large double bed, completely naked, arms behind his head and staring up at the ceiling. He was talking into the air. At first, she could not take her eyes off his groin. Her eyes flickered up and down his body. Then she realised what was strange. He had no phone! He was talking to the air!

She watched him get up from the bed and walk over to the wardrobe and start to select clothes. She slinked away from the door back into the lounge. She walked over to the window and stared out.

The blackness closed in around her mind. She still had no idea what was going on and she was still in this stranger's home. Things were out of control and had been since she had first met Joe. But at least she had a get out clause. She thought of the money she had stolen. All she had to do was get out of here. She felt a moment's guilt. That in itself was strange. She had not felt such an emotion for many, many years. She stifled it quickly. She must not get involved. She had to get away. She drew in a breath and spun around, ready to make a run for it. But stopped suddenly when she saw a fully dressed Joe studying her from the bedroom doorway.

Chapter 21 - Explanation?

"Going somewhere?" asked Joe.

Kate hesitated.

"No need to answer," he continued. "I already know."

He entered the lounge and flopped into a chair. He wore a loose shirt and jeans. His hair was still damp, and his feet were bare. She clearly saw the rings on the toes of his left foot as well as those on his right hand.

"You were going to get out, right? Not going to wait for your drugs?"

She stood still and did not answer.

"Look," he said. "I know how you must feel. You have no idea what's going on and these strange things keep happening. You feel that things are running away from you and that you are out of control. Your first instinct is to run. And on top of all that, you are confused because you find your body is no longer craving for your drugs. And that confuses you more, because until now, the drugs were your friend. And now you don't need them. And another thing is that your mind is now much clearer than before, and I am sure that you are having problems with those memories. Am I right?"

She stared at him, open mouthed. How could he know all that stuff?

"I... I..." She could not form words.

"The thing is, Kate, you don't need to worry about that. You don't need the drugs anymore. I cured you of that. You don't need to escape because you are safe here." He smiled at her.

She remained dumbfounded.

"I know you must have some pretty horrible memories you are dealing with. Why else would you be where you were when we found each other? But Kate, you don't need the drugs to deal with them. You're strong enough to handle it. You're stronger than you realise."

Another wave of blackness threatened to overwhelm her. Memories, horrible memories flooded forward. Tears fell from her eyes.

"I can't ..." she whispered. "Please, I need something to help me."

Joe rose from his chair and walked over to her. "It's okay, Kate. Don't panic. I'm here for you. It's going to be okay" He put his arm around her.

She found herself leaning into him. She moaned quietly. The horror and the darkness closing in all around her. She shut her eyes and gave in to it, spiralling down and down into its depths.

―――

Sometime later, she came back to the surface. Her first recollection was Joe's scent. She breathed it in deeply, savouring it. He smelled of shampoo, soap, and something indefinable that was clearly masculine. She felt him holding her and stroking her hair. He was mumbling something indecipherable about 'everything was going to be okay. And it was. She felt calm and relaxed, and let her arms wrap around him holding him tightly. It felt good.

A little while later she became uncomfortable with the closeness, and she pulled away.

He held onto her and smiled. "Better?" he asked.

She nodded.

"How about a warm, relaxing bath?" he suggested. He held up his hand to quiet her. "Don't worry, I'll give you some space." He wrinkled his nose. "I don't want to be personal, but I think you could use it as much as I needed it." He grinned to put her at her ease.

She looked up into his eyes and saw nothing but humour and concern. She nodded once again. He led her to the bathroom, pushed her inside, and shut the door behind her.

She felt emotionally drained and weak, but relaxed. For now, at least, the blackness had gone away. She looked around. The bathroom was spotless - all white and mirrors. The thought of a hot bath suddenly became very attractive. She inserted the bath plug and turned on the taps. As the hot water splashed and the steam rose, she slowly began to remove her clothes.

———

Later she was squeaky clean and dry, but naked. She looked at her discarded clothes in the corner. She could not put them back on. They were dirty and smelly. After all, she had been wearing them for weeks. She opened the bathroom door and peeked around intending to shout out and ask if Joe had any spare clothes. But as she did, she noticed a small pile of clothes just outside the door. She smiled, knelt and quickly grabbed them without opening the door any wider.

Once inside, she pulled them on quickly. There were jeans, T-shirt, socks, and some trainers that were too big for her. Clearly, they were his. But they felt comfortable and clean. She ran her hands over them. These were his clothes. They felt nice.

Dressed, she left the bathroom and approached the lounge. As she neared, she could hear him talking once again. But this time she could hear other voices. A man and a woman. It almost sounded like a party, there was laughing and giggling. She frowned. How long had she been in the bath? Had others come to visit?

She could not make out what the voices were saying, so she moved closer to the lounge door. When she reached it, she put her ear to it.

She could hear Joe's voice clearly, but the others were indistinct and sounded far away, which seemed strange.

"What have you guys been up to?" she heard Joe ask.

There was a faint, distant reply. "It's bad out here, Joe," replied a female voice. "Me and Mike are on R&R. Would you like to join us?" There was more laughter as her voice turned huskier.

Kate felt hot and flushed as she heard a groan from a man that was clearly not Joe. She could hear the woman breathing heavily. What the fuck was going on? It sounded like they were having sex!

"Sorry guys," replied Joe. "Not this time, I have a visitor."

The woman replied with a breathy, low voice. "That's okay, Joe. They can join too."

"Yeah," said the distant male voice. "Let's have some fun."

Fuck! They were talking about an orgy with her joining in! She was incensed. How dare he? The arrogance of the man. She burst into the lounge to confront them all. And was shocked to see just Joe lounging in a chair.

"What?" she exclaimed. "Where is everybody? I heard voices."

Joe looked at her. "You heard us?" he asked, a frown covering his face.

"Damn right I heard you," she exclaimed. "And I didn't like what I heard!" She span around when she heard a chuckle somewhere in the room. "What the fuck is going on? More bloody tricks I expect. You had better start talking fast, mister."

Joe sat up and leaned forward. "It's not what you think Kate. It's all fine. Let me explain. Sit down and I'll tell you everything." He glanced upwards. "And you guys, can it for now, but stay near. I might need your help."

As she sat, Kate heard more laughter and giggling.

"No problem, Joe," replied the breathy female.

"Yeah, no problem, Joe," echoed the male voice. "We'll be here for you as always."

Kate looked around again. The room was completely empty. Where were the voices coming from? They seemed to come from the air, from nowhere! It just wasn't possible. She faced Joe and waited.

Joe sat back. "Some of what I am going to tell you is going to sound strange and even impossible. What I can tell you is that it is all true." He paused and looked at her. "Okay here goes." He stopped, looked at her again and took a deep breath.

"I am what is called an Assisted telepath. What that means is that I use a device to boost my abilities." He held up his right hand. She saw the rings sparkling on his fingers. "I work for a group called the Alliance. Well, actually, I started it all about five years ago." He looked vaguely embarrassed. "The Alliance is at war. It's not a nice place out there, Kate." He gestured expansively. "When we first made contact, we were all ecstatic. And then it all started." He stopped.

Kate sat perfectly still. "What started, Joe?" she asked.

"The war. At first, we thought it was a mistake. People went missing. We thought it was something to do with the technology or a planet's native fauna. We are at war. But the stupid thing is we don't know why. We have tried to contact the enemy, whoever the hell they are. Nothing. They just don't want to know. We are holding our own, barely, but we can't keep it up. Pretty soon, we are going to lose. And when we do, all of this," he waved his arms around again, "all of this will be gone."

He stopped again. Kate was still unmoving. She said nothing.

"Of course, you don't believe any of this. Why should you? But I can prove it."

He held up his right hand again. He wriggled his fingers as blue crackling sparks danced up and down each finger. He turned and pointed a forefinger at the phone sitting in its dock. It turned on and music filled the room.

Kate had been about to laugh. Who was he kidding? Telepathy was science fiction stuff, she knew that. He was just spinning some bullshit yarn, trying to fob her off with some made up story. Then he wriggled his fingers and that all changed. Could there be some truth to what he was saying?

She opened her mouth to say something and then closed it. What if it was true? Could this be an explanation? Did it make sense?

Joe waved at the phone again and the music stopped. "Mike, Sammy, you still tuned in?"

A man's laughter filled the room. Kate looked around wildly. She could see nothing. "Of course we are, Joe," said the male voice.

"Stop that, Mike," said the female voice. "This is important." There was a pause.

"Kate, I'm Sammy. It's nice to meet you."

Kate sat open mouthed. She could not say anything.

"I know that it's hard to believe what Joe just told you, but I can assure you that it is all true. I thought the same as you before Joe found me and Mike. Let me show you."

Kate was suddenly frightened. Her eyes widened and she began to say, "No, I don't want you to show me anything….," when she started to feel something.

She felt the air grow warm and movement near her. Startled, she jumped and looked around again. There was nothing to be seen. But she could feel breath on her neck and could hear breathing. When she blinked, it was worse. With her eyes closed she could see things. She saw a body in dim light. It was a naked body of a man. A man who was moving very close and was very obviously aroused. She snapped her eyes open, but the view didn't go away! Along with the sensations, there was something else. She felt a thrill of arousal course through her veins, but it was alien. It was not her own arousal that she felt. It was someone else's!

"Stop playing guys" Joe spoke up. "That's not fair on Kate." He walked up to her and put his arm around her shoulders. "That's enough for now. I can handle it from here."

As soon as Joe touched her, all the sensations melted away. Giggling, laughing, and goodbyes melted into the air as the voices faded. Kate sagged into Joe. She couldn't take any more of this. It was all too much.

"Joe, I don't know what's happening," she said as she lifted her head to look into his electric blue eyes. "It's all too much for me. You scare me. I don't understand any of what is going on. Please, let me go," she pleaded.

Joe stared back into her eyes.

"Just give me money or the drugs so I can go back to where I belong," she wailed. "I can't take any more of this." Tears ran down her cheeks.

Joe realised that he had gone too far and kicked himself mentally. Of all the stupid things to do, introducing Kate to Mike and Sammy was a huge mistake. He was amazed that she could hear them. She clearly had an exceptional talent. And now he was going to lose her. What an idiot!

It was a full minute before he replied. "Kate, I don't want you to go."

She sobbed and dropped her chin onto her chest.

"Please don't cry. I'm really sorry I frightened you."

"I need to go.." said Kate through her sobs.

He had lost her. This amazing, talented, and beautiful girl that had somehow rescued him was going to leave him. He released her and stepped back.

"Okay, I understand. I know this is hard for you," he said with a shaky voice. "I won't stop you from leaving, if that's what you want to do."

He walked into the office and came out with a wad of notes clutched in his hand. He passed them to her and struggled to swallow the lump in his throat as she turned and shuffled out of the lounge, her shoulders still shaking with her sobbing.

Chapter 22 - Attack

Jim was over the moon. This was one of the happiest moments of his life. He took some time to savour it. After all, there weren't many of them anymore. Not since the car crash when he was 15. This is what he had been working for. All of his life, his damn brother had the upper hand. All of his life his brother had always been first, always the best. Well, not anymore. This time he had him. This time he was going to erase his brother from the face of the Earth! He had finally found him. And he was unprotected! It was a gift.

Wearing his suit, now fully charged, and with a silly grin plastered all over his face, he strode up to the door. He didn't bother knocking. Instead, he giggled as he brought up the tube and pressed the firing stud.

The howling blast of Silver Force sliced through the door like butter. Moving it around the frame he vapourised enough of it to allow him to walk through. The wooden frame burst into flames, around the entranceway which roared up the front of the building, even the brickwork was catching fire, as it was coated in black scorch marks and soot.

Kate was just entering the hallway when suddenly there was a loud crash, accompanied by an intense smell of burning. The door burst into a shower of sparks and flaming splinters of plastic and metal, which splattered onto the hallway floor.

Through the flaming doorway she saw a figure. As the smoke cleared and the figure stepped forward, she gasped in shock. It wasn't the fact that it resolved into a man who stood framed in the burning doorway. Or that he was covered in a mesh of wires, cables and glowing crystals, brandishing a metal tube. No, it was the fact that behind his manic grin, the man had the same eyes, the same build, and features as Joe. If she hadn't just left Joe in the lounge behind her, she would have sworn that he now stood in front of her, he even had the same long blond hair.

For a second their eyes locked. Then the man raised the metal tube to point directly at her.

"What the fu...!" she started to say, as Joe dived past her, pushing her backward holding up his left hand to deflect the beam aimed at Kate. She fell onto her backside hard, as the beam hit Joe's hand. She heard Joe scream in pain as the beam was deflected into scintillating shards to rebound and reflect up and down the tiny space. Rolling onto her stomach, she crawled forward and away from the screaming and noise with all of the speed she could muster. Up ahead was the door to the lounge. She shuffled into it as fast as she could and kicked the door closed. What the fuck was going on now?

She rolled onto her back and lay panting, her heart pounding inside her rib cage. She fought to calm herself and stop the panic rising in her chest as the adrenaline coursed through her veins. Fear threatened to takeover. She wanted to find a dark corner and curl up into a ball, just as she often did when taking the drugs.

The screaming and crashing from behind the door brought her to her senses. Joe! Could she hide here while Joe was being murdered? And just who was that look-a-like in the doorway? She looked wildly about the room. Maybe she could find something that could help.

Joe was a very strange man, but she could not deny that there was a connection between the two of them. From the first time they had met, he had been full of surprises, and a strangeness seemed to surround him. But as she lay there on the floor, she found herself admitting that she had feelings for him. Emotions that she had not experienced in years flooded forwards and tears ran down her cheeks. No. She could not run and hide. She had to help Joe if she could.

Jim was frustrated. It seemed that killing Joe was not as easy as it should have been. Yes, he had him trapped, but he turned out to be a slippery target. Again and again, he flashed Silver Force at Joe, and again and again Joe managed to dodge the lethal beam. It was like trying to catch a fish with his bare hands; near on impossible to do.

Joe realised that he was in trouble. He had known that his twin brother was mentally unstable, but never had he thought that he would try to kill him. He did not run and did not attack. He had to stand his ground in order to protect Kate. There was no way he could let Jim get any further into the house. He could not put her life at risk. And so, he stood firm, when he knew he could not win.

He had seen straight away that Jim was wearing some form of protective suit and was firing an energy weapon at him. There was not much Joe could do; he was defenceless. Desperately, he sent out a call to Alliance members for help. He was not sure if his call would be answered because he heard no reply. There was too much Psionic interference from Jim's energy weapon. He cried out in pain as once again the energy beam grazed an arm and spun him off balance. As he fell, he did the only thing he could think of. Rolling towards the corridor wall, he held out his right hand and invoked the command for his Assist to carry out. His form flickered, and in the blink of an eye, he disappeared.

Kate ran into the adjoining kitchen, looking around for something, anything that she could use as a weapon. As she scanned the room, her eyes alighted on the knife block. She hesitated as the memories threatened to take her again, but she pushed them back, stepped forward and grabbed the largest knife. She turned quickly and ran back towards the door. Maybe she was being stupid, but she simply could not run and hide like a frightened girl while Joe was killed. Gripping the door handle she drew in a breath and pulled the door open.

Jim gasped. Joe was gone! Had he got him? Had he vapourised him with Silver Force? He stopped firing and looked around carefully. Joe was tricky. Had he really got him? He would have to make sure. He stepped forward into the hallway, tracking the Silver Force weapon backwards and forwards. The corridor was practically destroyed, its walls blackened and smoking, strips of yellow metal exposed inside the walls, some melted and drooping downwards towards the floor. Black, thick smoke roiled at the ceiling and globs of hot plastic dripped down. Jim ignored it all. He was fully protected; heat and fire could not penetrate his screens. As he walked forwards, he could see nothing of Joe. Strange, he thought, and was just thinking that maybe he had killed him after all when he saw a door open.

Joe was still in the corridor. His final tactic had been to render himself invisible. Even though he knew he would not be able to hold it for long, he prayed it would be long enough. And it seemed to be working. Jim looked puzzled and had stopped firing. Joe watched as Jim stepped forward, peering around. He was just thinking that it was going to work when he saw the lounge door open. Kate stood there. Eyes wide open and a kitchen knife in her hand. Horrified, he saw that Jim had seen the door open and watched helplessly as Jim raised his energy weapon.

"Get back!" shouted Joe.

He could not let Jim kill Kate. Risking his life, he let his invisibility shield drop. Jim spun round, a wild look of glee in his face.

"Joe!" he spat. "Now I have you, no more tricks. You're dead, you're history. You'll never be better than me anymore!" He raised his arm and brandished Silver Force. "Say goodbye, you freak!" he screamed.

Joe could do nothing. He just lay on the floor and looked up at Jim sadly and waited for the end to come.

Suddenly Jim froze. His eyes widened and his mouth opened. He gulped like a fish and dropped his weapon. Joe looked on as Jim fell to his knees and toppled forward onto his face.

Behind Jim, Kate stood frozen, a look of horror plastered on her face as she focussed on the bloody knife she held in her hand. Over the crackling of flames, burning plastic and falling debris, the blood from the knife could be heard splattering onto the floor.

Kate's gaze flicked from the knife and locked with Joe's. They stared over Jim's body into each other's eyes. It was at that moment that something passed between them. Some emotion. Some 'thing', some connection.

"Kate," said Joe, getting up from the floor.

His clothes were reduced to burnt rags and were hanging off him, and burns covered his exposed flesh.

"Joe," said Kate. She did not move, but lowered the knife, blood still dripping from the blade. "What just happened?" She looked down at Jim's body and then looked back up at Joe. "Please tell me I didn't kill him." Tears streaked down her face.

"Kate," said Joe again. He reached her and took her into his arms. "It's alright, you had no choice."

"But, but.." she blubbered. "I killed him." She looked up into Joe's eyes. "Please, make it right. I can't go through that again.." Her voice shook as she sobbed. "I didn't mean to. I didn't want to. I can't....." She held her hands up to her head. "Noooo..." she screamed. "Not again."

She collapsed against him, moaning in pain and despair. Joe was taken aback. What was wrong with her?

THUMP. THUMP. Two very loud and earth rumbling bangs. He looked around and saw two Alliance troopers in full armour appear in the now very crowded corridor. The two instantly took in the situation and flanked Joe and Kate, weapons drawn.

"*Sorry we're late sir,*" said one into his mind. "*Just stay still, and calm. A full unit is on its way.*"

"*About time!*" was Joe's angry thought. "*The danger is over, check Jim, and douse these flames.*" He gestured towards the walls. "*And get a medic in here.*"

He then pulled Kate with him into the lounge and slammed the door shut with his foot. Once inside, he gently sat her in a chair and squatted down at her feet, wincing at the pain of the burns on his side and legs. He took her hands gingerly into his, ignoring the pain, and asked, "Kate, what's the problem? What's wrong?"

Kate was shaking uncontrollably, her slim frame racked with sobbing. "Oh, Joe," she cried. "I killed him!" She pulled her hands from his and hid her face. "But it's not the first time!" She continued sobbing.

"What do you mean?" asked Joe. He gently pulled her hands away from her face and cradled her head in his own hands.

She looked at him with tears running down her face. "Joe," she sobbed. "I'm not right in the head. I'm...." She stopped and looked deep into his eyes. "I'm a murderer! I've killed before!"

She broke down completely, wailing, rocking backwards and forwards, as the blackness consumed her once again.

Chapter 23 - Communion

Joe cradled Kate's head in his arms. His thoughts were in a turmoil. There must be some rational explanation, although he struggled to understand what that could be. Was she really a murderer? How could that be? He refused to accept it. He pushed through his Assist and soothed her with calm thoughts and mentally stroked her internal wailing. Shortly, her sobbing calmed, and she slumped into his arms.

A HAZPRO thumped into the room, ducking, and moving sideways to get through the doorway. *"We are secured, sir. Medics are on the way."*

Joe did not look up. He held Kate close

"Good. Is Jim...?" He could not finish his question.

The suited figure stood immobile, like a statue, but the head moved downwards, the exo-muscles whining as it moved to look at Joe.

"No sir, your brother is still alive, but needs urgent medical attention. We will transport him to the Complex as soon as the medics have checked him over."

Joe sighed in relief, he felt sorry for him. He was not mentally stable, and for some reason known only to himself, had been trying to kill Joe for the last 5 years. He was relieved for Kate's sake that she had not killed him.

"Thanks," he replied. *"Update the team back at the Complex and keep this place secure."*

The suited figure did not reply. It thumped away, the floor shaking as it went.

Joe turned his attention back to Kate. He had good news to tell her, but she was out of it for now, back in her black pit of despair. Also, he had to find out what was going on. Of course, he knew of her drug and alcohol addiction. That had easily been cured. He knew that she was running away from something terrible. He had sensed all of that quite easily, he had not probed deeper. That was something that usually was not done without permission. It could easily be seen as an invasion of privacy. Should he do it? He felt so sorry and sad for her and was desperate to help her. Whatever was going on inside her head certainly took its toll. The poor girl was in a bad way. And besides, he knew there was a connection, he knew that she felt it too. But something was in the way and that something would have to be removed.

He picked her up in his arms and carried her into the bedroom. There, he lay her on the bed.

He studied her. She was a beauty. Now that she was cleaned up, he could see the girl underneath the dirt and grime. She was slim, with raven black hair that framed her delicate and quite beautiful features. Kneeling by the bedside he placed his hand on her forehead, as he did so her eyes flickered open.

Kate opened her eyes. She felt his hand on her forehead. It felt warm and soothing. She could feel the warmer rings on fingers, with chains slightly tickling her cheek. A tear escaped the corner of one eye and trickled downwards as she turned her head and looked directly into Joe's eyes.

"Joe," she whispered.

He smiled back at her. "Hush," he said. "It's fine, you didn't kill Jim. He's still alive. The medics are on the way."

She closed her eyes and breathed out slowly. "Thank god," she whispered.

Another trickle of a tear appeared to run down her cheek onto the pillow. Joe held her face and bent closer over her. He studied her scrubbed clean face, her long hair was still knotted and tangled and had clearly not seen a brush for a very long time, but it was clean.

He could feel the connection. It was something that he had never felt before. It was real, he was sure of it. Just a few hours ago they had met in the back streets of Oxford and ever since then they had been together, although not always willingly on her behalf. He had cajoled her and persuaded her to stay and now he knew why. But he also knew that he had to be careful. He had her too far once already; she had been about to walk out. He mustn't do that again.

"You're safe," he whispered, his face just inches from hers. "The danger is over."

Her eyes flickered open, and she gave him a small sad smile. "It's too late Joe. It already happened." She closed her eyes again, more tears sliding down her cheeks. "I am so glad I didn't kill that man, but it doesn't matter. I don't deserve your good thoughts. Please, take me back where you found me and leave me there. I'm not worth it." She said this quickly without opening her eyes, her voice trembling slightly.

Joe sighed. He had to do something. He couldn't leave her like this. She was beautiful, amazing, talented and she had just saved his life.

"You saved me," he wiped a tear away with his finger. "You can't be that bad. I don't care what you think you've done. I just know one thing." He drew a breath. "There is a connection between us."

"You know nothing about me!" she exclaimed. "You dragged me here to this place, and all hell breaks loose. You show me parasite things" She shuddered as she remembered the coiling, roiling thing floating down the street. "You talk to people who aren't there and people who are even having sex, for god's sake!" She pushed his hands away and sat up. Her tone hardened. "I already told you; you scare me I don't know what's going on. And you talk about a connection" She pushed him away.

She was angry. Anger was good. Anger stopped her from thinking. Anger would help her through this.

Joe's heart sank. He couldn't lose her, he just couldn't. He shuffled back on the bed.

"I'm sorry. Things have moved far too fast for both of us." He looked away. "I don't know what to say to make you feel better and make you want to stay. All I can say is that you should stay and give it a chance. Let me show you what this is all about. Let me explain what's going on. And then, if you really want to leave, no one will stop you. I promise."

Her anger evaporated as quickly as it had come. She could see that he was trying hard. She sighed.

"I'm not worth it Joe. I'm damaged goods. It won't work. I'll more than disappoint you. I'll break things, I'll smash things, I'll argue. I'll do stupid things, I'll say stupid things. I'll do anything to prove that I am everything that's bad in a person. I am fundamentally flawed, horrible and nasty." As she spoke, her voice got quieter. "I deserve to be where you found me," she whispered.

Joe took both of her hands in his. "No, you deserve to be here. Will you trust me?"

Kate shuddered. She found that she wanted this, an end to the interminable loneliness and the endless fear, but she also knew what would happen. All of what she had said was true, she knew. It would all end in disaster and it would all be her fault, just as it had been all of the other times. She found herself longing for the blackness of not remembering, the dark that removed her memories. Because if she allowed them to surface, she would drown in them. She would be dragged under, and the pain would be unbearable.

"I don't know, Joe. I'm barely holding it together. I don't think that I can function without the drugs."

"I could help with that,' said Joe. "I know that there is something in your past that is hurting you and I'm not asking you to tell me anything." He held up his hand as if to push something back. "I can give you a block that will stop you from remembering."

Kate started to tremble as if cold. "Anything is better than remembering," she whispered her head down and face obscured by her cascading hair.

Joe knew that he wouldn't get a second chance and didn't hesitate. He laid his hand on her head again and closed his eyes. The two of them were as still as statues, neither moved, both with heads down and eyes closed.

Chapter 24 - Captured

Jim seethed. He had been so close! And somehow it had all gone wrong again. He had found Joe, stormed in and nearly killed him. That girl had stabbed him in the back! If he ever got out of here, he was going to kill her too. The bitch! Yes, she was definitely added to the list. He had been so focussed on Joe that he had forgotten the girl. Well, he wouldn't make that mistake again. Next time, he would be more careful. He would creep and skulk. Maybe use the invisibility screen at the start and then use Silver Force to cut Joe and the girl in half. He smiled at that thought, chuckling to himself.

He would have to do some more work on his suit too. It had been too flimsy and, although he hated to admit it, he had been outclassed by that big bulky red armoured thing when he attacked that building. His smile faded. Yes, he had a lot more work to do. But first, he had to get out of here.

He tried once again to raise his arms. He merely succeeded in rattling his cuffs. He was fastened down to a hospital bed by handcuffs attached to both wrists. He raged against his restraints, banging his head up and down on the pillow. He pulled at the handcuffs until the pain stopped him, blood trickling onto the floor from the broken skin on his wrists. He screamed and shouted and spat, spittle running down his chin as his screams turned into animal grunts and growls.

He could not get free. His wild eyes roamed about the room desperately trying to find a way out. There was nothing. He was alone in a stark white medical room. The door was shut. On his left, along the entire wall of the room was a low bench with shelves above it. The shelves were filled with all sorts of medical equipment, most of which were in boxes. On his right, there was a medical trolley.

He thrashed his head from side to side, spittle flying across the room. He screamed once again, and then lay back panting, trying to calm his seething rage so that he could think.

As he lay there, he let his head fall to the right, his eyes settled on the trolley. He noted the medical instruments. He was suddenly still, and the corners of his mouth rose in a rictus smile.

Chapter 25 - The Complex

Kate drifted to consciousness slowly.

She had no idea where she was and was completely disorientated for a while, and then realised that the sounds and smells could mean only one thing; she was in a car. Opening her eyes, she saw that she was lying on the back seat. All she could see was the back of the black leather seat in front of her and she could feel that the car was in motion as she was rocked back and forth gently. She found the motion was soothing, as was the soft murmuring of voices. She lay there, closed her eyes, comfortable and warm as the car rode over bumps and moved from side to side as it turned.

After a while, she became aware of the warmth of a hand on her hip. At least, that's what she thought it was. She could not be sure. Rather than be outraged, as she would have been a few short hours ago, she found that it was soothing. The warmth seemed to radiate from her hip, and she felt calm.

There was something at the edge of her mind. Something that she knew was not good, but it would not come into focus. Her thoughts niggled at it for a while, but to no avail. There was something there, but she could not get a grip on it, so she gave up.

She sighed contentedly and opened her eyes again.

"You okay, Kate?"

She recognised the voice of course. It was Joe. Memories flooded back suddenly, and she was afraid. Afraid of what? She remembered what had happened – leading Joe to the squat, the coiling parasite, the attack on Joe and stabbing that man in the back!

She sat up.

"What's happening?" she asked urgently. "Did you say that man I stabbed was alive? Please tell me that's what I heard."

"Yes," said Joe, smiling at her. "He is still alive. The doctors are looking at him now."

He was also in the back seat. It had obviously been his hand on her hip. She wasn't sure how she felt about that. But she sighed with relief.

"That's good," she breathed. She thought some more and remembered Joe leaning over her on the bed. "You said something about helping me?"

"That's right," said Joe. "I've given you a memory block. Don't worry." He held up his hand. "I didn't pry. I don't know anything about what was causing you so much pain, I just took it away for a while."

She was quiet while she thought about what he had just said. She supposed that's why she was a bit puzzled and confused when she awoke. A memory block? She was not too happy about that, but it was strange. She didn't know what he had blocked! That was obviously the point. So what did that mean? She didn't know what she was missing in her memories but there was still a vague sense of unease when she tried to remember. She thought that maybe she should stop trying, but wait a minute! A memory block? What the hell was that? Well, that was obvious, but she had never heard of it before, and how could he do it? Just who was he in the first place? She realised that she still had no idea who he was, where she was, and where she was going! Anger rose in her.

"You had better start talking, Joe, because this is getting creepy as hell. Just what the fuck is going on and where are we going?"

He looked serious. "Don't panic, just stay calm. I will explain everything. I said I would, and I will."

He looked forward through the windscreen. Kate noted that the driver was someone she had not seen before. A woman dressed in a white T-shirt who and dark sunglasses. She noted that they were driving somewhere in the country. Trees and hedges passed by slowly as the car moved gently along the winding road.

"It all started about ten years ago," he started. "I'm a twin, you've met my brother. He was the one you stabbed. We are identical twins. His name is Jim. We had always shared that something. We were very close when we were younger, always completing each other's sentences, always knowing things about each other, that sort of thing." He sighed. "Those were good times. But then it all changed."

He turned and looked at her.

"Jim grew more and more distant after we were involved in a car crash. Soon he was blaming me and our parents for everything that went wrong for him. He was angry, even violent." He sighed again. "Eventually it got too much, and my parents bought a house nearby and moved him into it. I didn't see much of him after that. I went away to university and while I was there, I stumbled on Psionics. Everything changed after that, and I haven't seen Jim since. Not until yesterday."

Kate interrupted him. "Wait! Yesterday? How long have I been asleep?"

Joe smiled across at her. "You've been asleep all night."

"All night? Oh my God!"

"Don't worry, it's okay."

"How did I get in the car? Did you carry me in?"

Joe nodded.

She went silent for a while as she digested this fact. "Where are we going?"

"We are going somewhere safe, somewhere I call the Complex."

"Oh." She was silent again.

"Remember I told you we are in a war? Well, it's true and it's not going well. People are dying. Our people."

He turned away, looking through the car window. Kate could see the sadness on the reflection of his face.

Kate was puzzled. She recalled that he had talked about a war, but there was no war that she was aware of. Unless he was talking about an African country or one of those obscure far eastern places that she had never heard of. This was getting ridiculous. The unexpected was happening again, and she was getting fed up with it.

"What on Earth are you talking about Joe? What war? Or are you making something up?" she snarled.

Joe smiled. "Oh, it's real, and it's not on Earth. In fact, it's not anywhere here." His smile faded. "It's up there." He pointed skyward.

Kate looked at him quizzically. "What a load of bullshit," she exclaimed. "What are you talking about?"

"You will see soon enough," said Joe, "In fact, we're here now, so I'll be able to show you."

As he spoke, the car turned into a single lane driveway and crunched to a stop on the gravel in front of a grand old country house.

Kate peered through the car window, looking at the house and its surroundings.

"So where is here?" she asked. "Is this house what you call the Complex?"

Joe opened the car door and started to get out. "Not exactly," he stated as the driver also exited the car.

Kate slid across the back seat and slipped out of the same door as Joe. She stood and looked up at the house.

"Impressive," she said, as she surveyed the stone-built facia.

It looked old and would probably have an ornate garden in the back. The driver walked to the large front wooden door and stood waiting. She was a slim, attractive woman standing in her jeans and her T-shirt. Kate noticed a flash of reflected sunlight from rings on her right hand.

Joe held out his hand and waited for Kate to take it. She hesitated but then slipped her hand in his. She immediately noticed the warmth and felt a tiny electric shock as her fingers brushed against his rings and chains.

"Okay," she said. "So, what is this Complex? Looks like a very expensive country house to me"

Joe led her towards the door, "It's our headquarters," he stated. "Let me show you and all will become much clearer."

He approached the door while the driver opened it for them. She stood to one side as Joe and Kate entered the house. Joe nodded to her as he passed.

"Thanks Sarah," he said.

As they passed through the entrance, Kate stole a glance at the driver's hand. Just as she thought, the rings on the driver's hand were connected with tiny chains, just like the set that Joe wore. What the hell did that mean?

They entered a large hall with a winding staircase on the left wall. So cliché, she thought to herself. Paintings were on all of the walls and an old grandfather clock ticked away against the right wall. It was all exactly what you would expect to see in this kind of house. It made no sense at all. She was about to say that this was no headquarters when Joe pressed a button on the staircase wall. As she looked, she could see a lift door. Ah, she thought. A lift taking them down into a secret lair!

The doors slid open, and Joe pulled her inside. As the doors closed, she turned to Joe and said "What's with the rings? You and that pretty driver girl have the same rings. Is that the device you were talking about yesterday?"

Joe smiled as he pressed a button and the lift started downwards.

"It's called an Assist," he said. "It's a device that boosts Psi abilities. Those of us that wear them are called Assisted. Remember when I told you back at the house that I was an Assisted telepath?"

Kate thought about what he had said. Psi what? Once again, Joe was making no sense. She supposed that she was getting used to it. The mad things that happened at regular intervals. Nothing was normal anymore, and everything was strange.

"Sure, I remember you flicking your fingers and music playing, but what the hell is Psi when it's at home?" she asked sarcastically.

"Psi is short for Psionics. It's a discipline of the mind and electronics. The idea is put the two together and you can do things that were not possible before."

Kate thought for a moment. "You mean like see parasites?" she asked, thinking about that floating, coiling dark smoky thing Joe had shown her in the street.

"Yes, exactly," replied Joe. "When I first discovered Psi, we were shocked to see things all around us that we couldn't see before. Turns out that we share this world with other creatures, and we had no idea about it." He smiled wryly. "That was when we started to realise that there were a lot of things to be discovered. And we made our big mistake." His smile faded into a grimace. "We should have left well alone. Or at least waited until we knew more about this new world we had just discovered." He sighed. "But no. We just couldn't help ourselves. We had to prod it with a metaphorical stick, lift the stone to see what's underneath. Big mistake."

She was about to ask, "What mistake?" when the lift shuddered to a halt and the door opened with a clang.

Through the opened doorway was a long corridor with metallic walls and strip lights disappearing down its long length, the end of which she could not see. But what really took her breath away was the figure standing in front of the doorway. It had no eyes.

Chapter 26 - Lee

3 years ago

Lee lay on his bed in his prison cell.

It was late at night and as usual, he could not sleep. The wing was as quiet as it could be, apart from the occasional shout from a prisoner, and the rattle of key chains as a guard walked past. Turning his head sideways, he once again surveyed his cell. There was a single bed, a single chair neatly placed under a tiny desk. On the desk were two books. He had read each one three times. In the corner was a small alcove containing the shower and toilet. The wall above his head held a barred window, through which he could just see part of a full moon.

He sighed and moved his head to look back up at the ceiling. Tomorrow would be the same as all of the other days. But, in his head it was different, because tomorrow marked his seventh year in prison. Three more to go, he thought. Three more years before he would be eligible for parole. And even then, he was not sure it would be granted. He may well serve out his entire 15 year sentence, given his crime.

The comparative silence was suddenly broken by a loud crack of noise which sounded like someone slapping their hands together. It was accompanied by a whoosh of wind and a flash of light that momentarily blinded him.

"What the fuck!" he shouted sitting up quickly.

He rubbed at his eyes. When he opened them, he was shocked to see a tall man wearing a long dark coat standing in his cell.

"Good evening," said the stranger.

He pulled the chair from beneath the desk and sat down. Lee was dumbfounded. He looked around to the cell door, seeing that it was shut. He looked back at the stranger.

"How the hell did you get in here? And who are you?"

The stranger smiled, his long blond hair falling across his face, hiding his eyes. "It's a simple matter of teleportation," he explained.

Lee swung his legs over the side of the bed but remained seated. "Teleportation?"

"Yes," replied the stranger. "It's the translation of matter from one place to another through the application….."

Lee cut him off. "I know what teleportation is. Are you saying that you teleported into my cell?"

The stranger nodded. Lee digested this fact for a little while.

"I didn't think that was possible. Yet here you are." He paused. "I can't dispute the fact that you are sitting in front of me."

He thought to himself for a while longer.

"So why are you here?" he asked.

"Straight to the point," said the stranger. "I have a job for you."

Lee laughed. "Look, I'm not even sure that this is real. I think that I may be dreaming. What could possibly motivate you to offer me, a convicted criminal, a job?"

"Good point," replied the stranger. "First, let me introduce myself. I'm Joe. I already know that you are Lee and that you are in here for murder." He paused. "Let me assure you that I would not be here offering you a job if I didn't think that you were not only innocent, but also had the abilities I am looking for."

Lee snorted. "I am not innocent. I killed all of those people."

"I know that," replied Joe. "But I also know that you didn't kill them because you are a sadistic murderer. You killed them because you felt that they deserved it."

Lee was caught off guard. "How do you know that?" he whispered.

Joe smiled grimly. "I know a lot of things. I know that they killed your wife and children. I know that you went after them, and you killed them."

Lee grew angry, listening to Joe's words.

"The bastards broke into my house, called us racist names just because we were Chinese. They killed my wife and my boys," Lee said bitterly. "They deserved what they got. I don't regret it."

"I know," replied Joe. "Anyone given the same set of circumstances would have done the same, especially given your set of skills."

Lee was startled. "Skills?"

"Let's not play games. You know what I'm talking about. You can find things, can you not? You found them easily. And once you did, you killed them."

"How do you know about that?"

"Like I said, I know a lot of things."

Joe crossed his legs and folded his arms. "Let's cut to the chase. You have a talent, a talent that I could use. Yes, you murdered those men, but who could blame you? I know that you are not a bad person. I know that you don't regret killing them, and I know that you would do the same if it happened again. Given all of that, I would like to offer you a job."

"The judge didn't see it that way," replied Lee.

"No," returned Joe.

Lee leant backwards against the wall. "Why would you offer me a job?" he asked.

"You've been busy while you have been in here," stated Joe. "How many degrees do you have now? Three?"

Lee nodded. "I have plenty of time."

Joe nodded back. "Psychology, Social Science and Philosophy."

"What of it?"

"You are clearly very intelligent. That and your talent makes you an ideal candidate for the job I have in mind."

Lee did not reply for a full minute. "And what is the job?" he asked.

Joe broke into a wide grin. "Second in command of my group I call the Alliance."

Lee coughed loudly and started laughing. Joe waited until he had recovered. It took little while. Once he had stopped laughing, Lee considered and was suddenly serious.

"You really mean it, don't you?"

Joe simply nodded.

"How big is your group?

"There are 48 of us so far, but more are joining all of the time."

"Not a big group then."

"No, but all of us have one thing in common. An innate talent to use various faculties of the mind."

"You're talking about extra sensory perception or ESP aren't you?"

"Well, that's one way of putting it, but essentially yes."

Lee thought about it. Could this be true? Could ESP be real? But wait! He had just seen a live demonstration. How could Joe have entered his cell? Teleportation must be real. And if it was, then this would be groundbreaking, a whole new science. The practical applications would be enormous. Not to mention prisons becoming useless! He grew excited at the possibilities. If this was real, he could not turn it down.

"Okay I accept. What now?"

Joe stood quickly. "Excellent!" he exclaimed. "And just in time, the guards are on their way."

Lee stood also. "They are?"

"Yes, they must have heard the noise of my arrival." Joe took one step towards Lee, so they were standing face to face. "Ready?" he asked.

Lee nodded. "What do I do...."

Joe brought up his left hand and gripped Lee's shoulder. The other he raised into the air. Lee saw rings and sparkling chains. He heard a key enter the lock of the door and then there was a flash.

A guard opened the door and surveyed the empty cell. He spoke into his radio.

"Raise the alarm, we have a breakout!"

Chapter 27 - Escape

Jim was happy. He was free!

Once he had calmed down, he had managed to free himself using the instruments from the trolley. He had been surprised that he had been left on his own for so long. But he had made good use of that time. His legs were not fastened, so he had been able to move the trolley with his foot into a position where he had managed to reach a short, sharp instrument with his right hand. It hadn't been easy, and had taken a long time, but eventually, he was able to pick the lock and free his hand. It was a simple task to free the other.

He had searched the room where he was imprisoned. He found some bandages, which he wrapped around his wrists to stem the blood flow. They were bruised and cut quite badly, but that was not important. What was important was that he had escaped. The freaks had underestimated him.

A further search did not reveal his suit. When he was captured, they must have removed it and stored it somewhere else. He was annoyed about this because he could have used its invisibility screen right now. He was also annoyed because it meant that he would have to rebuild from scratch, and that would take time.

He was wasting time. He had to get out before the freaks came back. He opened the door and peered out. It opened onto a long brightly lit corridor. Looking both ways, and seeing that it was clear of people, he stepped out. Picking a direction at random, he sneaked quietly and cautiously along its length. He noted as he went, that as well as regularly spaced doors, there were also regularly spaced alcoves, which he could use to hide as he moved along.

In one such alcove, he stopped panting heavily. He leaned back against the wall. The pain in his back was excruciating, he had to rest before he carried on. Trouble was, he didn't know where he was. It must be a large building, he thought. It was a place of long white corridors with no windows. Most of the doors were locked. The two he had peeked into were storerooms. Others had voices coming from them, so he had moved on.

He admitted to himself that he was lost as he gritted his teeth through the pain. But he wasn't about to give up, not when he had managed to escape his restraints. He would just have to keep moving. There was nothing else for it. Surely eventually he would find the way out?

He pushed from the wall and limped on trying to ignore the pain. He had to get out of this place.

As he wobbled down the corridor, he didn't realise that his wound had opened, and he didn't see the blood stain he had left on the wall.

Eventually, Jim found the way out. It had taken a long time and more than once he had to dive into an alcove or room to avoid being seen, each time twisting and hurting his back. But he had made it. Just one more obstacle to overcome. He had found a corridor that dead ended in a door that was clearly a lift. It was obviously the way out, it had the word, 'Exit', in big green letters on the wall above the door.

But how to get to it without being seen?

There was a freak standing in front of the door. He had seen many of them as he had wandered around this place. Typically, tall men and women, some with gold metal all over their heads. He had no doubt that the metal was some sort of device. Something like his suit, but not a weapon. Maybe something to increase their mental capacity. He would have loved to get hold of one and take it to pieces, so that he could figure out what it did and how it worked. But it was too dangerous right now. He needed to get out and re-group. Once back in his lab, he could rebuild. He already had a couple of new ideas, based on what he had seen. He had even managed to steal a couple of small devices. They were safely tucked away in a pocket.

Once he was out, he could experiment and try some new things. Then he would return. And when he did, he would blast all of these freaks to hell! But he would have to wait just a little bit longer.

The freak was still standing in front of the lift door when suddenly it opened with a loud dinging noise. He slid back quickly into another alcove. He could not afford to be caught again. He leaned back against the wall, trying to make himself invisible. The pain in his back ripped through him and he gritted his teeth.

As he hid, he didn't see both Kate and Joe stepping out of the lift.

He waited until he heard the steps and voices fade away and then shuffled as quickly as he could to the lift door. The 3 minutes he waited for the doors to open after pressing the call button stretched out interminably. He was sure that someone would open a door and see him at any moment. But he was lucky, the corridor remained empty, and no doors opened.

As soon as the lift arrived he dived in. He had done it! He had escaped! He allowed himself to gloat and was assured in the knowledge that he was better than these freaks. Sure, they had caught him, but he had escaped right away. They were useless, he was better than them, it had been an accident that they captured him. True he had underestimated Joe, but he wouldn't next time. And to top it all off, he had stolen some of the freaks tech. He could not wait to get back in his workshop. He would build something new. Something that he could bring back to level this place. They had made a mistake bringing him here. Now he knew where they were. Where they hid with all their secrets. He would get out of here and return, wiping out every last one of them. He grinned as he thought about it. As he did so the lift dinged, and the door opened.

Jim's grin faded. As the door opened, he saw a woman holding a weapon. The weapon was pointing directly at his forehead.

Chapter 28 - Enhanced

Kate shrank back into the lift. Her hand came up and covered her mouth, her eyes wild. Joe noticed straight away and grabbed her arm.

"It's okay. There is nothing to worry about." He tried to calm her.

"What the fuck is that?" she exclaimed, pointing to the figure that stood in the doorway.

The figure stood, its head moving slightly left and right and back again. It was a large, imposing black man who looked ordinary until you reached the face. Where the eyes and forehead should have been, there was a large, golden metal protrusion that bulged outwards and wrapped entirely around and over the head. The protrusion covered where the eyes should have been and went down as far as the nose.

The man spoke. "Don't be afraid, Kate," he said. "I understand that my appearance might be a little disconcerting." The corners of his mouth raised in a smile, "But it's nothing to worry about. My enhancement enables me to see quite well, and I can see that right now you are very scared. Please don't be. I won't harm you."

Kate peered at the man from behind Joe. "You can see?" she asked.

"Of course, probably better than you." The man held out his hand. "My name is Steve," he said. "I am Enhanced."

Kate gingerly took the offered hand. When she did, she felt the familiar electricity running up her arm and there was a feeling of a large mental presence. It was difficult to explain, but she could 'feel' a huge mental force pressing into her mind. She snatched her hand back.

"Enhanced?" she asked.

"Yes," said Steve. "Unlike Joe here," he gestured towards Joe, "I chose to have my brain augmented by this prosthesis." He lifted his hand to his head.

Joe interrupted. "Yeah, yeah, we all know yours is the superior method," he drawled. "Sorry, Kate. I should have warned you. You'll see quite a few of my people who are Enhanced like Steve here and quite a few who are Assisted like me."

Kate digested this. "So it's all okay?" she asked. "Steve is normal and not going to bash my head in?"

Both Joe and Steve laughed. "Definitely not," said Steve. "We don't believe in violence here in the Complex. Although, that has had to change recently."

"Let's move, Steve," said Joe. "I imagine we have a lot to do."

"Indeed," said Steve as he turned and led the way down the corridor.

Kate allowed Joe to hold her hand. She was kind of glad that he did so. She peered around as they walked while thinking of their exchange with Steve. Suddenly she stopped dead in her tracks, pulling Joe to a halt.

"Wait a minute," she said. "You just said 'my people'. What do you mean by that?"

Joe turned, looking a bit sheepish. "Oh," he said. "Didn't I tell you?" He waved his hand around. "I'm sort of the boss here."

Kate's jaw dropped, as Steve turned and nodded his metal encased head in agreement.

Kate looked incredulous. "You are in charge?"

Joe nodded.

"Really?" she said. "You?"

Joe nodded again.

"But I found you. You were in a right state, just like me." she added.

"All true," said Joe. "I did something stupid and paid for it in spades." He grimaced.

Kate this hard to believe. How could this be true? He had been completely out of it when she had found him and now all of a sudden he was in charge of a mysterious underground base full of people?

"So if that is true then why doesn't Steve call you Sir?"

Joe looked up at Steve and grinned, who grinned back.

"No need," replied Joe. "We all know who is who in the Alliance and we all know what we need to do. It's a sort of hive mind."

Kate was taken aback. "What the fuck are you talking about?" she asked. "All of this," she waved her hand around, "and these people and things?" She waved at Steve, who nodded. "It's just too much to believe. It's all too overwhelming." She put her hand to her head, a headache was starting.

Joe looked concerned. "Are you alright?" he asked.

"It's just a headache," she replied. "I can't think straight. All of this stuff is too much to take in."

Joe quickly looked at Steve then back at Kate. "Do you often get headaches?" he asked.

Kate rubbed her forehead and laughed. "All the time."

Joe looked concerned. "Kate, can we get moving? I'd like to get the doctors to take a look at you."

"What? No!" exclaimed Kate. "There's nothing wrong with me. Tell me more about what all of this," she waved her hand around again, "is about. And why the hell are you in charge?"

"Well, let's at least move along as we talk," said Joe, as he moved on down the corridor, beckoning Steve to come too. Kate started to follow.

"As I've already explained, it started five years ago," said Joe, as they walked. "That was when I discovered Psi, and I started to find others."

"You discovered Psi?" asked Kate. "That's electronics and mind control, right?"

Joe smiled. "Well, it's the connection between the mind and electronics. I stumbled across it and built my first Assist. With it, I started to reach out and found others like me."

"Others like you?" said Kate.

"Sure," said Joe. "I was surprised to find that there were lots of others like me."

"Like you," repeated Kate. "And what exactly is that?" She raised her eyebrows.

"A telepath," said Joe.

"Does that mean that you can read minds?" she asked. She thought for a second. "Wait a minute, have you been in my mind? Have you been spying?"

She started to think of all of the private things in her mind, the thoughts that she had, that she would never voice out loud and tell anyone. The things she wanted and yearned for and the things she had done. There was a sudden sharp pain in her head. She gasped and stumbled shooting out her hand against the wall to steady herself.

Joe stopped and stepped to her, grabbing her waist. "Kate!" he shouted.

Kate steadied herself against the wall. "I'm okay. I think," she said, as the pain increased. "Fuck, that hurts."

Joe was concerned. He looked at Steve and said, "I think that my mind block is breaking. Can you help?"

Steve gave a quick look at Joe. "Well, yes, but you know it won't last. What were you thinking?"

"I was trying to do the right thing, okay?" Joe snapped. "She needed help and I gave it. Now get over here and help."

Steve held out his hand to touch Kate's head. Through narrowed, pain filled eyes, Kate shrank back.

"What do you think you are doing?" She winced as she spoke. Drawing in a sharp breath with the pain.

"Don't worry, Kate," said Joe softly. "You need help. The mind block is breaking down and we need to do something quickly otherwise..." He didn't finish his sentence.

"I don't need help," said Kate, pushing away from the wall, "And I certainly don't want him touching me." She gestured to Steve.

Steve pulled his hand back. It was difficult to figure out his expression, thought Kate. No eyes, but she could see he wasn't happy. Maybe he was offended. Well, too bad. She didn't like the idea of him touching her. Besides, it was just a nasty headache. She jumped as Joe grabbed her hand. She looked down and saw his rings glowing blue. She tried to pull away but his grip was too strong and they fought each other momentarily.

"Get off, Joe!" she shouted.

He tried to soothe her. "It's okay, no one is going to hurt you."

Kate pulled her hand again. Although she had pushed away from the wall and was steadier, the pain was not getting better. If anything, it was getting worse. Her vision blurred and she suddenly felt frightened. What was happening? She couldn't see! She stopped struggling and rubbed her eyes with her other hand. It didn't help. Her vision went dark.

"Joe," she whispered. "I don't feel well. I can't see."

Joe pulled her close to him, his hand moving up her arm to her head. The blue glow appeared in her mind as she felt herself slipping into complete darkness, losing consciousness. The last thing she remembered was Joe and Steve catching her as she fell.

Chapter 29 - Intervention

Kate floated. It was dark but she felt warm and relaxed. It was as if she was on a soft cloud that cushioned her in its warm embrace. She breathed in and out slowly. She could hear murmurings in the distance, but they didn't worry her. They sounded soft and far away.

Gradually, she became more aware, and she realised that it was dark because she had her eyes closed. The voices continued and still sounded distant. She flickered her eyes open.

She was in a dimly lit room on a comfortable bed with blankets coming up to her chin. She turned her head to the right and saw shelves full of medical equipment. Turning her head to the left she saw a wall with a door, a chair, and a bedside table. She also saw that she was attached to a drip. Strangely, she was not worried or concerned. She sighed and let her eyelids slowly close.

She heard a door open.

"Ah, you're awake," said a woman's voice.

Kate opened her eyes again and saw a woman approach the end of the bed.

"Who are you?" she asked in a lazy drawl. "Have I been drugged?"

The woman was dressed in a white lab coat and long blonde hair. She was carrying something medical, and Kate noticed that she was wearing an Assist. She remembered that Joe had said that everyone would be wearing one. She supposed that meant that they were all telepaths.

"Nothing for you to worry about," she said smiling, as she walked to her bedside. "You are not well." She frowned. "Our beloved Joe has been a bit heavy handed. I've given you something to help."

"Whatever it is, it feels nice," said Kate. "Can I have some more?"

She stretched under the bed clothes, lifting her arms above her head. She noticed that her clothes had been removed but wasn't concerned. Whatever she had been given, it was good stuff.

She sighed again and brought her arms down by her sides, on top of the blanket.

"Joe told me about your addiction. I've examined you and I can tell you that the one good thing Joe did was to cure you of that particular affliction." She walked to the side of the bed and laid a hand on Kate's forehead. "I take it you are feeling okay?" she asked.

"Dreamy," replied Kate.

The woman smiled again. "Good. My name is Sally, and I'm one of the Complex doctors." She removed her hand from Kate's forehead and took Kate's right hand. "Joe has told me all about your encounters." She frowned again. "I must say that I do not approve of his methods and what he's put you through." She placed the medical equipment on the bedside table. "Although, I do approve of you." She placed Kate's arm across her chest. "You are a very special woman, did you know that? My examination shows that you have latent talent, although I can see that you have some psychological damage, not to mention the mess Joe made." She looked intently at Kate. "Are you listening to me, Kate?" she asked.

Kate looked up at her. She was listening, although she was having difficulty focussing. She felt relaxed and sleepy, and her eyelids were heavy.

"Hmmm.." she said softly.

It was all too difficult to concentrate.

Sally continued. "This is important Kate," she said earnestly. "Your psychological damage, together with Joe's meddling has left you in a precarious position. You need intervention to stop things getting worse." She paused. "Kate, I can help you, but it won't be easy for you."

Sally paused again. From the bedside table, she picked up a syringe. "Kate.," she said.

Kate opened her eyes.

"Kate, I need you to understand and agree to the intervention. This will help you be a bit more aware."

She injected some of the contents of the syringe into the drip hanging by the bed. In short order, Kate felt herself become a little more awake, exactly as Sally had said she would, but her limbs still felt heavy. She raised her head to look at Sally.

"Where am I?" she asked.

Sally smiled down at her again. "You are still in the Complex. Do you remember that I said I was a doctor?" she asked.

"Yes," said Kate. She dropped her head back onto the pillow. "You said something about intervention?"

"Yes," said Sally. "You need an intervention to stabilise your mental state. If we don't do it soon, the damage could be irreversible. I need you to understand and consent to the treatment."

"Damage?" asked Kate, she tried to rise, but her body was lethargic and heavy, she could only manage to raise her head again. "What are you talking about?"

Sally held Kate's hand again. "Take it easy," she said. "We are all here to help you. You are safe here."

Kate considered this. She recalled Joe had said something similar, and yet here she was in a hospital bed.

"I am not sure that makes me feel any better," she said, "Joe told me I would be safe, and look at me now."

Sally frowned. "Yes, our Joe has not been completely straight with you, nor has he done a very good job looking after you. I definitely do not approve, and I told him so."

"You did?" asked Kate.

"I certainly did," said Sally, her mouth drawn into a thin line. "He was not impressed. But I need to move on. You need to know that if we don't do something about your condition, you will not recover. You must understand and consent to the intervention."

"What is the intervention?" asked Kate.

Now that she was not so drugged, she was starting to feel afraid. Sally looked intently at her.

"I propose to fit you with an Assist." She held up her hand showing off the rings and chains. "It won't hurt at all, not physically, but it will mean that you will almost certainly have to live through some painful memories."

"No," whispered Kate. "I can't do that."

Sally took Kate's hand and squeezed it. "You can. You are a very strong young woman. The Assist will unlock your mind and give you access to all of your latent abilities, as well as all of your memories. It will also stabilize your mental state, which at the moment is essential to your wellbeing."

Kate started to cry, tears running down the sides of her face. A headache started across her forehead again.

"I try not to remember," she whispered. "It hurts so much, I can't bear it. Leave me be. Get Joe to take me back where he found me and pump me full of drugs." She moaned.

Sally looked concerned. "Oh, Kate, I am so sorry. You must be strong. You can do it, it's the only way. I don't want to take you back. You have so much potential." She hesitated. "You won't have to do it alone, I'll be there with you." She leant down and kissed Kate's forehead.

The door opened and Joe walked in. He stopped, looked at Kate and then Sally. He saw Sally's look of concern and the tears running down Kate's face.

"What..." he started to ask, but then stopped. He stared at Sally, who stared back. "It's that bad?" he asked.

Sally furrowed her brow at him. " Of course, it is you idiot," she said forcefully. She looked back down at Kate. "Kate needs help, and I said I would be there with her."

It was Joe's turn to frown. "Sally, you know that's dangerous. Are you sure you want to do this? You know I want you to because it's Kate, and..." He stopped and looked at Kate in the bed "But you don't have to, I can't ask you."

Sally gave a wan smile. "I think you have done enough damage already, don't you?" She beamed down at Kate. "I have examined her, and I can see that not only does she have a very high

Psi score, but she is also a lovely person with lots of potential." She drew in a breath. "She is worth fighting for."

"I know that," said Joe, "Please, do all you can for her." He looked down at his feet. "I need her," he whispered.

He hesitated, as though he was going to say more, but then he turned and left the room, closing the door behind him. The women looked at each other.

"He's alright really," said Sally, "Our beloved leader." She pulled a chair over to the bed and sat down without letting go of Kate's hand. "He means well, and is actually the best we have, and I know he thinks a lot of you."

Kate turned her head on the pillow to look at Sally. "What's happening?" she asked.

Sally looked earnestly into Kate's eyes. "Look," she said. "The bottom line is if I don't fit you with an Assist, you will never recover. The kind of things I am talking about are insanity, schizophrenia, psychotic break, vegetative state, or all of them. You will never be the same again.

You might even die." She paused. "On the other hand, with the Assist, you could be whole again. It will help you heal. But it will be painful. The fitting will unlock the full potential of your mind and will release all of your memories. It will force you to relive them. But if you can get through it, you will be fully healed. There is still some risk, but you are stronger than you know, and I think you can do it." She smiled thinly.

Kate's tears continued to flow, wetting the pillow. "I can't," she whispered.

"Yes you can," said Sally. "I'll guide you."

Kate closed her eyes. Her crying started to wrack her body as she let go, her headache slowly building.

"Please," she whispered.

Still looking into Kate's eyes, Sally asked, "Kate, do you consent?"

Kate trembled, still crying. She started to whimper softly. She looked back into Sally's eyes. She gave a barely perceptible nod. Her body shook with the crying, tears pouring down her face, the quiet wailing escaping from her.

Sally reached into her white lab coat with her free hand and pulled out the sparkling rings and chains of the Assist.

As she drew Kate's hand towards her, she looked deeply into her eyes. Kate stared back and watched through tears as Sally slowly pushed the rings onto her fingers, one by one.

Chapter 30 - Examination

"So, where have you been all this time?" asked Molly out loud, as she clipped an apparatus to Joe's head.

She was fussing with it, trying to make sure that it was fitted correctly. An Assist rattled around her fingers. She tutted to herself as it kept sliding out of position. The device was like a crown that encircled Joe's head, with a thick black wire connected to it, which trailed down and across the floor, where it snaked up underneath a bench that stretched across the entire length of one wall. The bench was covered with electronic equipment consisting of different sized screens, switches, lights, and dials.

Earlier, Naya, one of the Alliance doctors had dressed Joe's wounds. Most of them were superficial first-degree burns covering the palm on his left hand, his left arm and leg. They didn't require much attention, just some antibiotic cream and light bandaging which was now covered under new jeans and a T shirt.

He had been lucky. Molly didn't think that anyone else in the Alliance could have survived such an attack, and Joe had not only survived, but he had also done so when he was not fully recovered.

"No idea," said Joe. He was sitting in a medical chair in the centre of the room.

"I find that hard to believe," replied Molly as she stood back, satisfied with her work. "You must have some idea."

"Nope," said Joe. "All I can remember is blackness, then saving Kate from a gang of idiots, and then waking up with her."

Molly's eyebrows raised.

"Gang?"

"They were chasing her, I got rid of them."

Molly nodded, "and then you woke up with Kate?"

"It's not like that," said Joe. "Somehow, she brought me back."

"But you'd like it to be," said Molly, with a sly grin on her face, walking over to the electronic equipment and flicking a switch. The apparatus began to hum quietly.

Joe sighed. "Well, yes, of course. We clearly have a connection. But I'm not sure she sees it that way. This is all new to her and it frightens her."

"Well, of course it frightens her," said Molly, as she walked back to Joe. "She had no idea that Psi existed and what it means. And I bet you weren't subtle about it, were you?" She raised a quizzical eyebrow.

Joe grimaced. "Things kinda got out of hand," he said.

"I bet," said Molly. "However, I am more interested to learn how she brought you back, as you said."

"I can't explain it," replied Joe. "One moment there was blackness and the next, there she was."

She huffed, "not very informative." She made a small adjustment to the device on is head.

Joe spread his hands, lifting his shoulders as if to say, hell if I know.

Frowning, Molly moved back to the electronics and started throwing more switches and pressing buttons. She sat down in front of a screen.

"Jonas, you ready?" she asked.

Jonas sat in a chair in a corner of the room. He was Enhanced, the golden metal encompassing his head with yet another cable connected to his augmentation and snaking across the floor to the bench of equipment. He nodded.

"Whenever you are." His voice was deep and gravelly.

Molly turned to Joe. "Okay Joe, you know how this goes. I'll run my scan with Jonas to help out in case of any problems. From the scan, I will be able to tell if you sustained any damage to your mind. I'm sure I don't need to tell you that we need to make sure that you are okay."

"I'm fine," grumbled Joe.

"So you say. Let's find out."

She tapped her screen and the electronics started to hum louder.

At the time, both she and Joe did not notice how they had so casually dismissed his disappearance. Neither of them realised that they were being manipulated.

Chapter 31 - Kate's Nightmare

Kate stood, looking down upon her 15 year old self. "No," she said softly.

A small, warm hand gripped hers. "It's okay, Kate," said Sally. "It's just a memory, it's not happening now."

"But it did happen," whispered Kate as she saw her younger self trembling in her bed.

She remembered that she had delayed going to bed for as long as she dared, and then did not let herself go to sleep because she knew what might happen once she did. She watched on as her younger self kept looking at the clock. The electronic display said 2:20 AM. She remembered listening intently, she could hear the quiet of the house. Nothing was stirring, and that was good. She didn't want to hear anything. She wanted to sleep in the dark and the quiet, but too many times she had been awoken by the horror that happened every two or three days.

It was almost certain to happen this night. Her mother was at some conference or other that was so far away she had to stay overnight. Leaving Kate and her little sister, Bella, alone. Alone with their father.

She remembered the floorboard creaking outside her bedroom door and she saw her young self tense, her eyes wide and darting to the door. After a while, she had relaxed a little. Not yet. The door had not opened. She let out a trembling breath.

"I can't go through this again," said Kate quietly. She turned to Sally standing next to her. "Please don't make me."

Sally looked sympathetic and squeezed Kate's hand. "It's a memory and I'm here with you. No one can see us. We are not really here. We are just experiencing your memory."

Together, they stared at the trembling girl in the bed.

"No," said Kate." I can't."

"Yes you can. You must. This is the pivot point, the thing that changed your life forever and the thing that you try your best to forget by using alcohol or drugs. But you can't do that anymore." Sally moved to stand in front of Kate. "You must do this, Kate. You must confront your nightmare because if you don't, you will lose yourself forever."

Kate looked into Sally's eyes. "Please don't make me," she murmured, with a quivering breath.

"You can do it. You are stronger than you know, and I will be here with you. You won't be alone."

Tears ran down Kate's face, and Sally wondered if she had gone too far. She knew that this had to work. Because if it didn't, it would be both of them that would be lost. Lost forever in Kate's memory. They might never recover from this.

Chapter 32 - Sally

3 years ago

Towards the end of her night shift, Sally was exhausted. After 40 hours on her feet with just two 20 minute naps, she was about ready to drop. Walking down the length of the A&E department, she mopped her brow with the back of her hand. As she passed each bay, she mentally reviewed their treatments making sure that everything had been done for each individual to ensure the best outcome. When she reached the last of the bays, she blew out a breath of air. All was good, all of the patients were stable.

Reaching the doctor's station, she rounded the high bench and sat down heavily in an unoccupied chair opposite a computer screen. A nurse, Jennifer, sat next to her, typing away, updating a patients' record. Another, Ishita, stood at the bench leafing through brown folders and at the rear of the station Dr Tom Vance was leaning back in his chair with his chin on his chest, gently snoring.

Ishita, a tall, thin woman of Asian descent, looked up from her work.

"Tired, Dr Sal?" she asked.

Sally gave her a wan smile. "Am I ever," she replied.

Ishita smiled back. "And so say we all," was her reply. "Only an hour left on this shift. A hot bath and my bed are calling to me."

Sally nodded. "Just bed for me. I can't be bothered with anything else." She gestured to the sleeping doctor. "How does he do it? He's completely out of it."

"Tom could sleep anywhere," stated Jennifer without looking up from her screen. "Did I ever tell you about the time I caught him asleep on a trolley in the car park?"

"YES!" chorused Sally and Ishita at the same time. All three of them laughed together.

Jennifer continued. "What about the time…"

She broke off as the red emergency phone rang. Sally sat up as Ishita picked it up.

"Bristol A&E Resus," she stated, and then listened, writing notes on a trauma sheet. In short order, she said, "Thank you," and put the phone down. She turned to Sally, "RTA, 15 minutes away, major injuries to the legs and head."

Sally was galvanised into action. "Bay 4 is empty, get the trauma kit and call for an anaesthetist." She was up and out of her chair on her way to bay 4. "Get some more help down here, and someone wake up Tom," she called over her shoulder.

It didn't take long for the 15 minutes to pass and for the ambulance crew to crash through the doors. The crew were directed to Bay 4 and the patient was lifted from the trolley onto the bed. Sally stood at the bottom of the bed directing operations. She listened carefully as one of the crew members briefed them and listed all of the injury details and treatments administered so far.

The patient was a middle-aged man who had been riding his motorcycle and had been hit at high speed by a lorry. His injuries were severe;

both legs fractured, one wrist fracture, a portion of one arm had lost a lot of flesh and muscle, it having been trapped under the lorry wheels. He also had a head injury - the front of his helmet had been caved in.

Several doctors and nurses including Tom, Ishita and Jennifer were gathered around the patient attending to their various duties as directed by Sally. She was most concerned with the head injury. It was clearly serious as the patient was fighting them. He was shouting both from pain and confusion, as well as trying to wave away the help that her staff were trying to deliver. A clear sign of a brain injury.

"We need to put him under," said Sally. "Where is the anaesthetist?"

No one answered. She motioned to Jennifer. "Did you call the anaesthetist? Go and make sure that they are on the way. Tell them to hurry."

Jennifer moved quickly, disappearing beyond the curtain surrounding the bay. As Sally turned back she noticed that one of the staff attending had removed their surgical glove and had placed their bare hand on the patients' forehead.

"You!" shouted Sally. "What the hell are you doing?"

Many faces turned to Sally, questions in their eyes.

"What?" asked Tom.

Sally pointed at the figure at the head end of the bed. "Get them away from my patient."

Everyone turned to look at who she was pointing to.

"Excuse me," said Tom to the masked and gowned figure. "Who are you?"

The figure straightened up and faced the onlookers.

"He will be still now," he spoke with a male voice.

Sally was momentarily speechless. She flicked her eyes to the patient and noted that he was indeed still. He had stopped fighting the staff, his eyes looking up at the ceiling, blinking slowly.

She looked back at the ungloved figure who was meeting her glare with bright blue eyes.

"Move away from the patient," she said. "Who are you? You realise that you have broken protocol by removing your glove?"

All the staff looked back at the stranger.

The stranger lifted his ungloved hand and gazed at it. She noticed that he wore many rings. She was incensed. He did not reply to her questions.

"You have quite possibly put my patient's life at risk from infection. What were you thinking?"

The stranger moved away from the patient.

"He's calm now, you can carry on with your treatments." As he spoke he walked slowly towards Sally, who involuntarily took a step back. The stranger stopped.

"I'm not here to harm anyone. On the contrary, I am here to offer you a job."

Sally was taken aback and speechless for a few short seconds.

"Whoever you are, get the hell out of my department."

She turned to the staff gathered around the patient. They had all stopped what they were doing and were watching the events unfold.

"Someone call security," said Sally to the whole group. Several of them looked at each other, some looked at the stranger.

After a moment, one of the nurses said, "Yes doctor," glaring at the stranger as she strode out of the bay.

The stranger did not take his oddly bright blue eyes from Sally. "There is no need for security." He reached up and removed his mask and scrub hat. Long, blond hair fell forward, obscuring most of his face. "I'm Joe." He held out his hand.

Sally retreated another step again. "I don't care who you are. You have just put my patient at risk with your party trick. Leave now before security get here." She turned to her staff. "Get a mobile X-Ray in here, get another line in." There was another moment's hesitation and then they all carried on with their tasks, moving equipment and bustling around the patient.

"Can we talk?" asked Joe.

"Definitely not," replied Sally. "I'm busy. Just get out."

Joe ignored the response and instead took three rapid steps to take him right up to Sally. His hand snapped out and grabbed her wrist. Sally gave out a little squeak of surprise. She stepped back once again and pulled her arm to free herself. It was no use: Joe's grip was like a vice.

"Let me go." She was suddenly afraid.

This man was clearly disturbed and had somehow broken into the department, masquerading as staff. She wished security would hurry so that they could throw him out and she could attend her patient. It was just her luck that this would happen just before her shift ended.

"I'm not here to hurt you, I meant it when I said I'd like to offer you a job." Sally gasped as she heard the words inside her head. Before she could form the words for her reply, she heard the voice again. "We are communicating mind to mind. I can hear your thoughts. You don't need to vocalise them."

"What the fuck?" she thought.

"What the fuck indeed," replied the voice, which she realised must be Joe's. "It takes some getting used to, but it's so much faster than talking. Pretty cool."

"You can hear me thinking?" asked Sally.

"You bet. Interested in hearing about the job?"

Sally ignored the question. Her fear subsided to be replaced by shock. What had been an ordinary shift had turned into a nightmare. She was being accosted by an intruder who had interfered with her patient who was quite possibly dying. She would be held accountable; she was sure of that.

"*Your patient will recover; his injuries, while serious, are not life threatening,*" said the voice in her head.

"*What about the head injury?*" she found herself asking, even though it felt ridiculous to do so.

The reply was immediate. "*I am not a doctor, but I could see a large blood clot in his brain. I removed it and there doesn't seem to be any more bleeding. I also calmed him down by damping down his brain activity.*"

Sally looked at Joe with wide eyes, completely in shock now. This guy was talking bollocks! He removed a clot? What rubbish. Totally impossible without surgery. He was clearly delusional, perhaps high on drugs. What he said made no sense whatsoever. Once again, she felt afraid. What else was this idiot capable of? Did he have a knife hidden in his gown? Where were security?

She jumped as he raised his other hand and held it at full length, his palm facing the bed. She flinched as she saw a blue flash.

"*Come, let me show you.*" He pulled at Sally's arm, and she found herself being directed towards the bed.

As they neared the patient's head, she noticed that her team were just standing staring into space. They had all stopped working, their hands by their sides, some of them holding instruments, leads or tubes, but all of their eyes were vacant.

When they arrived at the head of the bed, Joe lifted her hand pulled off her glove and placed her hand on her patient's forehead.

"What's wrong with my staff?" she asked out loud.

"*Don't worry,*" came the replied thought. "*They are all fine. They are sort of asleep. They won't remember any of this.*"

"What?" asked Sally. "Just what the hell is going on? How are you doing this?"

There was no reply. Instead, he pressed her hand harder on the patient's forehead. Sally blinked and gasped. While her eyes had been momentary closed she had seen something. She closed them again and drew in a sharp breath. There it was again, an image. An image of a skull. She opened her eyes again and looked at Joe.

"What is this?" she breathed. He did not answer. Instead, he smiled. She stared into his blue eyes. "Was that my patient?" she asked.

Joe nodded. She closed her eyes again and saw the skull with an obvious fracture over the left eye. As she looked, she felt her vision move past the bone surface into the frontal sinus, through the orbital plate and into the frontal lobe. Here she could see the remnants of the hematoma.

"You did remove it!" she exclaimed. "How?"

"Well as I said, I am no doctor," replied Joe's thought, "But it was pretty obvious. I simply isolated the blood clot and teleported it out."

"Teleported?"

"Yes. It means moving things with your mind."

"Wow!" She was amazed.

"*So about that job,*" thought Joe. "*How would you like to be able to diagnose and heal your patients without the need for complicated and risky surgery?*"

Sally opened her eyes and was back in the bay with her staff, all standing still with Joe looking down at her, a small smile on his face. She thought about it for a while.

"You mean I can do this like you?"

"You bet," Joe replied out loud. He released her hand, and she hastily pulled it away, unconsciously wiping it on her gown. "Have you noticed that you often suffer from deja vu? Or that you are often able to correctly diagnose your patients without the full data? Or that sometimes you know who is at the door before opening it?"

"Well. Yes," she replied. "My mother used to say I was psychic because I always knew where she was."

She stopped. Why was she saying this? He had certainly showed her something that was beyond her understanding. She had never seen anything like it. She decided that it had to be real;

if not, she had no idea how he did it. And if it was real, then the possibilities were amazing.

"You see, you have some latent talent," continued Joe. "All you need is a little help. Come with me. Let me show you how you can develop your talents and use them to heal. Join my team and be my lead physician."

Sally internally deliberated. She didn't know this man. Even though he had showed her something exciting, something impossible, something with potential, something that could change everything, she did not trust him. Not one bit. How could she? He couldn't expect her to drop everything, her career, her life. She needed more, a lot more before she could make a decision like that.

"I'm sorry. Joe, is it? I have responsibilities. What you have shown me is pretty amazing, but I can't just up and leave everything behind."

Joe nodded. "I understand." He reached under his gown and produced a business card. "Take this. When you are ready, come and see us." He smiled. "You are going to love Molly."

Sally took the card. An address was written on it in small black letters.

Joe walked away through the curtain clicking his fingers once as he did so. Immediately all of the doctors and nurses surrounding the patient carried on with their work as though nothing had happened.

"Where did that stranger go?" asked Tom, looking puzzled.

The surrounding curtain parted, and a female security guard swept in. "Where is he?" she asked, panting.

Sally could not answer. As Joe had stepped through the curtain, she had seen him disappear. The whoosh of air was still wafting her hair. She looked back at the card in her hand. She placed it in a pocket and looked up.

"He's gone," she said all business-like. "Let's get this fella sorted."

Much later, as she lay in bed, she replayed all of the day's incredible events over in her mind. Despite this, her tired body and mind could not stay awake. As she drifted off, she knew that she would have to visit the address Joe had given her. Her last thoughts were: "Who is Molly?"

Chapter 33 - Death

Jim stood over the body of the woman he had just killed.

He was trembling, his eyes wide and frightened as he realised what he had done. For all his bravado, he had never actually killed anyone, and to find he had finally done it, was shocking. He was so shocked that he could not move. To take a life, he realised, was physically easy but was not easy on the mind. He was locked in place and could not think. He just stood there. He was surprised to feel tears running down his face. He wiped them away angrily with his hand. He was bigger than this. He was the best. He had just beaten an enemy. He should not be feeling this way, but he found he could not look away from her wide, staring, unblinking eyes.

As he stood, unmoving, he heard the lift doors close behind him. He had to move, but he could not. He had escaped, he had found his way out, but he had not expected this. He wanted to kill them all, but when finally confronted with the reality of killing he was surprised how much it had affected him.

The girl lay crumpled on the floor, wearing jeans and a white T-shirt, with her dead eyes looking up at him. He had to do it. There was no way she would have let him pass. She had been the final obstacle. He had to escape. So he had killed her.

As he rationalised what he had done, he began to feel better. The tears stopped and his bravado returned. He really was better than all of those freaks. He had just proved it. This girl had stood in his way and he had killed her, just as he would kill them all.

He managed to avert his gaze from the girl's eyes to look around. He was in a hallway of an ordinary house, albeit what was obviously a grand house, given the furnishings and its size. At the end of the hallway, he saw the front door. With a final glance at the dead girl, he walked towards it.

It was when he reached it and had gripped the handle that he heard the ding of the lift. Fear gripped him as he wrenched the door open and quickly stepped through, closing it behind him as silently as he could. He fervently hoped that whoever stepped out of the lift would only notice the dead girl, and not the front door closing.

Turning away from the door, he ran as fast as he could away from the house. As he ran, the pain in his back intensified and he could feel something tickling the back of his legs, but he dismissed it. He had to get away. He ran across the road into a wooded area, his breathing ragged as the pain made him slow down and he started to limp.

As he stumbled onwards, he was unaware that he was bleeding badly and was leaving a trail of blood behind him.

Chapter 34 - Bella

Kate screamed. She screamed and screamed and did not stop.

Sally wrapped her arms around her and shouted in her face, "It's okay. It was in the past. It's not happening now!" She held onto Kate tightly, desperately trying to calm her down and keep her from thrashing and flailing her arms.

Sally had been in Kate's memories, and she had seen Kate's trauma. She now knew why Kate behaved the way she did, and why she tried to repress these painful memories. She had never seen anything so traumatic. In all of her years as a doctor, she had never experienced anything as extreme as this.

She closed her eyes while holding onto the struggling girl and then snapped them open again as the images flooded in. Oh god, the blood, it was everywhere. Even she, with all her years of training and experience could not believe what she saw.

Kate's little sister, Bella, lying in her own bed. The knife from the kitchen protruding from her chest. Bella's eyes wide with shock, fear, and pain. The blood pumping from around the wound, spurting upwards, into Kate's face. Bella's gasping, gurgling sounds. Their father on the floor beside the bed, trousers around his ankles.

It was like something from a horror movie.

Kate had killed her own sister.

—

Joe's eyes snapped open. "Kate!" he shouted loudly.

There was a loud bang and the room filled with black acrid smoke pouring from the equipment on the bench. Molly was thrown backwards as her chair tipped, falling onto her back. In the corner of the room, Jonas grunted in pain stiffened and slumped in his chair.

"What's happening?" exclaimed Joe.

Kate was in pain, he felt it. He could hear her screaming inside his mind.

He sat up and sent out an urgent thought, "*Sally! Is Kate alright? I heard her screaming.*"

Sally's calming thought came straight back. "*It's okay Joe. I have it under control.*"

He breathed a sigh of relief. Kate was okay. Although, he could sense the turmoil in Sally's thoughts. There was clearly something going on with Kate, but he trusted Sally.

"*Alright but get in touch if you need me.*"

"*I will. You certainly know how to find em!*" she replied, with a shaky thought.

What did that mean? He signed off and directed his attention to his surroundings.

The room was in a mess. Molly was getting up from the floor, disentangling herself from the chair legs. She picked up her glasses and pushed onto her face. The equipment she had been sitting at sparked and smoked. Fans automatically engaged and were clearing the smoke from the room. On his right, Jonas was slumped over, half in and half out of the chair he had been sitting on. Some of the panels in the ceiling had fallen; one of them had landed on Joe's legs, others were just dislodged.

"Uhgg," said Molly as she stood.

"Are you alright Mol?" he asked as he tried to remove the headset.

"Leave the headset!" She spoke sharply. "You'll only break it!" She shuffled over to her equipment and looked at the screens and dials. "I thought so," she murmured.

There was a massive wump noise accompanied by a whirlwind of air, and a large, red metallic figure appeared in the middle of the room.

Molly held up her arm with her palm outstretched towards the HAZPRO figure. *"It's fine,"* she projected. She stumbled and steadied herself by gripping the equipment bench with the other hand. *"Everything is okay. Just overloaded."*

She turned and looked at Joe. "I have never..." She breathed in, "...never... seen such power."

She walked unsteadily towards his chair. "Your Psi score is off the scale."

When she was beside Joe, she raised her hand and held it over Joe's forehead. The rings and chains on her hand glowed briefly.

"Wow," she said, and set to removing his headset.

As she did so, she turned to the red figure and sent a quick thought, *"Get Jonas out of here and get him checked over. He'll be fine. He just took the brunt of the shock, that's all."*

The HAZPRO clumped to Jonas and touched his arm. Jonas and the armoured suit disappeared with a snap of air.

"It was Kate," Joe explained. "I heard her scream and knew she was in trouble. Something in me surged out of control." He looked around the room. "I'm sorry I made a mess of your lab."

She dismissed his concern. "Don't worry about it. I have others. You heard Kate, you say?"

Joe nodded.

"How is that possible if she isn't wearing an Assist?"

"Beats me. We have some sort of connection. I don't understand it."

Molly looked into Joe's eyes as she pulled up the headset from his head. "I hope things with Kate work out. But if they don't...."

Joe grinned. "You have Sally. And anyway, you knew that I had a high Psi score."

She ignored the Sally comment. "Yes, but not that high. Did you know that it's higher than it was before? The read-outs confirm it. And for the record, there is nothing wrong with your brain."

"That's a relief," breathed Joe, "But I kind of knew that. How do you explain the increased Psi quotient?"

Molly lifted the headset from Joe's head. "I'm not sure," she said. She paused and stared off into the distance. "Maybe some kinds of trauma increase the mind's resilience and make it stronger." She placed the headset on the bench.

"More research is required." She looked at Joe coyly. "I would love to join minds with you in order to kick off that research."

Joe grinned again and placed a hand on her cheek. His Assist jangled and sparkled.

"I think that Kate is the one for me," he replied.

Molly feigned a crest-fallen look. "Shame." She smiled and then frowned. "Seriously, we could do with finding out more about this. If we can boost our Psi, that would prove very useful. Particularly given what's going on right now."

Joe grew serious. "Yes. I've heard something about it, but I haven't been fully briefed yet."

Molly looked earnestly into his eyes. "It's bad, really bad. We need all the advantages we can get, and this may be one of them. I'm serious, Joe. This needs more investigation and research. And even though I am clearing you right now, there is no telling what might happen in the future. That increase in Psi. There must be a cost for that."

"Maybe," replied Joe. "But right now, from what I hear, we don't have much time."

"That's true. I remember the day when we lost you. You disappeared in a fire fight. No one knew where you had gone. Most of us thought you were dead, vapourised. And then you just turn up out of the blue. What's that all about?"

Joe stared off into the distance. "I don't remember, and that is frustrating as hell and does not make sense. This," he held up his hand with his Assist, "means I should be able to recall everything, but there is nothing. It's almost as though it never happened."

Molly put her Assisted hand on Joe's forehead again. Her head bowed as her rings glowed. Joe closed his eyes.

After a couple of minutes both opened their eyes and stared at each other.

"Nothing," said Molly. "Not a damn thing! And that really worries me. It shouldn't be possible."

"I agree," said Joe. "It makes no sense." He hesitated. "Nor does Kate." Molly pulled her hand away and looked quizzically at him. "What I mean is that I don't understand how or why I was drawn to her." He looked meaningfully at her. "But regardless, I am pretty sure she is the one for me." He smiled at her and lifted his hand to her cheek. "So until further notice, no joining. We need to treat Kate with kid gloves. She is new to this stuff, and she is a bit…" he hesitated, "…a bit head strong and flighty!"

Molly smiled. "So I've heard." She stepped away and started picking up items from the floor. "And speaking of which, I hope Sally can help her."

Joe looked serious. "So do I," he breathed. "So do I."

Neither of them realised the significance of what had just happened.

Chapter 35 - Assisted

Kate was still screaming. Sally held her close, her arms around Kate's waist, and was shocked to discover that she was screaming with her.

They were back in Sally's treatment room, and no longer in Kate's memories. Kate sat up in the bed, the blankets pooled around her as they dropped from her shoulders revealing her breasts. The screams did not go unnoticed. A massive, red armoured figure appeared in the room in a whirlwind of motion. Papers swirled and instruments clattered as they fell to the floor. Whump, whump went the red armoured Complex soldier as it took two steps towards the women. Then the door smashed to the side and two more unarmoured men rushed in.

Sally sensed the motion behind her and with an effort, outstretched a hand, palm upwards towards the doorway. The figures stopped, unsure what to do.

Sally slowly, so slowly, took control of herself and stopped screaming. She moved her other hand from Kate's waist and placed her hand gently over Kate's open mouth, muffling her screams. Kate's eyes were tightly closed and tears were streaming down her cheeks.

Sally took a deep breath. She moved her outstretched hand to Kate's forehead, the rings glowed briefly, and Kate's scream died on her lips.

"Holy Moly!" breathed Sally. She turned her head towards the figures.

"*It's alright,*" she projected, "*We don't need your help.*"

She replied to Joe's urgent thought, "*It's okay, Joe. I have it under control.*"

The two unarmoured men looked at each other. One shrugged, and they slowly left the room, closing the door behind them. The red armoured figure disappeared in a snap of wind. The two women were alone.

Sally severed the connection with Joe and turned back to Kate. "Shh," she whispered, "It's all okay. You're safe."

Kate opened her eyes. "What the fuck!" she shouted.

"I was there with you all the time, as I said I would be," replied Sally. "I know everything."

She looked meaningfully into Kate's eyes. They were face to face with just inches between them. Kate's eyes welled with tears.

"But you came through your trauma and you are okay. And now that you have, I can help you."

Kate's tears plopped down onto both her own and Sally's chests. Sally continued quickly. "Now that you have this," she took hold of Kate's right hand and raised it up into the air, "you can control these emotions and feelings. I'll show you."

"It's not possible," said Kate. "I am a bad, horrible person and I deserve to die."

"Stop that!" exclaimed Sally. "I'm not having any of it!" She breathed deeply again. "I know exactly why you feel this way. But you don't have to anymore."

She moved her right hand and intertwined her fingers with Kate's right hand. The women's' rings and chains jangled together. Kate looked at their hands and saw them flash. Without warning, she felt a tingling throughout her body along with a sense of calmness. She stopped crying and felt relaxed and warm.

"What was that...?" Kate breathed.

Sally smiled. "The Assist gives us control. It allows us to access all parts of our minds and to do things like remove pain, communicate over long distances, see things that others can't see and feel things others can't feel." She continued. "It also allows us to compartmentalise, sort and store memories. Even those we don't want to remember." She looked at Kate. "Kate, you don't have to be frightened and hate yourself anymore. You can simply file those memories away so that they don't bother you. Once you do that, you'll be back to normal."

Kate stared at her. "I find that very hard to believe," she stated. "I can never forget what I did."

She shuddered. But the feeling of wellness persisted.

"Don't worry," Sally replied. "I told you, I can show you how. It wasn't your fault. It was an accident. You were trying to protect Bella."

Kate did not answer.

"You're not a bad person," continued Sally. "I can understand why you think that you are, but it's not true. And I can show you how to file those memories away so that they don't bother you anymore."

"You made me live through all that again." Kate's face twisted in pain. "What sort of doctor are you and what sort of crap are you talking about?"

Sally grimaced. "I don't blame you for thinking that way. Try this…"

The rings flashed again. Kate felt her head clear as Sally directed them both inward, deep into Kate's mind. Together they could see everything inside Kate's mind; all her memories, her thoughts, and feelings. Everything was visible, but tangled like a spider's web, her memories intertwined and twisted in a mesh of connections.

"*Obviously your memories are not like a book or a filing cabinet, but we can arrange them like that if we want.*" She watched as Sally selected and moved memories around. "*In fact, memories are a complex set of junctions and connections - a network of interconnected neurons spread throughout the brain. This is far too difficult for us to follow and visualise, so I like to arrange them like this to make them easier to understand and to manipulate.*"

She watched as Sally arranged her memories, and then select and mark all of the horrible ones, consolidating them together.

"*Your bad memories are easy to find,*" she explained. "*They are so ingrained into your psyche because of their nature. So, I'm just collecting them together. And now I'll move them away into a corner away from the forefront of your mind.*"

Kate looked on amazed as Sally manipulated her memories with practiced ease.

"Now that they are over here out of the way, they won't intrude upon your normal day to day thoughts. They aren't erased - although we could do that if you wanted. They are a part of you, for good or bad, and they make you what you are today. But you don't have to suffer anymore by reliving them over and over. We can move them out of the way like this, so they won't bother you anymore."

Kate could see exactly that. The bad memories were still there but no longer taking over. She could see that effectively they had been removed. An enormous feeling of excitement, relief and surprise washed over her.

"Oh my God!" she shouted.

She snapped open her eyes. The two women were still in the same position, staring at each other. Sally was smiling. Kate had a shocked expression on her face. Suddenly, Kate moved forward and kissed Sally full on the lips. Although a little surprised, Sally accepted the kiss and said. "Why, thank you." She grinned.

Kate drew back, embarrassed. "I'm sorry. I don't know why I did that."

Sally continued grinning. "Don't be," she said. "I rather enjoyed it."

Kate flushed. Sally took a serious note.

"So you see; you are not just healed, but you now have access to new faculties." She nodded towards their still entwined hands. "The bad news is that you will need some training, but you will soon pick things up."

Kate recovered quickly. "This is just amazing," she said. "How is it possible? I saw what you just did, and I think…" She cocked her head to one side. "I feel really good." She stopped. "I can't remember when I last felt like this."

"That is so nice to hear," replied Sally. "I'm amazing at my job, even if I do say so myself." She gave a little laugh. "Seriously, it's all about this." She untwined their fingers and held up her hand, jiggling her fingers to show off her Assist. "Amazing bit of kit. It taps into our psychic fields, merges, and boosts them. Originally invented by our beloved Joe. You should have seen the first versions." She grimaced. "But now, I think that they look quite pretty really." She wriggled her fingers.

Kate looked at her own Assist. She could see that it was made up of five rings, one for each digit. Each one was joined by a short, delicate chain forming a complete circuit connecting each ring to its neighbour. There was one more chain that connected between the ring on her little finger and the one on her thumb. She flexed her fingers, the chains were just long enough to allow it.

"Of course," continued Sally, "you need the other half on your left foot in order to complete the set."

She carefully removed Kate's drip and then moved away from the bed and started scanning the shelves. "I have the other half of your set here." She picked them up and returned to the bed.

"I need more?" asked Kate.

"They come in sets," replied Sally. "You will need both and you should not remove either of them at all until I, or another Psi doctor, gives you permission." Sally gently pushed Kate back to a lying down position and pulled up the blanket to cover her. "Lie back down and I will fit them for you."

Once Kate was back down on the bed, Sally pulled up the bedsheet, exposing Kate's legs and feet. She selected her left foot and paused before pushing the rings onto her toes. She looked up at Kate.

"This will give you a bit of a rush."

"Rush?" asked Kate.

"Don't panic," smiled Sally. "It's not horrible."

She carefully pushed each ring onto each toe of her foot. When she had finished, she stood back.

"I don't feel anything..." started Kate. "Oh my God!" she gasped.

She had thought that she had seen everything, had seen all there was to see in this strange place called the Complex full of Psi-enabled people.

She was wrong. An electric tingle ran through her body from head to toe, causing her to arch her back. It was a mixture of warmth, tingling and a sexual thrill. She laid back with a small moan bringing her hands up to her red, flushed face. Slowly, the tingling subsided, and she relaxed, feeling more content than she had for years. Her lips turned up into a smile and a long sigh escaped from her. Her hands fell back to her sides and her toes curled upwards. Lazily she opened her eyes.

Sally was before her smiling downwards. She pulled the bedsheets down, covering Kate's feet.

"Good," she stated matter-of-factly. "You stay here for a while and recover. We wouldn't want our Joe to see you like this. At least, not just yet." Her smile widened as she broke into a grin.

"What happened?" whispered Kate.

"It's perfectly normal and nothing to worry about. It's an effect that happens when us women first have an Assist fitted. It's completely harmless and quite nice. For some reason yet to be discovered, the boys are not so lucky."

"It felt like..." Kate stopped, embarrassed. "Well, you know, it was a bit like...." She broke off.

"An orgasm?" asked Sally.

Kate nodded, her face all flushed.

"Exactly," said Sally. "When your Assist is first fitted, it taps into your Psi core. In doing so, it plumbs into the electrical activity of your brain and body. Over time, it will re-route and embed itself even further until it becomes a part of you. You will find that you have new senses and most of your existing senses are enhanced, many of which are connected in some way to your sexuality."

Kate stared. "But I'm not very....." She hesitated.

"Experienced?" Sally finished her sentence. Kate nodded. "I'm not surprised, considering what you have been through." She held up her hand. "Don't worry, those memories can no longer hurt you. Remember, we put them away." Looking down at Kate, Sally continued, "Experience has nothing to do with it. Let's just say that new opportunities are now open to you." She arched her eyebrows and then frowned. "However, I think I am going to prescribe some intensive training to help you manage your new faculties and help you keep your newly discovered emotions under control. Does that sound okay to you?"

Kate nodded gratefully. "I would appreciate that," she said, "I feel so different. I'm not sure how to be me."

Sally patted Kate's hand. "I'll be right back. You rest and stay where you are."

Kate closed her eyes as Sally walked away.

Sally shut the door behind her. Her smile faded and she shuddered. She leaned against a wall and blew out a lung full of air. She had never experienced such memories before and hoped she never would again. Although she had helped Kate block them, she had not done so for herself. She closed her eyes and saw images of blood. The knife jutting out from Kate's sister's chest, the feeling of horror and fear, the sounds of the screams and the final gasps of life-giving air and the staring eyes.

There was no getting away from it; Kate had been horribly abused by her father for years and when she was too old for him, he had started to abuse her sister. In an effort to protect her, Kate had tried to stab him, but instead had missed and killed her sister.

After that, there was no turning back. Kate had fled from her home, living on the streets, falling into a pit of despair, drinking alcohol and taking drugs. All in an effort to forget. Of course, it was all in vain. It was no wonder that she had been in a state. In fact, she thought, she was amazed that she had not tried to take her life. But there was one thing she had learned from being inside her mind - Kate was a very special woman.

One question remained. What was her connection with Joe?

Chapter 36 - Rescue?

Jim was running.

He ran at full pelt through the trees. Branches whipped his face and roots tripped him as he ran and ran through the wooded area. He was still emotional after killing that girl. She hadn't been a freak. She didn't look like a freak. She looked like an ordinary girl.

He was angry at himself for being so weak but kept running. His breathing became ragged, and the pain from his back was making it more and more difficult to keep going. He was sure that the real freaks were after him. They must be just behind, about to catch him at any moment, and drag him back into their dark evil place.

Soon, he could not go on. The pain was too much, and he couldn't breathe. He stopped, resigning himself to being caught and collapsed onto his side, near a large tree. His blood pooled behind him where his wound bled freely.

He lay there for some time, gasping for air. Presently, he was able to sit up and lean back against the tree. He knew that he was hurt. He could feel the blood running down his back and could see it all around him. He grew lightheaded and cold as he realised two things. The first was that he could not hear or see his pursuers and secondly, he could not go on. That bitch had killed him, he thought. Stabbed him in the back like a coward. And now he was going to die alone in this wood and without achieving what he had set out to do - to kill his twin brother.

He hated him. Oh, how he hated him. The favourite, the clever one, the better looking one - even though they were identical twins. It was not fair. He had never been recognised for his brilliance. His grades had always been better than Joe's - just a bit, but still better. But no one had ever said well done to him. It was always, 'why can't you be like Joe?', 'Joe is such a nice boy.', 'Joe works so hard and is always so polite'. Jim's face twisted in anger.

Well, he had tried. Tried and failed. Eventually he realised that he would never be like Joe, so he had stopped trying. He left home with a burning anger in his core. He left and made his own way in the world. Spending his time in his workshop, tinkering, and discovering, until he had thought he was ready. Ready to take on Joe and wipe that stupid smile from his face.

But Jim had underestimated him. He had not realised that Joe had been tinkering as well. But in Joe's case, it looked as though he had recruited an army. An army of freaks, for god's sake! Once again, Joe was better than him.

Anger and sadness were his only two emotions as he slowly slid sideways across the tree's trunk. As he did, his hand gripped one of the devices he had found in the freak's lair. His fingers rubbed over the exposed electronic components. He was too weak to notice the flash. And his body was far too weak to convulse from the small electrical discharge as the last moments of his life drained away and he fell onto his side.

Slowly, he closed his eyes for the last time.

As his eyes closed, he didn't see the ball of green light appear above the trees and slowly drift down to the ground in front of him. He never saw it expand and coalesce into a two metre sphere. He didn't see the centre turn black and expand until it became all black. And he never saw the figure step from within its centre that walked up to him and look down upon his body.

The figure was tall, and thin with red glowing eyes. It had no mouth or nose and a smooth matte white body.

A certain soldier back at the Complex would have recognised it.

Chapter 37 - Kate and the Enemy

"So I can't see her?" asked Joe.

Sally looked at him intently. "Don't think of pulling rank on me," she said forcefully. "Kate needs rest. She has been through some intense trauma and needs to recover. And I don't want you going in there dribbling and lusting all over her. She needs sleep and time."

"But is she alright?" he asked earnestly. Sally nodded. "And she's outfitted?"

Sally huffed. "Yes Joe, she is now Assisted. But I don't want you bothering her just yet, especially Psionically. She needs to get used to it and she needs training. She does not need you frightening her, she is not ready,"

Joe sighed in relief. "That's good," he breathed. "Don't worry, I'll do exactly what you say. I won't bother her. I'm just relieved that she is okay." He looked at Sally intently. "And you, of course."

Sally arched her eyebrows. "I'm glad to hear it. I'm pleased that you are concerned for all your staff, not just Kate." She shuddered. "I can tell you that it was one of the worst cases of trauma I have ever had to deal with. It's no wonder that she was the way she was." She paused. "In fact, I'm surprised that she has not tried to take her own life. Underneath it all, she is a very strong girl."

Joe considered for a moment. "I suppose you aren't going to tell me anything about it?"

"Definitely not!" retorted Sally. "That is entirely up to Kate and not me. When she is ready, she will tell you if she wants to." She lowered her head and looked up at him through her eyebrows. "And that means that you leave it to her and you don't push or probe." She let her displeasure show.

Joe grinned and held up his hands. "Don't worry, Doc. I'll follow your instructions to the letter."

"You'd better," she replied. "Now, I have other things to do."

She turned and started off down the corridor. Joe also turned and sent out a mental call.

"*Steve. What's happening? Give me an update.*" He walked down the corridor in the opposite direction. As he did, he mentally conversed with Steve.

———

Kate awoke from sleep suddenly. For a moment she did not know where she was, and then it all came back to her. As she lay on her side, she smiled. Her mind felt clear; no headache, no longing for drugs and best of all, no blackness. She closed her eyes and let herself doze. For the first time in years, she felt relaxed. She could let her mind wander wherever it wanted, knowing that it was safe to do so, and that she was safe. There was nothing for her to worry about.

Sally had been nice, she decided. She had helped her, and it was because of her that she was feeling good now. She must thank her properly, she thought. She realised that she hadn't actually said those words. She remembered kissing her and she felt embarrassed, her face grew warm.

She clenched her hand and felt the newly fitted rings. She wriggled her left foot and felt the foot rings. She had an Assist. She supposed that it had been given this name because that's exactly what it did - assist. Assist her Psi ability, whatever that was. As far as she was aware, she had none.

Her thoughts drifted to Joe. She liked him, she thought, although she was very wary about him. He had introduced her to a world of strange things, most of which she did not understand. But at the same time without this Assist - she wriggled her toes again - she would still be in a state.

It was the smell that alerted her first.

As her mind wandered and drifted, she slowly became aware of a peppery smell. It was gentle at first but gradually became stronger. Her nose wrinkled and her thoughts stopped drifting. What was that smell? She opened her eyes. She saw nothing unusual, just the side of the bed and the wall painted white. As she lay there the smell grew stronger still. It was not unpleasant, but it was unusual, and it was becoming overpowering as it filled the room. Annoyed and perplexed, she rolled onto her back. She screamed.

Standing over her, next to the bed, was a humanoid figure with red glowing eyes. Its skin was completely smooth and white, with two metallic protrusions sticking up above each shoulder, like gun barrels. Although it was tall and menacing, it did not move. Kate shrank back and scooted up the bed to get as far away as possible. As she did so, she fell over the side of the bed, onto the floor. She stopped screaming and grunted in pain as she hit the floor shoulder first. The figure loomed over the bed and looked across it and down at her but still did not move towards her.

With a loud clap and a whirlwind of air, a giant, red-suited figure snapped into existence. She realised that she had seen one just like it before. It was exactly like the one she had seen in Joe's place all that time ago.

There was no warning, no sizing each other up. The red armoured soldier took two giant steps and crashed into the humanoid. There was a huge bang and clatter as they both fell to the floor. As they fell, they clipped the bed and it flew at Kate. Lying on the floor, Kate lifted her hand to protect herself. There was a blue flash from her Assist and the bed stopped dead and dropped to the floor with a crash, before it hit her. Kate's eyes opened wide in shock and surprise.

As the two figures struggled and rolled on the floor, the door crashed open.

"Kate!" shouted Joe as he ran in and slid across the floor towards her.

He collided into her and flung his body over hers, shielding her from any flying debris. Over his shoulder and through his hair, she saw a beam of shimmering red slash across the ceiling, burning through it and showering them both with falling plastic, metal, and cement. There was a deafening crash and the beam flickered out. There was a repeated thudding and then a scream of metal on metal. Joe's arms tightened around her, and a shimmer of light surrounded them. "He's protecting me," she thought, and she gripped him tightly around his back, her eyes wide in fear and confusion.

There was more crashing and banging and then an entire wall disappeared in a burst of light and flame. Two more red armoured soldiers appeared in snaps of wind and threw themselves into the fray. She heard a roar of wind, and the air grew stiflingly hot. The ground shook as one soldier was thrown across the room to crash through the wall where the door used to be. After three repetitive loud booms, each one rattling her teeth, there was a sudden silence.

Joe lifted his head and looked into her eyes, mere inches between them. She felt his panting breath on her cheek.

"You alright?" he whispered.

She nodded, "I think so, I was asleep," she said as though she needed to explain.

The air around them shimmered and then flashed as dust and concrete fell from the ceiling. It slid around them as though sliding across a bubble.

"I know," he said gently as he lifted one hand and brushed a lock of her hair from her face.

They stared into each other's eyes. Kate could feel his mental presence. She could sense his concern and worry. She reflexively moved the fingers of her hand and felt the rings and chains grow warm. She could feel her mind move forward and past his eyes into his. Once there, she felt a wash of emotions and thoughts crash into her senses. There was the worry and concern that she had already felt, but there was more, much more. There was anger, such anger as she had never felt before. He was angry that she had been in danger and could have been killed. There was anger that somehow it had happened when he had been nearby. And there was anger that they had been caught off guard, that their most secure and defended base had been so easily discovered and invaded. They had been invaded, for fuck's sake! She had a glimpse of his fears and doubts. She saw his excitement when he had first discovered Psi and his overwhelming dedication and work, he had put into this organisation. How he had sought out others like him. How he had realised that those that he found were society's outsiders, some even diagnosed with mental conditions and locked up in hospitals. He had found them, helped them, and recruited them all and shown each one that they were not ill or damaged; instead, they were special. She now knew why Sally had referred to him as 'our beloved Joe'. She also saw that deep down, he was hiding things. He was terrified of what was happening around him, of this baffling war. And even deeper still, she saw for the briefest of moments her face. Joe was hiding, or trying to hide, his feelings for her.

Their connection ended abruptly. She was back in her own head, staring into his eyes. They said nothing but she could hear movement in the room.

An understanding passed between them. A realisation of something. Something had happened. Something not planned, but that they had both hoped for in their own way, at some point in their lives.

"All clear" a voice boomed, breaking the moment.

Joe's head flicked around to take in the devastation.

"No need to vocalise anymore," stated Joe. "We are all Psi-enabled here."

Kate was startled to hear the soldiers reply, loud and clear in her mind. *"Sorry Sir."*

Joe moved. *"We can get up now."*

She heard his voice in her head. He started to get up off her, but she grabbed him and pulled him back. They looked into each other's eyes again.

"You know what just happened?" she asked, not used to the mind talking or whatever they called it.

Joe nodded. *"Yes, we were attacked."* His words echoed inside her head.

"Not that. Us."

"Ah. That," he said out loud. "Let's just say that there is a definite connection." He smiled and pulled away.

This time she let him. "It's not over, mister," she said to his back as he rose. "That was definitely something."

Joe paused and nodded. She felt his affirmation slide into her head.

Once up, Joe looked around the room. It was chaos. Plaster, concrete, bits of metal and dust covered the floor. Fused lumps of slag and black streaks covered the one remaining wall. In one corner molten metal glowed, radiating heat into the room. There was hardly anything recognisable left. And in the centre was the creature that had attacked Kate. It was clearly dead, its eyes no longer red, but dark. One arm was missing and there was a huge smoking hole in its chest. Next to it was a HAZPRO suit with its head caved in. The other two HAZPRO figures stood nearby, their weapons levelled at the enemy on the floor.

Sally ran in, jumping over concrete blocks and metal bars. She veered around the crumpled and crushed bed and made straight for Kate, completely ignoring Joe.

"Kate," she burst out breathlessly. "Are you okay?"

Sally knelt beside her, holding one hand to Kate's head, and running the other along her body. There was a look of concern on her face.

"Here, let me cover you up."

She held her hand up in the air to catch a blanket that appeared with a snap. She draped it over Kate. It was only then that Kate realised that she was wearing nothing.

Oh, for fucks sake! she thought. What next? Here she was lying on the floor naked! And Joe had been on top of her! And why was she worrying about that when she had just been attacked? She should be cowering in fear.

"*Don't worry,*" Sally's words were in her head. "*It's the aftereffects of the treatment. Your emotions will return to normal soon.*" She resumed running her hand up and down Kate's body as her Assist began to glow. "*Hmm, nothing broken*" She lowered her head, closing her eyes. Her Assist glowed purple. "*No other damage that I can detect. Just some scrapes and scratches.*" She looked up and smiled at Kate. "All good. No problems. How do you feel?"

"I feel okay, I guess," replied Kate. "Embarrassed? Especially with what happened with Joe.."

"We'll get to that later," replied Sally. "Let's get you out of here first."

She pulled Kate up to her feet, making sure that the blanket covered her. Together they walked out, Sally shielding her from the two bodies on the floor.

Joe watched them leave and then looked down at the crushed head of the HAZPRO on the floor.

"Who was it?" he asked of no one in particular.

Mike, who was in one of the other HAZPRO's replied, *"Erica. She was nice, she's just come back from Arcadia."*

Joe sighed. Another of the Alliance dead. He remembered Erica. He had recovered her from a mental institution in the southern United States. She had been interned there for three years when he had found her. He recalled how happy she was when she finally understood that her illness was no illness after all and that she had a talent and it should be celebrated. Once fitted with her Assist, she became a valued member of the Alliance. And now she was gone. She had been killed protecting Kate. She had performed her duty right to the end.

He turned to the dead enemy, which was still smoking. This was the first time he had seen one close-up. He examined it closely noting the smooth alabaster white outer layer, and the metallic and electrical components sticking out of the hole in its chest and arm socket. It looked like a robot and he would have sworn that it was save for the red liquid trickling out of the many cuts and grazes all over its body. Was it an organic robot? But then why all of the metal inside it?

He turned away. *"Get this mess cleaned up and get this dead thing,"* he indicated the dead enemy figure, *"to the labs. I want our best scientists working on it immediately. Tell them to get a report ready ASAP."*

With one last look at Erica, he exited the room. *"See to it that Erica is recovered properly, and her body looked after."* He sent a last command.

Chapter 38 - Alex

3 Years ago

Alex worked at the University of Arizona in Tucson Arizona. He was a leading research scientist in the field of dark energy. For the last six years the Defence Advanced Research Projects Agency: DARPA, had been funding his research.

Observations by astronomers around the world, had shown that rather than the universe's expansion slowing over time, it was, in fact, accelerating. When first discovered, it had been completely unexpected. Astronomers had been trying to explain this expansion since 1988, and so far, there were numerous theories but none had been proven. Dark energy had been coined as a place holder to describe this observable expansion effect. Although it was generally accepted that around 68% of the universe was dark energy, no one knew what it was.

Alex was part of a small number of scientists across the world who ascribed to the theory of quintessence, which described dark energy as a field or energy fluid that filled all of space. His entire career had been devoted to proving this theory by detecting and directing this energy field. And now, with the DARPA funding and his hard work, he was finally getting somewhere.

Alone in his laboratory, he was ready to run his latest experiment. The equipment had taken four and a half months to assemble and, according to his latest equations, should be able to detect the energy field. If he could show that the field existed, he would be one step closer to tapping into it and maybe one day directing it. Not only that, but he would also be able to secure further funding. His DARPA sponsors were starting to get itchy feet. After six years, there had been nothing to show for their money and he was starting to get hints that they may withdraw it and mothball the project. He couldn't allow that. Not when he was so close.

Sitting at his workbench, he scrutinised the numbers scrolling down the screen in front of him. The experiment had been running for two hours, which he gauged should be enough time.

He looked with pride over the top of the screen at the mess of wires and electronics spread all over the bench. The entire bench of equipment was designed to measure the different energies collected from the detector which it grouped into categories, one of which was dark energy.

Rolling his wheeled chair over to another bench equipped with another screen, he signed in and started the analysis program. This bench was equipped with yet more electronics including a scaffolding of metal work equipped with four mesh dishes pointing in the directions of the compass, its many components made up his latest attempt at a detector.

He was pleased to see data and charts move on the screen as the numbers started to add up. Rubbing his hands together in anticipation, he then selected the final analysis programme. As he stabbed the return button on the keyboard, he was startled to hear a voice behind him.

"It's not going to work."

Alex spun around in his chair, the wheels skidding and the back of it crashing into the work bench. He was surprised to see a young man with long blond hair standing a few paces away. He watched, speechless, as the man gazed around the lab. The stranger then started to casually move between the equipment benches, lightly touching various components.

Alex was suddenly angry. "Who the hell are you and what are you doing here?" he spluttered.

The young man stopped, turned, and stared back at him. Alex noticed that he had very bright blue eyes.

"My name is Joe," said the stranger calmly, "and I'm here to offer you the chance to prove your theories."

Alex almost laughed hearing the ridiculous reply. At 55 he had spent most of his adult life at various institutions working on dark energy projects. What could this youth know about it? He was barely out of school. He got up from his chair and walked over to a desk upon which sat a phone. He intended to call security to have this interloper removed. He lifted the handset and started to punch three numbers with his forefinger. The first two clicked and he heard a tone with each number in the earpiece. When he went to punch the third, the phone was gone. His finger missed and stabbed thin air.

He stared blankly at the spot on the desk where the phone had been. In his left hand, the handset was also gone. He was holding nothing up to his ear.

"I can't let you call security just yet," came a voice behind him. "We haven't finished our conversation."

Alex whirled around. "What the hell is going on?" he shouted.

The stranger stood before him. He was dressed in loose, faded jeans and a black T shirt underneath an open, long, dark coat. His long blond hair reached his shoulders with much of it falling across his face, but the bright almost luminous eyes peeked intently at him.

"There is no need to be concerned," said Joe. "I came to see you. I'm interested in your work. I think that we have something in common."

"Just what the hell are you talking about?" asked Alex, a little calmer. "How did you get in here? Where is the phone? And anyway, why should I listen to you? Who the hell are you?"

Joe smiled. "I will explain all in due course," he replied. "First, I want to talk about dark energy. You are close, very close. What would you say if I told you that all of your theories were correct and that it was possible to detect and direct the dark energy field?"

Alex was dumbfounded. Who was this young man? How could he know anything about dark energy? And more relevant, why should he believe anything he said? After all, he had obviously broken into his lab. He couldn't possibly know anything. He was probably just some kid playing games.

"If you don't leave right now, I will go get security myself and have them throw you out." Alex said firmly.

Joe sighed. "Of course, you don't believe me. Why should you? Maybe a demonstration?"

He held up his right hand. Alex caught a glimpse of something metallic and he flinched, raising up his arms to ward off an attack.

Joe smiled. He wriggled his fingers. A blue spark leaped between them. There was a noise coming from the desk behind Alex. He spun round and watched mesmerised as a pen lifted slowly and drifted past him towards Joe, who caught it in his raised hand.

Alex gulped a couple of times like a goldfish. "How.... How did you do that? Was that some kind of trick?"

"No trick," answered Joe. "I tapped into the energy field and manipulated it. You call that field dark energy. I call it something else, but it doesn't matter what it's called. Your theories are correct. There is an energy field all around us. It pervades all of space. With the right equipment, it can be manipulated. The only thing you are missing is the mind."

"The mind?" stuttered a shocked Alex.

"Of course," replied Joe. "The mind or conscious thought operates at the quantum level and can therefore interface with the field. You probably hadn't made that connection because you are a physicist concerned with the non-biological universe. You've been correct all along. If you had worked with a psychologist or a philosopher, you might have made the connection." Joe smiled again. "Or maybe not."

Alex didn't know what to think. He was in complete shock. He had no idea what to do. Was this Joe talking sense or garbage? Was this still some game he was playing? But then how did the pen move? Thinking about it, he had seen magicians on stage do something similar. It was an illusion. The pen was on a fine, practically invisible thread.

"You are talking complete garbage and you are trying to fool me with your tricks. Well, young man, you will find that I won't fall for any of it. I'm going to get security." He turned and started to walk towards the door.

"That's a shame," Joe shouted after him. "We could do amazing things together."

Alex kept walking. He reached the door and grabbed the handle. When he pulled the door, it didn't move. It seemed as though it was locked, although he didn't recall locking it. He twisted the handle back and forth and pulled harder. It wouldn't budge.

"Let me try and convince you one more time," came Joe's voice. "If you still don't believe me, I'll leave. Well, actually, I'm pretty sure you will believe me."

Alex did not reply. He pulled at the door with all of his might, but it did not budge. He turned and faced Joe who stood in the middle of his lab.

"Have you locked this door?" he asked. He was starting to get angry again.

"I've manipulated the atoms in the door frame so they have bonded with the door. You won't be able to open it."

Alex just stared at Joe. "That's impossible," he stated. "Unlock the door now."

Joe did not reply. He raised his right hand again, this time the blue glow engulfed his hand. He flicked his hand towards one of the workbenches. A ball of blue fire streaked from his hand and struck the bench which promptly exploded sending glass shards and bits of metal flying through the air. The sound was deafening, causing Alex to cover his ears. Great flaming globs of material hit other benches, the air screamed, and a fire roared into life as Alex dropped to the ground. Acrid smoke started to fill the air as the bench and everything on it burned in a white-hot intense heat, which also caused the paint to bubble on a nearby wall and melted the ceiling tiles.

"Holy shit!" screamed Alex, as he cowered on the floor, arms covering his head and ears.

As parts of the ceiling crashed down, he squinted through half-closed eyelids towards the middle of the room and saw Joe standing silently. None of the burning material had touched him, nor was the smoke reaching him. It was like he was in the eye of a storm. The air around him appeared calm and clear as he surveyed the destruction. Through watering eyes, Alex saw that Joe was completely unaffected. Nothing had touched him, nor could it, he realised as he heard a small explosion and saw a flaming piece of metal crash into something invisible two feet in front of Joe. It hit and then slid vertically downwards until it dropped to the floor. Alex saw that there was a ring of flaming debris around Joe and he understood that Joe was being protected by an invisible screen. It was at that moment, as he breathed in the smoke and a coughing fit wracked his body, that he knew that this was no trick. Joe had been telling the truth.

He was unaware that Joe walked over towards him and laid a hand on his shoulder. He didn't hear or feel the whoosh of air. He didn't feel the floor change from being hard to soft. He didn't feel the change of temperature from hot to cold and he didn't see the light change from bright to dark.

He didn't feel or see anything because his eyes were tight closed against the smoke and his body was convulsing with coughing. He lay on the ground, unaware of anything save for the pain in his eyes and throat as he coughed and retched. Presently, he recovered enough to open his eyes and roll over onto his back. Through watering eyes he saw a smiling Joe standing over him.

"You'll be okay," said Joe.

Alex looked around, squinting with blurry eyes. He was shocked to see that it was dark. Where was he? Then he saw the glow and heard the flames. He was outside! How had that happened?

Joe leaned down and pushed a small card into Alex's shirt pocket. Alex tried to raise his arms, but he was too weak and exhausted.

"If you want to learn more and join my team, come and see me. My address is on that card." He nodded towards Alex's chest. He stood, and then slowly walked away. Alex watched as the figure receded. He rolled onto his side and saw the building that held his lab burning.

His life's work was destroyed. He could not believe what had just happened, a few minutes ago he had been about to prove the quintessence theory, and now his entire building was a flaming ruin. Anger surged in him. The young man called Joe had taken away everything away from him, he had nothing left. It had taken years to get this far, he couldn't contemplate starting over. And besides DARPA would definitely pull the funding now. His anger evaporated to be replaced with sadness. It was over. This wasn't a setback, it was a disaster.

But wait! What had he just witnessed? He had seen Joe move things, lock a door, make things disappear and then set fire to the building. How had he done that? Could there be some truth to what he had said? Had he really manipulated dark energy?

As he watched the building burn, he pulled out the card from his pocket. An address was printed in black ink. He didn't recognise the city, but he did recognise the country - England.

Chapter 39 - Kate is Amazing

Kate was with Sally in another consulting room. She was beginning to realise how big the Complex was. It had taken them a good five minutes of walking to get here. During the journey, she saw a lot of people. Some were running and some seemed to be panicked. As they walked and they passed them, she found that she could sense emotions and sometimes even hear thoughts.

"Where was Joe?"
"What the hell was that?"
"We've been attacked!"

There was a sense of urgency and disbelief from most of them. One or two were angry, and some were frightened, but most were determined and grim, with their mouths set in thin, tight lines and their brows furrowed.

As they continued their walk, Kate found she could not only sense their emotions, but she could see them! The corridor was full of colour streaming from heads as they made their way purposefully backward and forward. The colours bounced around, rebounding from the walls and the roof. The further they got from their source, the dimmer and more diffuse they became. It was like coloured smoke but smoke you could see through. She recalled seeing pictures of a festival a long time ago where people were throwing coloured chalk or dust into the air and at each other. It was like that, but the colours were brighter and clearer. The tunnel had become a riot of shades and brightness as they walked through them, passing through reds, blues, greens and yellows. Kate's eyes were wide open as she took all of this in, as they entered the new consulting room.

Once Sally closed the door with a click, the colours and thoughts faded until they were gone.

"Phew." Kate blew out her cheeks.

Sally looked at Kate quizzically. "Problem?" she asked.

"No," replied Kate. "It's just nice to be out of all of the noise."

"Noise?" asked a puzzled Sally, then her eyes widened. "You don't mean noise as in voices.

You mean thoughts!" She walked up to Kate and gripped her upper arms. "You could hear them?"

Kate felt a bit embarrassed. "Well, yes."

Sally pushed Kate backwards. "Sit here." She directed Kate to the side of the medical bed and Kate sat, pulling the blanket tightly around her shoulders. "That's pretty impressive, if you can hear them already. It normally takes a couple of days."

She released Kate's arms and turned away, walking to a wall of drawers and cupboards.

"It was the colours that really surprised me," said Kate.

Sally stopped walking, her head snapped round. "You saw colours?" She could not conceal the shocked look on her face.

Kate was taken aback. She saw a diffuse blue streamer streak from Sally's head. She could feel Sally's confusion and concern.

Seeing the worried and slightly frightened look on Kate's face, Sally smiled, turned, and walked back to her.

"I'm sorry," she said. "I didn't mean to frighten you. You surprised me, that's all."

Kate relaxed a bit but she could still sense Sally's concern. The blue pulsed and turned purple.

Sally noticed Kate was staring above her head. "Can you see them now?" she asked.

Kate nodded.

Sally frowned. That should not be possible, she thought. For the last minute or so she had been shielding her thoughts. She should not be radiating anything that could be picked up by anyone or any device that she knew of. That being the case, what was Kate seeing? Was there someone else nearby? Or maybe a leaky circuit? Yes, that must be it she decided.

Kate's words broke into her train of thought. "No, it's you."

Sally was shocked again. "You can hear me?" she said out loud incredulously.

Kate nodded again. Sally drew in a sharp breath. She stared at Kate with wide eyes.

"But I have my mind block up. Nothing can get in or out." She then thought, *"I am thinking of a dog, can you hear that?"*

"You're thinking of a dog," stated Kate.

Sally's mouth described an O shape. "Oh, Kate. That's incredible!"

Kate was not convinced. "Well I'm not really trying, it just happens. Why? Isn't it normal?" She frowned.

"It's most definitely not normal!" exclaimed Sally. "What you have just done should not be possible. I have never known anyone who could read thoughts through a block. Kate, you're amazing!"

"I am?" asked Kate.

"Most definitely." Sally threw her arms around her and gave her a hug. "This is big, really big. This could be the next big thing. This could give us a huge advantage in the war. We need to figure out how you do it."

Kate pulled back a little, clutching the blanket closer, "I'm not sure I want to be involved in the war. That sounds dangerous and scary." Her expression was concerned.

Sally realised that she might have gone too far in her excitement. She didn't want to frighten her. She was starting to really like her and hopefully they would be friends, but the war was serious. Much more serious than Kate knew. They were losing; people had been killed and they had just had an attack inside the Complex. How that had happened, she did not know. She hoped that Joe was figuring that out and doing something about it. But what Kate had just done could be important. It was something new and needed more investigation, of course. It could be a whole new aspect of Psi. There was no telling where it might lead, she could only hope that Kate would understand.

"I do understand Sally, but I can't help but be a bit scared about the war and even the investigation you just thought of," continued Kate.

Sally could not keep a startled look from her face. "Wow Kate, that is truly amazing. I wasn't even thinking in words."

Kate nodded.

Sally removed one of her arms from around Kate and put a hand on her forehead. Her rings glowed. They both closed their eyes. Kate could feel delicate tendrils of thought probing her mind. Presently, Sally removed her hand and looked into Kates eyes.

"Your Psi is a lot stronger than it was before. There is a different quality to it. It feels bigger and stronger with a new texture that I haven't felt before."

"Is that bad?" asked Kate.

Sally smiled. "Not at all." She stepped back, letting go of Kate. "Let me check out those small cuts and scratches and get you something to wear. Then we will go and see a friend of mine."

Chapter 40 - Kate, the Enigma

Kate was feeling better than she had in years. All her scratches and scrapes had been dressed and they were no longer stinging. Her soul-crushing memories were put away so were no longer dictating her actions and mood anymore. And she was finally wearing something that fitted her. Sally had left the room and returned a few minutes later with a selection of tops and trousers as well as underwear. Best of all, they fitted, and she finally felt comfortable. She had chosen a pair of plain grey tight-fitting trousers and a white T shirt with the words 'I run on caffeine' printed across her breasts.

With some embarrassment, she recalled her last conversation with Sally.

"Are you feeling alright after the attack?" Sally had asked

"Yes. What was that thing? It was staring at me." She paused. "It was scary." She shuddered.

"I have no idea. It's pretty bad that it got into the Complex. I hope that Joe can find out what's going on." Sally projected worry tinged with some fear. She changed the subject.

"So, what happened when I came in to get you? You said something about Joe?"

Kate made a conscious effort to send a thought. *"Well, it's just that for a moment Joe and I connected and I could see everything."*

"Everything?" asked Sally.

Kate was impressed with herself. She had managed to communicate with her mind! *"Wow!"* she thought.

"You'll find that this sort of thing will come naturally." Sally thought back. *"I must say you are a fast learner, but I expected as much. So, spill, what happened when you and Joe connected?"*

"It was like I could read his mind," thought Kate. *"I could see or read, or feel emotions, even some that were hidden."*

It was Sally's turn to be impressed. *"That sounds like what we call a Deep Link. It's rare. I have only known it to happen with a few of us who have met someone who they are strongly attracted to.*" She raised her eyebrows. "*Are you strongly attracted Kate?*" she asked with a mischievous smile on her face.

Kate clamped down on her thoughts. "That's private. How the fuck do I stop people from reading my thoughts?" she demanded.

"You'll learn that you don't need to, we are all friends here," replied Sally out loud.

"I don't care who anyone is, I don't want people prying where they shouldn't," replied Kate.

Sally had agreed to help her, but first she had wanted to visit her colleague and friend, Molly.

So here she was, sitting in a medical chair, as Molly fitted some sort of headset on her head.

Sally had introduced her to Molly as an original developer of all the Psi-enhancing equipment. Kate decided that she liked her. Of course, Sally would always be special since she was the one who had fitted her with her own Assist. That was an experience that she would never forget. The moment Sally had shown her how to compartmentalise her memories so that they would no longer rule her life. The relief that she had felt had been indescribable, and she would never be the same again. She would be grateful forever.

Looking at Sally, Kate could sense her excitement. She wasn't thinking in words, but Kate could read them nevertheless. Sally was hoping that Kate could help end the war. Kate was dubious about that. She gave a little push and found herself inside Sally's mind. She could read her thoughts as plainly as though she had spoken them. A bit shocked, she pulled back. She looked down and tried to keep within herself, vowing that she must stop looking into other minds.

Molly, who was adjusting the headset, tutted as it slipped forward.

"Are you alright, Kate?" she asked, lifting Kate's chin with a finger so that her head was level.

The headset consisted of a ring of metal which fitted around the head, adjustment screws enabled it to fit differing shapes and sizes. Wires from various positions on the ring converted into one thick cable which trailed downwards and across the room into a panel of switches and dials. Molly was in the process of moving the adjustment screws, making sure that it was a perfect fit for Kate. She moved the headset back into the correct position.

Kate nodded, the headset sliding back and forth causing Molly to tut again.

"Please keep still," she told Kate.

"Did you just sense something?" asked Sally. She noticed that Kate seemed to be embarrassed. "Is something wrong?"

Kate raised her eyes and looked at Sally. "I'm sorry, I didn't mean to pry. I couldn't help it."

A puzzled look crossed Sally's face. "You mean you just read my mind? I don't have anything to hide." She gave Kate a big smile. "After all, you and I have been pretty close."

"Well, I know you said that you and Molly were friends, but I didn't know that you were… Well, you know," Kate stammered.

Molly and Sally looked at each other and they both laughed.

"Do you mean that she is gay?" asked Molly.

She had stopped trying to adjust the headset. Sally and Molly were grinning.

"Of course she is, everyone knows that." Molly turned back to Kate, returning to her adjustments. "Now, keep still while I get this right."

"It's not a secret," stated Sally. "Down here, there is very little that we don't know about each other."

"It's just that…." started Kate. "Well, I kissed you!"

Molly's eyebrows shot up. "Well, now. That sounds like fun," she said turning her head to look at Sally and then back to Kate. "Keep your head still." She continued to work on the headset. "Nearly done."

Sally grinned. "You sure did, and it was very nice. Don't worry, Kate. I know that you have a thing for Joe. I'm not about to rip your clothes off. I've seen you naked already, remember?"

Kate flushed and Molly snickered.

"Well," said Molly as she stepped back, eyeing her handiwork, "when you two can stop oversharing, we can get started."

Sally picked up a chair and carried it over to place it next to Kate's medical chair, and sat in it. She reached over and took Kates right hand. Kate's eyes widened.

"Is this going to hurt?" she asked, suddenly worried.

"Not at all," replied Sally. "I'm here for moral support."

Kate looked at Sally gratefully. "Thank you," Kate said. "And I really am sorry if I have offended you. It was just a bit unexpected."

Sally smiled back. "Not a problem. You and I have a very close connection given what we went through. You didn't offend me in the slightest."

Molly rolled her eyes. "For goodness sake you two, get a room!" She sat at a terminal which was next to a bank of lights and switches. "Can we please get on?"

Kate looked over at Molly. "Can you tell me what you're doing again?" she asked.

"Of course," replied Molly pushing her glasses back on her nose. She sat back in her chair and spun it round so that she faced Kate and Sally. "With the help of this equipment, I am going to probe your mind to read and measure your Psi abilities. From this, I will be able to produce a map of your brain which will allow me to trace your Psi centres, which in turn will allow me to access each one in order to determine their individual function and strength. Sally has told me that you can read through a block. I've never seen this before, so I am very interested to see what your brain looks like." She picked up another headset placed it on her head and started to make adjustments. "That is, of course, if you agree?"

"I won't pretend to understand any of that," returned Kate. "But as long as it doesn't hurt, then I'm okay with it." She squeezed Sally's hand and Sally squeezed back.

"Good." Molly spun back around to face her equipment. She flicked two switches and readjusted her own headset. "Just sit back and relax. You will feel me inside your mind, but it won't hurt. It should only take 10 minutes."

Kate did as she was told. She squeezed Sally's hand again, let her head sink back onto the chair's headrest and closed her eyes. She heard Molly flick some more switches and, presently, she could discern a faint hum from the machinery.

"Here we go," she heard Molly say. "Just relax, Kate."

Kate did just that. After a couple of minutes, she heard Molly. "Kate, can you relax your block?"

Kate opened her eyes and lifted her head. "Block? What block?"

"The one that's stopping me from entering your mind," replied Molly, turning and facing Kate.

"I don't know how to do that if you mean what I think you do. Sally was going to show me. I don't want people prying into my mind without permission. But she never got round to showing me."

Molly looked as though she didn't believe her. "Well, you sure have one hell of a block now," she exclaimed. "I can't get anywhere near you."

"Kate's right," said Sally. "I haven't had time to show her how to block." She looked back at Kate from her chair and grinned. "There is a certain young man who she doesn't want to know what she thinks of him."

Kate flushed. Molly looked back and forth between the two of them. She frowned and spun back to her instruments.

"But this shows a block." She pointed to a display. "And it's the strongest block I have ever seen." She tapped her teeth with a fingernail. "How can that be?" she asked herself, as she picked up a clipboard and a pen.

She scooted along the instruments and started making notes, all the while mumbling to herself. Sally and Kate looked at each other.

"Is there a problem?" asked Kate.

Sally was still holding Kate's hand and she gave it another squeeze. "I'm sure Molly can find out what's going on. She's the best at this business. She was one of the first that Joe recruited. Together, she and Joe built this Complex." She waved her other hand around to indicate the room and beyond.

Kate felt an inexplicable pang of jealously. "Really?" she asked.

"Oh, yes," replied Sally, oblivious. "Apparently Molly was on the verge of discovering Psionics just as Joe had. When they started to work together, there was a meeting of minds, and they developed the Assist."

"Did they?" Kate replied coldly.

"She is very clever." Sally turned and looked at Molly, who was frowning and leaning over her clipboard. "She is also very talented." Sally was smiling a look of adoration on her face.

Kate suddenly realised something. She looked at Sally and pushed into her mind ever so gently.

"You love her!" Kate exclaimed.

Sally was grinning when she turned back to Kate. "Is it that obvious?" she asked, knowing the answer. "Molly and I have been an item for the last 6 months."

Kate wasn't sure why she felt a huge sense of relief. "*I've got to get a grip,*" she thought. "*This is ridiculous. I hardly know him. I'm not some 16 year old girl anymore. I need to control my emotions.*"

As she voiced her thoughts, both Sally and Molly snapped their heads around to look at her. Seconds later, the door opened, and a man poked his head around. It was someone Kate had not seen before.

"Everything alright?" he asked. "I heard someone shout."

Molly waved her hand at the man without looking at him. "It's fine Diego. We can handle it."

Diego seemed a little puzzled, hesitated, and then left the room, closing the door behind him.

"We just heard your thoughts, Kate," said Molly. "In fact, I wouldn't be surprised if the entire Complex heard them also." She winced a little. "That was loud."

"It was?" asked Kate. "But I wasn't trying to shout. And I thought you said I had a block. Doesn't that mean that no one should have heard anything?"

Molly frowned yet again. "Yes," she said, thoughtfully. "You're an enigma." She got up and approached her. She walked up to the chair and looked deeply into Kate's eyes. "Let's try something different. I think physical contact is called for." She looked at Sally's hand gripping

Kates. "Is that alright with you?" Molly asked Kate.

Kate nodded, her eyes wide. It was happening again. She had no idea what was going on. It left her feeling uneasy and frightened.

Molly reached out, gripped Kate's other hand and pushed her mentality into Kate's mind.

Chapter 41 - The Meeting

"Oh, for fuck's sake!" exclaimed Joe out loud.

He sat at the head of a large table in a meeting room with other Complex members. There was Steve at the opposite end of the table, his metal forehead glinting from the artificial light. There were no windows, of course. After all, they were several storeys below the ground.

On his left sat his chief scientist, Alex, an older man whose recent Psi discoveries and innovations were proving invaluable in the fight against the enemy. The rings and chains of his Assist sparkled as he twirled a pen. In front of him were sheafs of papers and a tablet which was displaying the internals of the humanoid that had attacked Kate.

On his right, his second in command, Lee, sat with his arms folded across his chest, a serious expression on his face.

Around the table, four other members of the Complex sat looking down, avoiding eye contact, shuffling papers, or playing with their tablets.

They could all sense Joe's frustration. There was Naya, a doctor standing in for Molly. Molly was, of course busy. There was Simon, who represented the military portion of the Alliance. He was a dour, frowning man who was always serious and never smiled. Behind him, sat Prisha in her wheelchair. It was felt she should be here because of her insight into the enemy's fighting tactics. And finally, there was Ahmed who represented staff generally and usually attended meetings to present staffing issues and concerns.

All were Assisted apart, of course, from Steve who was the only Augmented person in the room. He sat still, emitting an aura of calmness.

"You're telling me that Jim has escaped and that you think he killed Sarah. And on top of that, we have been attacked!" He was almost shouting now and rose from his chair to stand at the head of the table. "One of those things got inside the Complex, despite all our defences, all of our detectors and the rest of our technology. It got in and it attacked Kate!"

Now he was shouting. Some of the people in the room winced as Joe inadvertently radiated his anger.

"It's not good enough!" he shouted as he continued. "Just what have you all been doing to allow all of this to happen? It's a major disaster!"

Lee raised his hands. He also talked aloud. "Please calm down, Joe." He stood and continued out loud. "First of all, I would like to say that we are all really pleased to see you back. We all missed you. We thought you were dead." He paused, everyone around the table nodded their heads. "We are all as annoyed, and as angry as you. What's important now is that we figure out what's going on and come up with a plan." He placed his hands palm down on the table, the chains of his Assist rattling on the wood as he sat back down.

Alex had stopped twirling his pen and nodded. "*I too am pleased to see you back, Joe, but recriminations and shouting won't get us anywhere,*" he sent. "*What happened has happened. The important thing is to consider our options and to ensure that we are not as vulnerable to attack as we so obviously were.*"

Joe sat down. He knew that they were right. He realised that he was struggling to contain his emotions.

"We should also add to your points." Steve's thought was clear and sharp. *"Where and why did you disappear, Joe...?"*

Joe nodded. "Okay," he said aloud. "We have a lot of things to discuss." He sat back. "Who wants to start?"

An hour later the meeting had progressed. Decisions had been made, and tasks were being assigned.

They had dispatched a team to find Jim and were expecting a report soon. They had also increased the security patrols, and doubled the number of Psi Sensitives, whose job was to scan for any nearby disturbances and Psi attacks.

Lee had given a full report on both dead humanoids, which was very shocking to say the least. The one from Arcadia had proven to be identical to the one that had somehow gained access to the Complex and attacked Kate.

"So basically, these humanoids are creatures that have been made?" asked Joe

"Sort of," returned Lee. "It looks like they were once alive, in a biological sense, but they have been hollowed out. All of the internal organs were removed and replaced with mechanics and electronics. The only organ remaining is the brain, although that too has been heavily modified. Weapons and defences have been built in, and the skeleton has been reinforced with various materials, some of which are unknown to us." He knocked his pen against his teeth. "Someone or something has taken a biological entity and rebuilt it to make a very effective weapon. And the fact that we have captured two that are the same seems to indicate that they are starting with a common biological being." He sat back. "Looking at the highly modified brain, we can see that before all of this invasive work, the being they started with was probably intelligent." He looked down at the table.

They were all horrified. Someone or something had hollowed out a living, intelligent being in order to repurpose it for war. Not only was it immoral, but it was also abhorrent. What kind of intelligent being could do that to another?

The conversations continued. They were fast, conducted as they were via thought alone. Thoughts being that much faster than words, the meeting was far more productive than conventional meetings; in addition to the main conversation, emotions and additional, extraneous thoughts were also projected, considered, and evaluated.

It wasn't long before Joe was angry again.

"What do you mean, she let it in?" He was practically shouting.

In the last five minutes, several reports had been delivered to the meeting cohort. Each one more alarming than the other, until Joe was no longer the only one angry and outraged. The whole of the gathering was projecting thoughts of alarm and concern. It started with a report from the team monitoring the Complex and the surrounding area for anything untoward. In particular for any Psi activity.

Two instances of extremely intense Psi activity had been recorded. One in the Complex, the other nearby. The first was obvious - it was the attack on Kate. The second was not - it

351

occurred outside in the woods nearby. A team had been despatched to investigate. Their report was inconclusive. Traces of blood were found, along with residual Psi energy. The blood had been analysed and it was discovered to be a match for Jim. Jim was nowhere to be found.

A further report presented a completely unsubstantiated theory that the humanoid that had attacked Kate did not, in fact, attack her. Instead, it appeared to be attracted to her in some way. Maybe it was scanning her or, even worse, maybe she had let it in. Joe simply could not accept this. It was pointed out that Kate had sustained no wounds and that when the soldiers burst in to defend her and the Complex, the humanoid was standing still and staring at her. It could have killed her instantly, instead it did nothing. This pointed to collusion, said the report.

And finally, to top things off, another report from Arcadia, an important jumping off point, told of a superior force overwhelming their troops deployed there. All Alliance members were being evacuated via teleport.

It was disaster upon disaster, with no explanations. And as usual, the Alliance was completely in the dark.

"So," said Joe out loud. "Let me sum up." He ticked off items on his jewelled fingers. "One: Jim has escaped, is injured, and is missing. We don't know where he is or how serious his injuries are, although the doctor who treated him said that his wound was serious. Two: There was some very high Psi activity outside the Complex, which may or may not have something to do with Jim, because he could have been in that area. And we don't know why or what this Psi energy was about. Three: We have been attacked in our very own base. The attacker was very interested in Kate, and we don't know why. I cannot accept that Kate is in league with the enemy. Four: Suddenly we are being overwhelmed on Arcadia, where we have been holding our own for weeks now. Five: We still don't know who the enemy is, although, at long last we do know something about their soldiers who appear to have once been intelligent beings who have been 'hollowed out' in what must have been a horrible and diabolical process to be repurposed in order to fit the enemy's requirements."

Joe stopped and looked around at everyone. "Have I got this right? Have I missed anything?"

Steve's head moved from side to side "Yes," he projected in his calming deep voice. "There is a number six. Where have you been, Joe?"

All eyes snapped to look at Joe.

Joe looked uncomfortable. "I'm not sure," he radiated confusion and blankness. "All I know is that Kate brought me back. She found me and somehow there was a connection." He frowned. "I remember the battle and then nothing until I woke up with Kate."

Prisha snickered.

Steve dismissed her with a wave of his hand. "It could be that what happened to you is the crux of the matter, the pivotal point if you like, since all of this has started happening since you came back. Maybe we should be devoting time to understand it more." He nodded at Joe. "You have been examined by Molly?"

Joe affirmed. "Yes, she found nothing."

"Nothing at all?" asked Steve

Joe thought a little. "*She did say that my Psi score is higher than it was before.*"

There was silence around the room.

"*Higher?*" Alex looked alarmed and broke the silence. "*How can that be?*"

Joe shrugged.

Steve continued. "*I think that this is significant and should be investigated urgently.*" He nodded at Joe again. "*I think that you need to get Molly to look deeper*"

"*Okay,*" said Joe, "*I take your point. You may well be right. What's important is that we start to figure out things quickly. So, here's the plan.*" He turned to Lee. "*Lee, I want you to assume command of the investigation of both the humanoids and the Psi energy bursts.*" He turned to Alex. "*Alex, how are the new weapons coming along?*"

Alex sat up straight. "*On that point, I have some good news. Production has just started. The HAZPRO suits are being retrofitted. We also have new screens, something I've been tinkering with for a while.*" He lifted his chin radiating pride.

"Good," answered Joe. "Carry on with that, and I want the new screens up over the Complex ASAP."

Alex nodded as Joe turned to Simon. "Simon, I want you to personally take charge of our retreat from Arcadia, and I need you to come up with new tactics against the enemy now that we know a bit more about them."

Simon projected agreement.

"Meanwhile," continued Joe, "I will go and see Molly as Steve has suggested." He compressed his lips into a thin line. "Let's hope she can find something because, at the moment, things are looking pretty bleak"

Chapter 42 - Fuse

Kate, Molly, and Sally were still in Molly's examination room. Kate was still sitting back in her medical chair, her eyes tightly closed. Molly was on her left, standing close and gripping her left hand. She too had her eyes closed, her head back, her face towards the ceiling. And finally, Sally was sitting in a chair on Kate's right, holding her right hand, her eyes also closed.

The three of them had been motionless like this for a full five minutes. At one point, the door had opened, and someone popped their head round, clearly wanting something, but seeing the three of them in deep concentration, they had changed their mind, withdrawn, and closed the door quietly behind them.

While outwardly still, a lot was going on inside Kate's mind. All three of them were together. Molly had been right - the physical contact had allowed her to enter Kate's mind. She was exploring and cataloguing, as well as measuring and weighing what she found. As she did, Kate could feel her probing, and sense

Molly's mumbling. Sally mentally held Kate close and reassured her with her presence.

"Don't worry, I've gone through this myself. My Molly is good at her job. She's the best."

Kate found that it wasn't painful or uncomfortable, but it was very strange to have someone else inside her head. At times, it was embarrassing as Molly lightly touched sensitive areas, particularly as she brushed passed the core of her sexuality. As Kate cringed, Molly moved on, continuously sifting, and examining.

"It's a bit like being naked in front of lots of people," thought Kate.

"It certainly is," Sally's thought answered. *"But you get used to it. As telepaths, there is not much we don't know about each other. You'll find that it's amazing. It brings us all closer together. There is no chance of a spy being in our midst, no chance of anyone who is not working towards the same goal. We all know and love each other. Of course,"* she continued, *"there are some drawbacks. There isn't much privacy, but after a while, you'll find that you will embrace it. It's a new way of living and being together."*

After what seemed like a long time being examined by Molly, Kate sensed surprise coming from her.

"*Without my machinery, I can't tell what your Psi score would be, Kate,*" Molly sent a thought, "*but I can tell that it would be very high.*"

"*What does that mean?*" asked Kate

"*Your Psi score is a measure of your Psi power and control. The higher the score, the more power and strength you have. For example, the higher the score the further you could communicate mind to mind. Every one of us has different strengths and abilities, boosted by our Assists.*"

"*Er, okay,*" Kate thought back.

"*But what is really interesting is this, down here.*" Molly indicated an area deep down through several layers.

"*It is?*" asked Kate.

"*Yes.*" Kate imagined Molly tapping her front teeth. "*I have never seen anything like it.*"

"What is it?" asked Sally

"I have absolutely no idea," replied Molly "And that is annoying me no end, believe me."

Kate had no response, and Sally radiated surprise.

"It obviously has something to do with your block and may be where other, new faculties reside or are generated from," Molly mused. "It's a new development in Psi evolution and I need to understand it." She projected frustration and annoyance. "Kate, do you think that we could get you to drop your block so that I could continue my examination with my systems?"

"Considering that I have no idea how I'm doing it, I am not sure," was the reply from Kate. "But I'm willing to give it a go if it helps."

"It most definitely will help," exclaimed Molly. "Sally, I am relying on you to help Kate."

Before Sally could respond, Molly withdrew from Kate's mind.

"*She's a bit direct and matter of fact,*" thought Kate

"*She is.*" Sally thought back. "*She can't help it. It's how she is.*"

Kate recalled her moment of jealously when she thought that Molly and Joe had a relationship. "*You love her, right?*"

"*I do,*" replied Sally, radiating feelings of comfort and satisfaction.

"*I'm happy for you.*"

"*You know,*" responded Sally, "*you might have something going with Joe.*"

"*I don't know how I feel about him really,*" replied Kate. "*He frightens me.*"

She recalled all the strange and scary things that had happened since she had met him. But she also realised that if it weren't for Joe, she wouldn't be here now with Sally and Molly. She wouldn't be cured of her drug addiction, and she wouldn't be able to file away her awful memories. She wouldn't be feeling as good as she did right now - even if she did have something in her brain that Molly didn't understand.

"But somehow, I also have to be grateful that we found each other." thought Kate. "Because if it hadn't happened, we wouldn't be here today." She squeezed Sally's hand. "And if I wasn't here, you wouldn't have helped me with my memories. I won't ever forget that." She pushed her thoughts of thankfulness at Sally.

Sally gasped. "Whoa Kate, not so loud and hard." She winced physically and mentally. "You have no idea how strong you are. You seem to be getting stronger by the minute!"

"I'm so sorry," Kate thought feeling ashamed and appalled that she had hurt Sally.

"It's okay," Sally thought back. "Just take it easy, that's all." She let her emotions fill Kate's mind. "I am so glad that I could help you. It was touch and go for a minute. Thank goodness for Assists, eh?" She held up her hand with its chains and rings.

Kate held up her hand with her Assist and held it next to Sally's.

"Mine is different to yours," she said aloud.

"What!" exclaimed Sally, also out loud. She examined Kate's hand closely. "Molly," she shouted. "We have a problem."

Molly, who was back at her console, whipped her head around. She instantly understood what Sally was concerned about, thoughts ripped back and forth between her and Sally in less than a second. Then, Molly disappeared and reappeared next to Kate with a crash and whoosh of air following her.

Kate had no time to react; she had barely registered the fact that her Assist was different to Sally's. She saw that one of her rings was larger and another was red instead of gold like the rest of them. She was about to say something when Molly flung her arms around her and then there was blackness followed by a bright light, causing her to close her eyes in pain.

The two women were in a tangle on the floor. As Kate tried to recover, she felt Molly disentangle herself and move away.

"I'm sorry Kate," Molly was breathless." I needed to move you quickly to somewhere safe." Kate realised that Molly was not using her mind to communicate.

Kate struggled to her feet. "Wha..." she started to say.

"There's no time, Kate," interrupted Molly. "Just do what I say and do it without hesitation."

Kate half opened her eyes. The bright light hurt, but less so. She staggered. "Wha.." she started to say again.

Molly interrupted again. "Kate, remove the Assist from your hand slowly and place it in this box."

Now that Kate could finally open her eyes, she saw a box on a table in front of her. Its sides were thick, at least an inch thick. Eyes wide, Kate quickly scanned the room now that she could see. It was empty apart from the table in the middle. She also noticed that there was no door. How could that be? How did they get in? The walls, ceiling and floor were the same dull, metallic colour, and she could see gold metallic strips inside of them. She suddenly remembered Joe's flat, where she had seen the same metallic strips in the hallway.

She turned to Molly to see that she had stepped away and was standing against the far wall.

Kate gulped. "But Sally said to never remove it. Where are we?"

Molly gave Kate a desperate look. "I know, but please, do as I say," she implored.

Kate held up her hand and looked at her Assist. The red ring was now black, and she noticed that the others were also turning red.

"Please hurry," begged Molly. "If we don't get rid of it soon, we are both dead!"

Kate was completely confused and hesitated.

"KATE, DO IT NOW!" shouted Molly

Kate jumped at the shout. She instinctively followed Molly's instructions. She removed the rings one by one, noticing that some were warm to the touch. Once removed, she placed it in the box.

There was a bang and the lid appeared on the box. Then it disappeared with a snap of wind.

Seconds passed and then Kate heard Molly sigh. "Phew, that was close."

Kate looked across at Molly. "Where did it go? Where are we? What happened?"

Molly walked back to Kate and grasped her shoulders. "Thank you for doing what I asked," she said, relief evident in voice. "I'll explain everything. But first, I must get you back to my lab. I didn't have time to explain before. I got us both here using teleportation. Have you heard of that before?"

"Well, yes," replied Kate. "But only in movies. Is it a bit like the Star Trek transporter?"

Molly smiled. "Sort of. It's moving objects using the power of the mind."

Kate was starting to recover from what had happened and was trying to process it all. Yet again something had happened which she did not understand. Yet again she was being told stuff that made no sense. Where was she? Why was she here? And what had just happened? Could she trust Molly? She had brought her here and got her to remove her Assist. Sally had told her to never remove it. What was going on? It made no sense, and she was starting to get annoyed with the just not knowing. It was all starting to get to her. Every time things started to make sense, something else came along to show that she understood nothing. She was now fully immersed in this world of Psi, all these strange people in this strange place with strange things happening. She did not understand any of it. But as her thoughts raced, she realised that there was one thing that, although she did not understand, she could get hold of and be thankful for. It was Sally. Sally had been with her when she had relived her horrible memories. It was Sally that had helped her, and it was Sally that had looked after her.

"I want Sally," she blurted.

Molly looked puzzled and surprised. "Okaaay," she said. "But first I need to get us out of here." She looked around. "You may have noticed there is no door." Kate nodded. "Only one way in and out - a teleport jump."

"Take me to Sally," replied Kate bringing her hands up and gripping Molly's shoulders.

The two women stood each gripping the other's shoulders, eyes locked on each other's. Molly shrugged and they both disappeared.

Chapter 43 - Resurrection

Jim felt as though he was floating.

For some time, he was content to let his thoughts drift aimlessly, but eventually, he remembered. The seething anger returned as he recalled being trapped inside with the freaks. He remembered escaping and, with regret, killing the girl outside the lift. He quickly squashed that feeling and allowed the anger to take over again. He remembered running through the woods and then, he remembered dying.

Well, he thought he had died. It had not been unpleasant; it was just like drifting off to sleep, the pain gradually diminishing along with his thoughts until there was nothing.

But if he had died, then where was he now? He puzzled over this thought for a while and then decided it was beyond him. Maybe he was in heaven, maybe he hadn't died after all or maybe he was in hospital drugged up to the eyeballs. That would explain why he couldn't feel his body or move. He couldn't even open his eyes - all he could do was think. Perhaps he was paralysed from his injuries; his anger surged until it was all-consuming. He hated them. All those freaks under that house - he hated every single one of them and wished that he could kill all of them. For a while he could think of nothing else, such was the depth of his anger.

Presently, he calmed down somewhat and started plotting. What could he do? What should he do once he was out of hospital? Certainly, he needed better weapons and defensive screens, that much was obvious. But how to build them? He would need to go back to the drawing board and try to come up with some new designs. Even through his anger, he was not afraid to admit that Joe had been busy. Jim did not shy away from the facts. He had been outclassed by the freaks. Not just outclassed, but so far behind the curve in terms of equipment that he found it hard to believe. Well, that was not going to happen again. Yes, when he got out of here, he would get started on some major redesigns straight away. When he attacked, he would be prepared. He would not be beaten again.

"*Joe and his freaks deserve to die,*" stated a voice.

"Oh yes," seethed Jim. "*Every last one of them.*"

"*You need better weapons,*" replied the voice.

"*You bet,*" vocalised Jim in his mind. "*But I have some ideas, I just need to get out of here and get started.*"

"*What if you had them now?*" asked the voice

With a jolt, Jim realised that he wasn't talking to himself. Someone else was here. Someone was in his mind. Afraid, he raised a mental block that would keep them out.

"*Answer the question,*" said the voice, not affected by his block.

He was shocked. Nothing could get through his block, not even the freaks. Although, thinking about it, he was not entirely sure about that, not after what had happened recently.

"*Answer the question,*" said the voice again.

There was no recrimination or anger in the voice; it just repeated the question.

"*Who are you?*" asked Jim.

"Not pertinent," replied the voice. "*Answer the question.*"

Jim was perplexed. What was going on? Who was this asking him questions and why did his block not stop them? Was this a trick by the freaks? Was he being questioned? Had he been re-captured? Maybe he wasn't in a hospital after all.

"*I'm not answering any of your questions,*" he thought.

While he did so, he assembled a blast of mental force that, once sent, would kill instantly. It was exactly what he had done to the girl outside the lift. He built it and nurtured it, increasing it in size and intensity. He moulded it with imaginary hands into a round hard ball of energy, and then he squeezed. He squeezed with all the power of his mind until it was as small and dense as he could get it and then he hurled it outwards towards the voice. In his mind he grinned, supremely confident that whoever was behind the voice would be dead. He imagined one of the freaks slumping to the floor and wondered if it might even be Joe.

He was shocked to his core to hear, *"Your efforts are pointless. Answer the question."*

Jim started to feel fear. Whoever or whatever was directing the questioning had deflected his bolt with a casual ease that hinted at something with great power. In the backwash of force from his mind bolt, he had glimpsed a mind of enormous capacity. A mind of granite hardness that was as cold as frozen helium, and completely devoid of emotion. He realised immediately that he was dealing with something completely unknown, something he had never encountered before. It didn't take a genius to connect the dots and to understand that it was alien.

Deep within his mind he whimpered. He was going to die. There was no way he was going to escape this time. While in the freaks' lair, he had sensed powerful minds, and although he would not admit it, he knew that Joe's mind was more powerful than his. But still, with his know-how and technology, he had been confident that he could beat them and finally get rid of his despised twin. This was different. The mind he was dealing with here was so much more powerful than anything he had ever sensed before. He felt like an ant under a microscope.

"Please," he whined.

"Answer the question," came the rock hard thought once again.

The mind behind the voice was relentless. He realised that it would not stop until he answered. But how to answer? What could he say that meant he could escape with his life? Was there any answer that would help? Would it make any difference? He gathered himself together. He was not dead yet.

"What are you offering?" he thought back.

"Will you accept help?" asked the voice.

Jim considered. Obviously, a mind this powerful could easily kill him, and yet it had not. It wanted something from him. And if it wanted something, he had a chance. He could play along and see where it led. He might get out of this yet.

"If I say yes, what would you do?" he asked.

"With your affirmation, we propose to equip you with the tools to enable you to achieve your goal," came the reply.

Jim thought furiously. Suddenly, he had hope. This could be good, very good. Was this being really going to give him the weapons he needed to defeat Joe? 'No' was clearly the wrong answer. If he said no, then he would be of no use to this being. The mind he had glimpsed had not one single iota of emotion; it would dispose of him without any remorse. He was clearly going to have to say yes. There was no choice. But could he get more out of this situation? Could he get what he wanted and take the advantage? Maybe even turn the tables on this being, get the upper hand. But before he could answer, the voice spoke again.

"There is no room for hope," it said mercilessly. "You will be equipped to enable you to achieve your goal, nothing more."

Jim realised that he should not be surprised. Clearly, his thoughts were wide open and could be read with ease by a being of this power.

"*Yes!*" he said. "*I want you to help me to achieve my goal. I want pay back. I want to make Joe and all of his freaks suffer. I want to kill them all!*"

The voice replied immediately. "*There will be pain,*" it said.

A startled Jim started to say, "*wait!*" But he had no time. Before he could form the word fully, pain crashed in all over his body as it was disassembled.

Unable to move or see or even scream, he felt the excruciating agony of his body being ripped apart as it was restructured around his living brain. His limbs were lengthened, his internal organs removed, his bones replaced. Nerves, arteries, and veins were severed and discarded as he was transformed. And throughout it all Jim remained conscious, knowing what was happening but powerless to do anything about it.

The transformation took some time. Throughout it all, Jim remained awake and aware.

Chapter 44 - The Twins

It was exactly noon when Joe walked through the main door of the hospital into the reception area. He strode confidently up to the main desk.

"I need to visit two of your patients," he told the petite receptionist.

"Names?" she asked, without looking up as she continued to read a gossip magazine.

Joe crossed his arms on the high rise at the front of the desk and leaned forward. "I don't know their names, but I'll know them when I see them."

The receptionist looked up.

"Excuse me?" she asked, noticing him for the first time.

She saw a tall slim man wearing a long black coat. His hair fell across his face obscuring his eyes but not his winning smile. She smiled back. He was handsome, she thought to herself as her eyes flicked to his left hand to automatically check for a wedding band. She saw none and her smile widened.

"If you give me their names, I'll see what I can do for you." She fluttered her eyelashes at him, trying not to look too coy.

"The thing is, I don't know the names," replied Joe. "Would it be okay for me to visit your wards?"

"Well, that's highly unusual," replied the receptionist. "I'm afraid I can't allow you to visit without a name. Are you next of kin?"

Joe leaned further forward. "The thing is, I know that there are two people in your hospital that need me, so I need to find them."

He unfolded his arms, exposing his right hand. She noticed immediately that he wore several rings and she briefly wondered if he wore his wedding band on his right hand instead of his left. She watched, mesmerised as he lifted his ring-adorned hand a couple of inches off the desk, his palm facing her. She saw a tiny spark that flicked from his thumb and tracked from finger to finger. When it reached his little finger, everything went dark.

Joe stepped away from the desk and walked over to a nearby wall, where a map was displayed. Behind him, the receptionist stared blankly ahead, completely still.

Having learned the location of the wards, Joe entered a lift and rode up to the 3rd floor. Before the doors opened, he closed his eyes and concentrated briefly. When the lift dinged and the doors slid open, he exited and turned left. Any of the visitors, doctors and nurses that saw him no longer saw a tall young man in a long black coat. Instead, they saw whatever they expected to see. Hospital staff would invariably see a visitor. Visitors would see a nurse or a doctor. It was perfect camouflage. If ever questioned, no one would have seen or noticed anyone who didn't belong.

There were six wards on this floor. Joe's patients should be in one of them. As he walked, he expanded his consciousness forward and examined all the beds as he passed the entrances to each ward. When he reached the sixth, he had still not found his targets. Unperturbed, he about-faced and walked back to the lift. Once inside, he studied the buttons. He noticed one labelled SB1 and below that another labelled SB2. Cocking his head to one side he considered for a moment and then stabbed the SB2 button.

This time, when the doors dinged open, he saw a typical basement. It was darkly lit by long open strip lights, many of which were flickering. Pipes ran along the ceiling with cables tied to them. The floor was dusty and clearly had not been cleaned for a long while. At intervals there were boxes stacked against the walls, some collapsing under the weight of those on top of them. A reel of cable and a broom leaned against the wall opposite the lift doors and a plank of wood lay across the floor. Stepping out into the corridor, Joe paused, turning his head back and forth.

He stood still for a good ten seconds. Then he turned left, stepped over the plank of wood, and walked slowly down the dimly lit corridor. As he made his way, there were many times when he had to step over or around boxes, bundles of papers, empty cans and even at one point an entire wooden pallet. It was apparent that even though it was neglected, the basement had regular visitors. Joe could see many footprints and scuffs along the way. He didn't need to use his faculties to locate his objectives, all he had to do was to follow the dusty prints.

It did not take long before he stood before a locked metal door. The lock was no obstacle; he flexed a small mental projection and the lock opened with a loud snick. Opening the door, he stepped inside.

As soon as he did so, his senses were assaulted by the smell. It was so bad that he almost took a step back. But he gritted his teeth and fully entered the room. He had expected this. Breathing through his mouth, he surveyed the room.

There were no windows since they were underground. The room was lit by a single naked bulb hanging from the centre of the ceiling. On one side of the room there was a single plastic chair and a small metal desk with nothing on it. Next to the desk was a toilet and a sink. The toilet had overflowed onto the floor. Joe realised that accounted for the smell. On the other side of the room there were two single beds, both covered with dirty sheets and a single blanket. The two occupants of the room were sitting together on one of the beds, arms around each other. Both were dressed in filthy medical gowns, and both were looking up at Joe, their eyes wide with fear but partially hidden behind, thick, matted, greasy hair.

"Hello, you two," said Joe with a smile. "I've been looking everywhere for you."

Two identical, dirty faces stared up at him. Neither said a word.

Joe continued, "My name is Joe and I've come to take you out of here."

The two girls did not reply, just continued to stare at him. "I'm not here to hurt you. On the contrary, consider this a rescue."

The girls swivelled their heads and looked at each other, then turned back and stared at Joe, they seemed to be a little less fearful.

"You do want to get out of here?" asked Joe.

Two heads nodded simultaneously.

Joe was about to reply when he heard a distant dinging sound. Immediately, both girls jumped off the bed and scrambled to hide underneath it. Steps could be heard getting nearer as someone approached the room. Joe moved to one side and turned to face the open doorway. He waited.

Presently, a large man in a doctor's coat stood in the doorway holding a tray with two bowls and two glasses of clear liquid, presumably water. He saw Joe and stopped so suddenly that one of the glasses tipped over, splashing its contents all over the tray and over the sides to drip onto the floor.

"Who the hell are you? And how did you get in here?" he asked angrily.

Joe replied, "None of that matters. What matters is why you have locked up these two girls."

The doctor was dumbfounded and spluttered, "That's none of your business. Leave right now before I call security."

Joe approached him slowly. "And just how are you going to call security. Doctor!" he shouted the last word. "You've locked these two girls in this room, in squalor, for no reason at all."

He stopped nose to nose with the doctor, the tray pressed between them.

The doctor tried to back away, but Joe gripped one of his arms. "What's your explanation? Doctor!"

"They are barely human!" he said righteously, "Hardly more than animals. They can't speak, and they are dangerous. If they are set free, they will run riot, like letting lions out of a zoo." As he said it, he lifted his chin and looked down at Joe. "Who the hell are you to know anything about it?"

"He's a bad man. Please let us out of here," came a voice from underneath the bed.

"See!" exclaimed the doctor. "Gibberish! They don't have the intelligence to form words or learn how to speak properly."

Joe looked at him with pity. "You moron. Didn't it occur to you that they have their own made-up language? I can understand what they are saying perfectly. Why would they want to communicate with you, their captor? These two girls," he gestured behind him, "are so much more than you know." His face twisted in anger and disgust. "Why am I bothering to explain? Get lost."

He released his grip stepped back and waved his hand at the doctor, who flew backwards out of the room to crash against the far wall in the corridor, the tray contents crashing around him. The doctor gave a grunt when he hit the wall. He slid down it and collapsed in a heap, unconscious.

Joe turned and squatted down so that he could see the girls under the bed, who were watching warily.

"He was indeed a very bad man. He won't hurt you anymore." Joe knew that there were other reasons he had locked the girls up. "And yes, I'll get you out of here." He knew that they would understand him.

"How did you make him fly?" asked one of the girls in their strange grunting, guttural language.

Joe grinned at them. "Well, I just wished it to happen. And with the help of this," he held up his right hand showing off his rings, "my wish came true."

The girls looked entranced. They turned their heads to face one another, After a brief moment they nodded to each other and crawled out from under the bed and stood facing him. Standing upright, Joe could see that they were younger than he had thought. Both had long dirty matted blonde hair that hadn't seen a comb in months. He could also see, just as he expected, that they were identical twins.

"Well now," he said. "It's nice to meet you. I came to find you so that I could take you away from this place. I have a job for you."

"Getting out of here is all we want," replied one in their strange language.

"Of course," said Joe, "But suppose I told you that you were special? You can communicate with your minds, can't you?"

They looked at each other and then back at Joe. Both of them nodded.

"That is a very special ability that not many people have," continued Joe. "I would like to invite you to come with me and join my people. They all have special abilities just like you. You wouldn't be alone or different anymore. You would have a home and a family. What do you say?"

The twins looked at each other again and then back to Joe again.

"We have never had a family," said one twin.

"You'll have a very large family if you come with me," replied Joe.

One of the twins pointed a finger at Joe's hand. "Can we have one of those?" she asked.

Joe laughed. "Absolutely," he replied. "You'll have one each."

They turned and gazed into each other's eyes again and then turned back to Joe.

"We accept. Please take us away."

Chapter 45 - Rebirth

Jim was no longer human.

The pain had gone on for a long time. It had taken him to breaking point, and then beyond. It had pushed him over the edge. Jim had gone insane.

When the pain had finally stopped, a blackness had descended upon him, and he had lost consciousness. Later, he had woken to find he was no longer himself. Although he could feel his body, he could not control it. He felt himself get up from a platform and stride over to a wall. He could see perfectly as he approached a large, mirrored section.

What he saw moving towards the mirror both horrified and elated him at the same time. He saw a large, matte white, human shape. Equipped with long and powerful limbs, it strode quickly to stand in front of the mirror. Jim looked back at himself in his new body. Its smooth white skin was flawless, its bright, lidless red eyes staring as it stood stock still allowing him to view every inch of its massive form. It had no nose, mouth, or hair, it was naked and was completely devoid of any genitalia.

He giggled madly as he watched his body moving by itself running through a series of movements that were clearly designed to test the flexibility and range of all of its joints. As it did so, Jim felt like a passenger; all he could do was look on as its powerful limbs moved smoothly back and forth and around. It was impressive, he thought to himself. Its strength was obvious, its massive muscular frame spinning, turning, and stretching as it exerted itself through various stretches and contortions.

Throughout all its exertions, he felt no tiredness, muscle twinges or pain. He felt only the smooth power of its limbs. He also realised that he did not seem to be breathing observing that his massive, muscled chest was not moving

Presently, his body stopped all movement and stood still in front of the mirrored wall.

"*Integration complete,*" said the voice in his mind.

Jim's body turned and moved towards the opposite wall. He watched as the platform he had been lying upon sank into the floor and the wall he approached opening inwards to reveal another room. A machine sat at the centre of the new room. Giant metal struts pointed down from the ceiling hanging above a four metre raised circular platform. Thick black cables swung down from above to connect into racks and racks of electronic equipment that covered the far wall. A loud humming filled the air and lights flashed on various panels. The room was completely empty. There was only the equipment.

As he strode towards the machine, the voice continued, *"Your brain has been integrated with new equipment and weapons. You will shortly be transferred to a contested location. Once you arrive, you will be given limited control. Your objective will be to become familiar with your new equipment by leading the final assault on the enemy."*

Jim had difficulty focussing. *"Integrated?"* he asked.

"As requested, you are now equipped with the weapons and systems to destroy your enemy."

"But I didn't ask you to replace me!" shouted Jim at the voice. "I'm not me anymore!"

"Irrelevant," replied the voice calmly.

"It's not irrelevant for me," Jim continued shouting. "My body is gone! Replaced with this big, ugly thing, and I can't do anything! I can't move! I can't do anything! I can't do anything!"

"Your body was inefficient and had ceased to function. It has been discarded and replaced. Your new body is equipped with all the weapons and systems you need to carry out your function. As already stated, upon arrival at the contested location you will be granted partial control, allowing you to familiarise yourself with your new equipment and abilities. You will lead the final assault. If successful, you will be transported to your home planet to lead the assault on the enemy's headquarters."

Jim was giggling madly again as his damaged mind flipped and he remembered Joe and his freaks.

"Yes!" he replied. "Can I kill them all?"

The inscrutable voice replied, *"That is your function."*

Chapter 46 - Arcadia

Simon was not happy. As the military commander of the Alliance, he had been asked by Joe to supervise their retreat from Arcadia. It was not going well.

He stood on the distant world they called Arcadia, his forces beaten back by hollowed out humanoids. Organic robots that had once been sentient beings but had been repurposed to become mindless remote-controlled soldiers. He felt sorry for what had been done to them - how they had been completely wiped clean of all their individuality, their ability to think and to be aware. It was the most horrifying thing he could think of that could be done to a sentient being. He wondered briefly if there was any awareness left.

But at the same time, he hated them. The Alliance was leaving Arcadia, retreating from an overwhelming force. They were being driven off planet and it did not sit well with him. Arcadia, while not a particularly pleasant planet - its noxious atmosphere could not support any life, was a key planet. It was a staging post. It was important.

When Joe and Molly had built the first teleporters, they discovered a massive problem. That problem was range. These miracles of engineering could transport people and material over vast distances in an instant. But there was a limit to their operating distance. And it just so happened that Arcadia was exactly half the distance to another world. And that other world was not like Arcadia at all - they had found a second Earth. A beautiful, lush world, capable of supporting humans, and best of all, it was empty of all sentient life. They called it Kaunis, the Finnish word for beautiful. It was a small planet orbiting the star Epsilon Tauri about 147 light years from Earth and it was full of birds, mammals, fish, and reptiles, all of which were small. Strangely, the largest animal was the size of a dog. There was nothing bigger. The Alliance zoologists loved it. A whole new ecosystem for them to study with a puzzle for them to get their teeth into. Why were there no large animals? Studies had only just begun when the enemy appeared on Arcadia. Once the enemy took Arcadia, Kaunis would be out of range forever.

To Simon, this was unacceptable. And yet, there was absolutely nothing he could do about it. He gritted his teeth as he watched the last of the Alliance staff file into the transporter, making their way back to Earth. He promised himself that they would return. As soon as they could, they would take Arcadia back. It would be the enemy's turn to be driven from Arcadia.

As he watched, a thought called him.

"Sir, enemy contact North of Sector 1. It's something new." Simon identified the caller as one of his few remaining troops, guarding the withdrawal.

A shocked Simon thought back, *"Explain."*

The thought returned immediately, *"Sir, it's like the humanoids, but bigger. A lot bigger."*

Simon pondered for a few seconds then relayed his instructions. *"Do not engage, withdraw ahead of the enemy to base 1."*

He did not like the sound of this at all. Something new could not be good.

He turned to his guards - two soldiers encased in the new HAZPRO suits standing silently behind him. *"Set the charges,"* he instructed them. As the two behemoths strode towards the transporter, he contacted the outlying soldier again. *"Relay what you can see,"* he thought at them.

The soldier complied, and Simon could see through the soldier's eyes. With his HAZPRO suit's visor set to maximum magnification he could just make out many of the humanoid enemy figures moving slowly forward. Scanning along the line he saw what the soldier had contacted him about.

Another much larger figure strode along with the others. Focussing his attention on it, Simon felt the hairs on the back of his neck rise. It was easily twice the size of the rest, both in height and proportions. Its massively muscled arms swung back and forth as its huge thick legs pistoned up and down, propelling it forward with gigantic strides. It made the others look like ants milling around their queen. There was something about its motion that manifested power and control.

As he watched he saw the gigantic figure raise its left arm and wave it across down the line of approaching figures. With a chill, Simon realised that it was directing the others. It was not just a bigger version, it was in charge.

Simon withdrew from the soldier's mind. "*Continue withdrawal,*" he instructed, "*And while you are doing so, keep eyes on this new thing, whatever it is. If anything changes let me know.*"

He turned to the Transporter and watched his two guards fixing the explosives around the base. He smiled grimly to himself. When the enemy arrived, they would be in for a big surprise.

Chapter 47 - We've Been Had!

Striding down the corridor, Joe pinged a thought to Molly, *"Hi Mol. I'm on my way to see you, got something to sort out."*

Molly replied instantly, *"Snap."*

Joe projected puzzlement.

"Bit of a situation with Kate," Molly thought back.

Alarmed Joe asked, *"What's going on? Is she okay?"*

"Don't panic, Romeo," came the reply from Molly, *"She's alright, I just need to stabilise her Assist."*

Joe was puzzled even more. *"Why? What's wrong with her Assist? What do you mean?"*

"She's outgrown it." Joe sensed Molly's surprise and annoyance. *"I'm going to have to give her a Mark Five."*

"*Outgrown it?*" exclaimed Joe. "*How is that possible?*"

"*You tell me,*" replied Molly. "*She's your girlfriend.*"

Joe picked up on her worry and concern behind her light-hearted thought.

"*I thought that the Mark Fives weren't ready?*" He projected his own concern.

"*They aren't,*" replied Molly. "*But I have to do something. She just fused her Mark Four.*"

Joe was amazed and worried at the same time. He knew that Molly was making light of the situation. But he also knew that this was serious. The problem was twofold. If Kate had fused her Assist, then it was no longer operating. That was bad, very bad. Once an Assist was fitted, it should not be removed until the wearer had adjusted fully to it. That process usually took several weeks. He had seen first-hand what happens when it was removed too soon. He recalled in the early days, when he and Molly were experimenting with the first Assist models, how one had broken.

It had been fitted on a man called Samir. The very first Assists were delicate. One day, Samir had knocked it against a table corner. While Joe was building a replacement, Samir had fallen into a coma. He never recovered. Two days later he was dead.

The other problem was the Mark Fives. The latest revision of the Assist was still in development, and not yet ready for general use. Giving Kate a Mark Five could be dangerous. It was not fully tested, and it was possible that some of its effects could damage Kate's brain. But given the first problem, he realised that they had little choice. Giving her another Mark Four would be a waste of time; if she fused one, she would fuse another.

Fusing was the term used when someone's Psi powers were too strong for the Assist to handle. Its tiny circuits were burnt out and the build-up of Psionic energy usually caused an explosion, which in some cases was powerful to kill both the owner and those around them. Joe knew that overloading a Mark Four would require a lot of Psionic energy and when released, could easily be enough to destroy the entire Complex.

Joe broke into a run, *"I'll be there in 5 minutes,"* he thought at Molly.

Molly laughed. *"As if I need you,"* she thought back. *"I know what I'm doing. I'm not sure what you can do to help. Or do you just want to hold Kate's hand?"* She radiated humour.

"This is not the time for jokes," projected Joe harshly. *"This is serious, Kate could die!"*

"Not with me looking after things," replied Molly angrily. *"You don't have to tell me how serious this is, I just saved the entire Complex from being blown up! Let me do my job. You know I'll do my best for her."*

Joe felt ashamed after his outburst. *"I'm sorry Mol."*

"That's okay. Joe, I get it. I really do. I will keep you updated."

"Okay," replied a relieved Joe. *"I'm still coming. I have something else to discuss with you."* He stopped running, slowing down to a brisk walk.

"Which is?" asked Molly.

Joe took a deep breath. "We must find out more about why I can't remember what happened to me after the attack. Steve thinks it's important, and I think he's right. I've been ignoring it up until now, but now I see that something is wrong. It should be impossible for me to not remember. Something happened and we need to find out what it was. It could be important."

"I've been thinking something similar as well," replied Molly. "Whatever happened affected your Psi score too, remember? I don't know why I wasn't more concerned at the time, but now you've brought it up, I can see how important it is and I can't understand why I didn't investigate further."

The two of them, in rapport with each other, did a collective gasp. They both understood at the same time that this was not normal behaviour for either of them. They should have been curious. They should have grasped the significance of their discoveries and investigated. Instead, they had dismissed them and carried on as if it were nothing. In their connected minds, they stared into each other's eyes, their mouths forming an O of understanding.

"We've been had," said Joe.

"We've been manipulated," replied Molly.

Chapter 48 - New Screens

Alex looked on his work with satisfaction. As the Alliance chief scientist, it was his responsibility to improve their defences and weaponry. Joe and Molly, the original developers of the Assist and Augmented technology, were constantly improving and perfecting their devices. But they were not enough in a battle with the enemy. They simply did not have the energy reserves, the range, or the power. Nor could they protect the wearer from hazardous environments.

Hence the HAZPRO suit, with its weapons and screens. Alex and his team were responsible for its development, and, like Molly and Joe, his team were constantly working on improvements and modifications.

One of the key areas that needed work were the screens. After all the suits were big and presented a large target. They needed to be able to survive a direct hit, preferably several. Prisha's recent encounter had proved the inadequacy of their current defensive technology.

Since then, Alex and his team had been working tirelessly, providing incremental upgrades to all the suit's battle systems. These upgrades had allowed them to hold their own. Barely. But all of that had changed. Once again, they were being outclassed. Their recent losses and subsequent withdrawal from Arcadia had shown what that meant. Deaths of Alliance members and the loss of an important staging post.

What was needed was more than incremental upgrades. They needed a step change; something new, something bigger, something that would give them the edge and enable them to drive the enemy back.

Easier said than done. Once again, Joe had led the way. He and Molly had been working on the Mark Five Assists, which used a different technique to tap into the energy field. This new technique delivered more power to the wearer. Joe and Molly were interested in miniaturisation and integration with the mind. Alex's requirements, on the other hand, were all about raw power which he needed to drive his screens and weaponry. Simply put, the more power he had at his disposal, the stronger his screens and weapons.

Today was the culmination of months of hard work. He and his team had taken the Mark Five power technique and had integrated it into the screen generators covering the Complex. His team was still working on retro fitting the HAZPRO suits, which was proving more problematic given the size limitations. In the Complex he had room to spare, the generators and power receptors could be any size he wanted, within reason. But clearly that was not possible in the HAZPRO suits - space was at a premium. Joe and Molly were the experts in miniaturisation, but he needed the power that only a large installation could provide. Getting the right balance for the suits was proving difficult.

With a flick of a switch, the new screen generators burst into life and covered the entire Complex with their impregnable force. He knew of nothing that could penetrate them, not even a nuclear strike. Of course, this meant that while the screens were impenetrable, nothing else was. Only the buildings, people, machinery, and anything within the screens would be protected, while everything outside of the screens would be vulnerable.

Shockwaves and physical forces would be dispersed along the screens entire surface, energy attacks would be deflected, and radiation blocked, while gases would be unable to pass through it. Leaving just one problem - breathable air. Fortunately, this was easily fixed. The Complex was also equipped with numerous air tanks and air generators. Everyone inside would be perfectly safe.

He rocked on the back two legs of his chair and put his hands behind his head, a huge grin on his face. He sent out a quick thought to Joe and the defence crew.

"*New screens are up. Nothing can touch us now.*"

He was supremely confident as the many congratulatory thoughts came back.

He would soon be proven wrong.

Chapter 49 - The Mark Five

Joe burst into Molly's lab to see Sally and Kate holding onto each other tightly, their arms wrapped around each other as they stood in the middle of the room next to the examination chair, with a bemused Molly looking on.

"*What's going on?*" He directed the thought at Molly.

"*Bit of a love fest,*" came Molly's reply. "*It seems that Kate trusts Sally more than anyone else here, not that I blame her.*"

Joe understood. It had been Sally that had helped Kate when she had fitted her Assist. It made sense that she would trust her above everyone else.

"*Got it,*" replied Joe. "*I can't get involved with that now. We have some urgent work to do.*"

"*You got that right,*" was Molly's thought. "*Sal, I need you.*"

Sally kept hold of Kate but turned her head from Kate's shoulder to look at Joe and Molly, both of whom had moved close together, foreheads touching.

"*I'm in,*" Sally's thought replied.

There followed an intense session of thoughts as their minds merged into one. Being meshed so closely together they thought and acted as a single entity, all of their individuality replaced by a single coalesced mind. In this state, they lost touch with the outside world as they reviewed what they were calling the manipulation problem.

Completely unaware of the interaction between the three of them, Kate said out loud, "Thank you Sally for being here."

When Sally did not answer, Kate looked up from Sally's shoulder, and saw that she was staring away across the room. She followed her gaze and saw Joe and Molly locked together, staring into each other's eyes with their heads touching. She felt a brief pang of jealousy, noticing how close they were standing and opened her mouth to shout something at them when she suddenly stopped. She closed her mouth and frowned. She could no longer see any colours flowing from their heads, and she could no longer hear their thoughts. It felt as though something was missing.

She recalled what had just happened and supposed that it must be because she was no longer wearing her Assist. Molly had made her take if off and then caused it to disappear. She also realised that Molly had not explained her actions, despite saying that she would. As she recalled the recent events a throbbing pain started at the front of her forehead.

"Sally?" asked Kate.

As she spoke, she tried to direct her question as a thought. She waited for a reply but received none. All three figures barely moved and were oblivious to what was going on around them.

Kate started to get angry. They were ignoring her. Didn't they realise what she was going through? Molly had said that she would explain but had not done so. Her anger built and built. She could feel her face flush and felt a wave of adrenaline-fuelled heat pervade her entire body until she could contain it no more.

"SALLY!" she screamed. Her head throbbed with more pain as her body shook with emotion.

Sally instantly snapped her head back around to look at Kate. At the same time, Molly and Joe broke their connection and also turned to Kate.

"Kate," said Sally, a look of concern on her face. "I'm so sorry. We were discussing something very important, but we shouldn't have forgotten you."

Joe and Molly walked over to Sally and Kate, who were still in an embrace.

"Too fucking right!" shouted Kate. She unwrapped herself from Sally and pushed away, staggering backwards. "What the fuck is going on? Why did Molly ask me to remove my Assist? You told me to never take it off. Molly made me, and then she made it disappear, and no one is talking to me." She turned towards Molly and Joe. "And then, you two are stood over there, cuddling like nothing has happened." She stopped, out of breath.

"I don't feel right," she continued in a small voice.

All her anger evaporated as the pain in her head overwhelmed everything else. She brought a hand up to her face.

All three Alliance members had a look of concern on their faces. They all started talking at once.

"I'm sorry Kate," said Sally, moving forward to lightly touch Kate's arm.

"Mol, get the new Assist," said Joe urgently, who also moved forward to help Kate.

"Get her in the chair," said Molly, who spun around and ran over to a work bench.

Kate allowed herself to be led to the chair and laid back in it, rubbing at her forehead. "Ow," she said. "It hurts."

Sally reclined the chair and moved down to Kate's feet. She began to unlace and remove her left shoe. Joe stood by Kate's side and gently took her hand in his.

"I'm so sorry," he spoke earnestly. "We should have been looking after you."

Kate squinted up at him through the pain stabbing through her head. "Well, you are doing a pretty shit job of it!"

Joe grimaced. "Yeah, you're right. We'll try to do better."

Kate did not reply. She scrunched her eyes tight shut and started to breathe in and out in short, shallow, breaths.

Joe looked around. "Mol!" he shouted.

Molly was on her way back with the Mark Five Assist in her hand. "I'm here," she replied, as she arrived next to Joe.

Molly watched as Sally gently removed the other half of Kate's Assist from her foot. Once Sally had finished, Molly removed Kate's right hand from Joe's, and started to push the rings onto her fingers. Kate opened her eyes and watched as each ring was slipped on.

"What's that?" she asked, referring to a part of the Assist that was different from the one she had removed just a short while ago.

"This is a Mark Five Assist, it's a bit bigger than your old one," replied Molly. "I'm sorry that I frightened you earlier. I knew that you were special, but I didn't realise how special." She smiled as she pushed another ring onto a finger. "Your old Assist was a Mark Four, the fourth generation of the technology. Once you were fitted with it, somehow new areas of your mind opened up and you literally outgrew it. It couldn't handle the power flowing through it. If we had left it fitted, it would have exploded, killing you and those around you. So, I ported you to a safe room and got you to remove it. I then ported it away into space where it could do no damage."

Sally took over the explanation, "Because you already had an Assist fitted, together with the treatment you had, it's essential that we fit you with a new one as soon as possible. That's why you have your headache - you're starting to have a withdrawal reaction. You need this new one fitted now." She sighed. "We should have been paying more attention and attended to this straight away. I'm very sorry. It's no excuse, but Joe came to us with an urgent problem, and all three of us forgot."

After pushing the final ring onto Kate's little finger, Molly continued. "This Mark Five should be able to handle you. You've noticed that it has this extra part?" She held it up as far as the chains would allow. Kate saw that it was much larger than the rings. It looked like a golden bangle with delicate swirls inlaid into its surface. The swirls were made of a darker material and wound around and along the inch wide surface.

"It's a bracelet that clips around your wrist. We couldn't get the extra componentry into just the rings, so we came up with this. It's still very pretty, I'm sure that you agree. The other half, the one that goes on your foot, has an anklet."

Molly completed the fitting as she closed the bracelet around Kate's wrist with a click. Once done, she reached into a pocket and pulled out the other part of the Assist and walked down towards Kate's feet.

Kate watched. "When you fit the foot piece, will I have a…" Her voice trailed off.

Sally understood immediately. "Yes, Kate, you will."

"What are you talking about?" asked Joe, as he took Kate's hand from Molly.

"I don't want Joe here," said Kate forcefully.

Sally nodded. "I understand." She turned to Joe and said firmly, "Out you go Joe, we need some privacy."

Joe looked annoyed and flicked his gaze from Sally to Molly and back to Kate. "Oh," he said. He looked back up at Sally. "Okay I get it."

He sighed, squeezed Kate's hand, and then let it go. He wheeled around and walked out of the room.

Once the door clicked shut, Molly started pushing the rings onto Kate's toes.

Standing outside in the corridor, Joe smiled to himself as he heard Kate shout out, "Oh My God!"

Chapter 50 - Jim on Arcadia

Jim was having fun.

For the last hour, he had been striding towards some low white buildings which he knew were the freaks' base. All around him were miniature versions of himself. Well, not miniature, just smaller than him. He towered above them being at least twice their height. Thinking about it, he wasn't sure how big his new body was. With no terms of reference, it was difficult to say. But if he assumed that the miniature versions were normal height for a human, then he must be at least three metres tall.

But the best part of the miniatures was that they followed his lead. If he waved his arm to the left, they moved to the left. If he waved his arm to the right, they moved to his right. He had spent a good ten minutes doing just that, giggling madly to himself as he got 1,000 mini-mes to move backwards and forwards, left and right. He loved it. The feeling of power was immense. That, and his new body gave him an overwhelming sense of raw strength and control.

It was later, when he and his army moved forward, that he had discovered the weapons.

It was not much of a fight; the freaks in their red armour were retreating before him. They were doing it in a controlled manner, moving from cover to cover, laying down covering fire as they went. Leapfrogging their lines backwards towards their base. Some of the covering fire hit his troops. Whatever they were using, it was lethal to his mini-mes. When it hit, a mini-me went down and didn't get back up.

His own large, lumbering body made it difficult for him to dodge any energies or projectiles aimed at him, but he soon found that it didn't matter. His body seemed to be made of different stuff than the mini-me's. Rays of force just splashed across his frame, and projectiles ricocheted away. He felt invincible. When he had raised an arm to point at one of the retreating red figures, he was surprised to see the flesh of his forearm split open and retract, allowing the short barrel of a weapon to slide out covered in red flecked mucous. It unleashed a bolt of force and an area of ground ten metres across was instantly vapourised. He used it again and again with glee.

Wondering what other weapons were built into his body, he raised his other arm. He was awed to see the skin of his arm bulge outwards until another barrel burst its way out of his forearm in a shower of red sticky mucous. A stream of projectiles streaked outwards from the its thick muzzle, disintegrating everything in their path. This was everything he had dreamed of. He was all powerful. Nothing could stop him.

As he and his mini-mes drove forward, chasing the retreating red figures he shrieked with delight. Approaching the low white buildings, he saw that the freaks were retreating inside the largest. What idiots! Did they think that the building would protect them? His army would level it with them all inside, there was no way they could escape. Firing at the last of the retreating red figures, he was disappointed to see that he had missed again and again. They were like scurrying ants. They were difficult to target.

Soon there were no red ants to fire at - they had all disappeared inside. He giggled at his ant analogy, as he and his mini-mes continued their march and surrounded the central building. They all stood waiting for his direction, but he waved them back. The final kill would be his. He would kill them all. He approached the entrance, ducked down and stepped through the doorway.

Inside, was a single large room, full of machinery and equipment arrayed around a central, raised dais, but no little red ants. Puzzled, he walked towards the centre of the room. He noticed that the dais was connected by massive cables to various cabinets that circled it at regular intervals. Where did all the ants go?

He took one more step forward and the entire building erupted in flames as it exploded.

Chapter 51 - Kate Explores

When Kate awoke from her slumber, she was assaulted with a barrage of thoughts, voices, and emotions. She screwed her eyes tight shut and her brow furrowed as she fought to make sense of what was happening. A cacophony of thoughts crashed and battered at her own, threatening to drown hers with their intensity and volume. She struggled to think clearly, to control what was happening and to force the thoughts out of her head. As she fought for control, she felt a tingle in the fingers of her right hand, the hand fitted with her Mark Five Assist. She concentrated on the tingle, unconsciously tapping into her Assist control centres, allowing her to construct a mental barrier around the core of her own thoughts. Once built, she expanded it until all of the external thoughts were blocked and outside of her head.

She breathed a sigh of relief, relaxed, and opened her eyes, which was a mistake. When she opened them, the world exploded in colour and blinding light. Crying out in pain, she instantly closed them tight. She recalled seeing colours before, but not like this. The colours were now so bright and vivid, so much brighter than they had been before. She kept her eyes closed and she tapped into her Assist once more. She wasn't sure what she was doing, but she knew that it was the right thing to do. She was sure that she should be able to control what she saw just as she had with the outside thoughts.

She tried to remember what Sally had taught her. Focussing her attention inward she found that she was able to visualise all the compartments and recesses of her mind.

It was like viewing innumerable rooms in a vast building, with each room having a different purpose and reason for being. Of course, this was only a visualisation of a massively complex interconnected web of experiences, memories, and faculties. Visualising them as rooms helped her make sense of the boundless complexity of her mind.

Using this newfound ability, she was able to identify areas responsible for the visualisation of Psi energies. She was surprised to see how numerous they were, but even more surprised that she could see them expanding as she examined them.

Observing the new centres and loci opening and growing throughout her entire mind, she realised that the Mark Five Assist was having a much greater effect than her previous Assist. She could literally feel her consciousness expanding and inflating as the interface, the connection, grew stronger. She wondered what all of this meant and how it would affect her. She hoped that it wouldn't change her, and that she would still be herself. Just better.

Focussing back on the visualisation centres, she easily identified the one connected with her sight and controlled the input to make it much more manageable. She opened her eyes.

She was still in Molly's lab. The chair in the centre of the room had been fully reclined to make a comfortable bed and she had been covered with a blanket. There was no one else in the room. She lay quiet for a while processing what had happened. As she did so, she could feel more new areas opening in her mind, like doors being unlocked. They had always been there but had been inaccessible because she did not have the key. Now that she did, she could feel every door being opened and flung wide one by one.

She didn't know what was behind each door, just that now they were open, she could access them whenever she wanted. She was wary of doing so, and before she did, she needed to make sure that it was safe. She needed help. She knew that Molly was the one to help her. After all, wasn't it Molly who said that she had built the Mark Five?

Rather than call her, she closed her eyes and let her consciousness expand beyond her body, through the walls of the room, through the corridors and other rooms until she could view the entire Complex. With her increased abilities, she could identify every single member of the Alliance. It was easy to find Molly. She was with Joe, and they were deep in a very intimate mind link. Moving her perception in close, she observed both, without being detected.

Chapter 52 - Steve

3 years ago

Entering Tower Hamlets Cemetery Park at the Hamlets Way entrance, Stephen Abayomi stalked his victim. He had been following him along Southern Grove that skirted the park along its eastern edge and watched as the lone figure dressed in jeans, white trainers and a black hoody had turned right and entered the park. Looking back over his shoulder he saw the rest of the gang silently egging him on. Some raised their fists in the air, two raised knives and one a Glock handgun; all looked on expectantly.

Turning back to follow his victim, Steve kept his distance and continued to follow. His victim followed the path and took a left turn to the northern edge of the park. After a short distance he came to a bench and he sat and took out his phone, he began scrolling and tapping, completely oblivious of his stalker.

Steve slipped into the bushes and trees and made his way parallel to the path so that he approached his victim from behind. Of course, his victim had brought it upon himself. He should have known better that to come into the Snake's hood uninvited. Everyone knew this was Snake territory and everyone knew that they would not tolerate outsiders. Steve had been chosen as the one to administer the punishment.

When he was just one step away, he silently drew his knife from his pocket. Quickly, he took the final step and thrust the knife between the slats of the bench and into his victim's lower back.

The victim shrieked in surprise and fell forward onto his face, his hands breaking his fall and then grasping around to clutch at his back.

Far down the path, a shout erupted from the gang members as some of them cheered and screamed their approval. The victim rolled onto his back, one of his hands still behind him.

Steve stood up straight. His 6 foot 2 muscled frame must have looked menacing to his victim. The victim's eyes opened wide, and he tried to move away, his heels making ruts in the gravel as he tried to push himself backwards.

Steve did not move. He watched as the man bled out and frantically tried to get away. A pool of blood oozed from under his body as he flopped down, one hand beneath him still trying to stem the blood flow.

"This is Snake territory," said Steve. "If you live, tell your bros to keep out." He turned and sauntered back to his gang mates.

As he turned, he put the knife back into his pocket, keeping his hand hidden for long enough to find his phone and press a three key sequence.

Once he was back with his gang, the masked group gathered around him cheering, slapping him on his back and clapping. There was lots of laughter and the gang moved as one, away from the park down Hamlets Way, some walking, some on bicycles. The kill was the talk of the group as they ambled down the street together. Cans of beer were pulled from a backpack and passed around. Some members sipped, others chugged the whole can in one. One even poured an entire can over his head much to the amusement of the others.

As the group turned left into English Street, the front members stopped so suddenly that some in the rear bumped into them. One, on a bike, fell off and yelped. At the other end of the street, a man leaned casually against a lamp post.

At first no one said anything, then the shouting and jeering started. The tallest and biggest youth in the group turned to Steve and asked, "How come there's a white boy in our hood?"

Steve shrugged. The tall leader, turned to the rest of the members. "We need to teach this white boy a lesson. No one comes into our hood without our say so." There were cheers and raised fists as the whole gang sauntered purposefully towards the stranger. Those with bikes threw them to the ground and followed suit.

Once they reached him, they surrounded him, and the leader approached. The stranger had made no move, he was still leaning casually against the post.

"What you doing here, white boy?" asked the leader.

The stranger looked up. "I'm not interested in you. I want to talk to him."

He lifted his arm and pointed. The leader turned and followed the pointed finger to see Steve. He laughed and turned his attention back to the stranger.

"You in my hood. You speak to me, not my boy."

The stranger was staring from beneath long blond hair at Steve. He flicked his outstretched hand and all of the gang members found themselves thrown backward to land heavily on their backs - all, that is, except for Steve who remained standing.

"Steve," said the stranger. "Can we talk?"

A shocked Steve looked around and saw all of his mates on the floor. Some of them were starting to get back up on their feet, anger in their faces. He looked back at the stranger. "What was that?" he asked.

The stranger smiled. "I just gave them a little push. Call me Joe."

"Bullshit," replied Steve.

By now all of the gang were back up. They all looked to their leader for direction. The leader was the first up and moved towards Joe, a gun pulled from his pocket and his arm raising it.

Joe flicked his fingers, and the gun flew from his hand, flying through the air to land on the other side of the street with a loud clatter. The leader howled with pain as the gun was ripped from his fingers. He didn't know it, but two of them were dislocated. He cradled his hand to his chest, a look of white-hot fury burning in his eyes as he turned his head sideways.

"Get 'im!" he snarled to the gang.

The whole gang charged forward, some stepping around Steve who remained motionless.

Another flick of Joe's fingers saw the whole charging mob flying backwards again, this time much higher and much further. There were grunts and cries as bodies hit the ground or landed on top of each other. They were not so quick to get up. There were several moans and groans as some struggled to get up. Some lay back winded and two did not move; they had hit their heads and were unconscious.

"Go away," said Joe to the leader, "I only want to talk to Steve."

The leader struggled to get back to his feet. Still cradling his hand to his chest, he looked wide eyed at the stranger. "How did you do that?" he asked warily.

"It's not your concern," replied Joe.

The leader turned to look at Steve. "You know him?" he asked.

Steve slowly shook his head. After witnessing the impossible, he was shocked into speechlessness.

The leader looked back at Joe and seemed to be considering his options. He looked around at the rest of the gang, many of which were still on the ground.

"Okay white boy, you win this time, but I see you again and I'll kill you." He turned to Steve. "You come see me later. You have some explaining to do."

He glared at Joe again, turned and walked away. The rest of the gang fell in with him, some of them dragged and hauled the two unconscious members with them.

Steve and Joe stood looking at each other. Steve was the first to break the silence.

"Just what the fuck happened? And who the hell are you?"

Joe stood up straight and brushed at his long black coat. "I've already told you - I'm Joe." He stepped towards Steve, but Steve inched back. Joe stopped. "You have nothing to fear. I just want to talk."

"Talk about what?"

"I have a job for you, if you are interested."

Steve was taken aback. This is not what he expected. "A job?" he asked, "Why would I want a job?"

"Well now, why indeed?" Joe seemed to consider his next words. "I know that you live alone and have no friends. I know that you hate being in your crew, and I know that you want to get out but can't see a way to do so."

In the distance a police car wailed, drawing closer. "You're wrong," replied Steve.

Joe smiled again. "Really?" he asked. "You didn't kill that boy earlier on. You were careful with that knife. You made sure there was lots of blood, but you didn't hit any major organs. And then you called the police."

Steve was shocked once again. "Bullshit!" he blurted, trying to cover his reaction. How could the man know this?

"Do I need to prove it?" asked Joe. "In your right-hand pocket, next to your knife, you have a burner phone. You've programmed it so you can hit certain keys and it will text the police a message. You've done this so you don't have to kill anyone. You aren't a killer. How many times have you done it, I wonder?"

Steve was now panicked, his heart pounding behind his ribs. This stranger had it all figured out. If he told anyone, he would be finished. He could not afford to show weakness in the gang. What could he do? His mind raced, trying to figure it out and come up with a plan to get out of this. Lots of possibilities came to mind but none that he thought would work. Then, he had it.

"How much?" he asked.

Joe laughed. "I don't want your money. I want you" He gestured towards him.

Steve went silent again. His mind raced. In the distance he heard the police car siren stop. "So I take the job or you tell on me?"

"Not at all. You take the job or not, it's up to you. If you say no, I'll walk away."

Steve knew it was not that simple. If he said no, he would still have to explain to the gang what had happened and why this mystery man wanted to talk to him. And he could think of no explanation that would satisfy them. He realised that he was done. Playing for time to think he asked: "How did you do those tricks? You some sort of ninja?"

Joe held up his hand, it was adorned with rings and chains. "Jewellery?" asked Steve. "You rob a store?"

Joe replied. "Nope. This is a device." He wriggled his fingers. "It allows me to tap into an energy field and then direct that energy. You saw the result."

Steve digested this for a full ten seconds. "I saw you do some crazy shit, but I'm not sure I believe you."

"Of course, you don't," sighed Joe. "No one ever does."

He snapped his fingers and disappeared. A startled Steve gasped and then jumped when a hand tapped him on his shoulder from behind. He spun around to see a smiling Joe.

"What the fuck!" Steve exclaimed.

"Make a decision," said Joe. "I've got other stuff to do instead of playing games."

Steve knew he had no choice. He could not go back to the gang now. He would be branded a snitch, a traitor. They would turn on him without a second thought. He was as good as dead.

"What's the job?" he asked.

"Does it matter?" asked Joe. "Don't answer. Suffice it to say I need people like you, and I have a new device that you might be interested in testing for me."

Joe handed him a card. "Come and see me here as soon as you can." He turned away and walked off down the street.

Steve watched him until he had rounded a corner. He looked down at the card. It was plain with an address printed in black letters. He looked around, checking that he was alone. Taking the phone and knife from his pocket, he looked at them both and then dropped the phone on the pavement. He crushed it with his booted foot. Walking over to a drain, he dropped the knife between the grill, and watched it disappear into the water below. Certain that it could not be found, he broke into a run and raced to the train station to get a ride to Oxford. He knew he did not have long before the gang found him.

Meanwhile, in the park, an ambulance had arrived. The paramedics were loading their patient into the back.

"You were lucky," said one to the boy lying on the trolley. "The knife missed all your major organs and arteries. It's a miracle really."

Chapter 53 - Joe's Memories

Molly and Joe were examining Joe's memories.

The brief discussion between himself, Molly, and Sally had confirmed what they had thought. They had, indeed, been manipulated. But by who? It was imperative that they found out.

Since this revelation, Joe knew that they needed to find out more quickly. If they had been so easily controlled or affected without it being detected, then it was clearly the work of a master operator. And if it was the enemy, then they were in serious trouble. So he urgently asked Molly to assist him so that they could figure out what was going on. She of course agreed, understanding the seriousness of the situation. Once she knew Kate was sleeping, she joined him in another of her labs.

In this lab, there were two single beds next to each other. Various cupboards and shelves held equipment on the two side walls. The beds were situated with their heads on the far wall from the door. Like all of the rooms in the Complex there were no windows. Each bed had a chair and a bedside table.

Molly and Joe were lying on each bed both on their backs, their eyes closed. Outwardly still, they were both working hard. They were meticulously examining Joe's memories.

In their mind link, they reviewed and catalogued his memories for the last few days frame by frame, looking for anything out of the ordinary, anything that looked strange. They were focussed on the last moments of a battle. A battle where Joe had gone missing.

Unaware that they were being watched by Kate, they relived the engagement.

Inside his HAZPRO suit, Joe led his expeditionary force forward. The twin moons of Arcadia rose in the West, casting their wan light over a barren desert. The thin air moaned across the plain, stirring up mini dust devils that died as quickly as they were formed, whipping up the sterile regolith. Given the lack of oxygen in the atmosphere, it was not surprising that the entire planet was devoid of animal and plant life.

Across this landscape, Joe's group of five moved towards a cluster of silver domes, which were clearly not natural. This was to be Joe's first encounter with the enemy. There had been other encounters, but since no Alliance members had returned, no one knew what had happened. All they knew was that they had been the subject of unprovoked attacks several times. They had no idea who the enemy was, or why they had been attacked. All that was known was that no one returned. This time was different. This time they had discovered what looked to be an enemy base, albeit a small one. This time, they had the upper hand, the element of surprise.

Even so, Joe was not in a hurry to attack. He was sure that the whole thing was a misunderstanding, a communication breakdown. He was convinced that if he could just open a dialog with whoever they were fighting, it would all be resolved. Who knows, maybe they could join the Alliance and they could work together?

Making up the five members of his team were Simon, the military commander of the Alliance, Mike, and Sammy, two members of the Alliance who had been amongst the first to be recruited by Joe, and the final two members were affectionately known as the twins. Two sisters, Doortje and Eline, with an incredibly strong psychic connection specialising in languages. They would be indispensable translating any communication should they make contact.

"Remember," Joe sent out a thought to the group, *"no one makes any aggressive action. Our priority is to make contact."*

The five suited figures assented as they loped towards the buildings.

"Shields up, Power up XO-assist," Joe spoke to his suit, which replied, "Confirmed. Power envelope now at 420 minutes."

He knew that the rest of the group were doing the same as he maintained an open mental connection with each one of them.

"Simon, scout forward," he directed.

The suited figure of Simon powered forward. In three long, high leaps he was 100 metres ahead and some 500 metres from the nearest dome building. All of the remaining team readied their long, tri-barrelled weapons as Simon slowed his advance. He covered another 50 metres, knelt, and sighted down his weapon.

"No movement," he reported. "No signatures in infra-red or ultra violet. Nothing discernible on any Psi band." He waited for the rest of the team to catch up and join him. "It's too quiet," he directed at Joe.

Joe agreed. "You think it's a trap?" he asked.

"Could be," was the reply.

"Maybe if we take some pot shots at that building?" suggested Mike. "See what happens."

"We could," replied Joe. "But I want to make contact if we can. We need intel."

"Sure, but we don't want to become another statistic. We don't want to be another team not going home," commented Sammy.

"True," replied Joe. "We proceed with caution. Simon? Your recommendations?"

Simon considered. He didn't like any of this. Approaching an enemy encampment with no cover. There was no way of knowing how many enemy combatants there were in those domes. Nor if they had dug in, planted mines, or set any other traps. Or maybe the domes were empty and abandoned.

"We approach from different directions, slowly with half our force. The other half stay back in case of trouble."

Without hesitation Joe replied, "Agreed. From now on, Simon is in charge. Everyone follows his orders."

"Sammy and Mike, you're with me," ordered Simon. "Joe and the twins, hang back. Keep a 100 metre distance between us. Sammy, you approach from the West, Mike from the East. I'll go straight down the middle."

Joe watched as Mike, Sammy and Simon approached the domes from their allotted directions. All was quiet. Maybe it was an abandoned installation. There was certainly no sign of the enemy.

"*I think that they are oxygen breathers,*" came Eline's thought. "*Why else would you need buildings if not to keep your atmosphere in?*"

"*It might not be oxygen,*" commented Mike.

"*I guess not,*" replied Eline, "*but we haven't come across any species that does not breathe oxygen, so I think that it's a safe bet.*"

"*I think you're right,*" replied Joe. "*The buildings are all separate so they must have individual airlocks, although I can't see them from here. Simon, do you see any entrances to any of the buildings?*"

Simon's thought was instant. "*Nope, and that's not a good sign.*"

"*It isn't?*" asked Sammy.

"*No,*" replied Simon. "*These buildings may be a decoy. If they have no entrances, then what purpose could they serve?*"

Joe considered for a few seconds. *"Okay Simon, continue your approach with caution. Do you think we can find out if it's a decoy or not?"*

"Affirmative," came Simon's thought as he slowed to a walk. *"Mike, Sammy, approach from your directions slowly."*

Joe watched as the trio continued their course towards the domes.

"I count 11 domes altogether. So far, no entrances," Simon commented.

"11 is an unusual number," said Doortje. *"It may have some significance. For example, maybe they have 11 digits on their limbs."*

"Now about 10 metres away, still no sign of an entrance. The domes seem to be made of some sort of material like concrete. They have what looks like a rough texture." Simon gave a running commentary.

"Same here," echoed Sammy and Mike.

"What do you think?" Joe asked Simon.

Simon had stopped his approach and thought furiously. He scanned the domes and the surrounding area. No signs of any movement. It did not make any sense.

"Scan all," he told his suit.

While he was waiting, he sent a mental probe towards the nearest dome. He was surprised that it was blocked at its surface.

"I've got a Psi block on this building!" he radiated, and then immediately, "Infra-red signatures detected," his suit informed him.

"DECOY!" he mentally shouted. *"Retreat!"*

He jumped backwards. His suit assisted him, and he sailed 100 metres up into the air. As he flew upwards, his suit displayed red dots on his HUD. He grimaced as he saw that there were 21 of them.

Mike and Sammy also jumped, mimicking Simon's manoeuvre. But Joe and the twins crouched and brought their weapons up ready for action. Scanning around, Joe could see no sign of the enemy. He was about to instruct everyone that they were to hold fire unless they were fired upon first, when the ground beneath his suit collapsed and fell inwards. His heavy suit tumbled forward and down into the collapsing ground.

Joe was not concerned for his safety. He was fully protected inside his suit, it would ensure that he would be safe. Sure enough, the suit detected the fall and immediately fired attitude jets to orient itself upright. Once upright, Joe directed the suit upwards such that he hovered above a rapidly enlarging hole. As the ground continued to fall inwards in an ever-increasing circle of destruction, Simon, Mike, Sammy, Doortje and Eline moved back keeping pace with the collapse, but staying a good 10 metres away from the rim.

"What's happening?" asked Sammy.

"I don't like it," replied Simon. "Continue to fall back, keep weapons at the ready. Joe, you are awfully exposed up there."

"Don't fire unless I order it," stated Joe, still hovering above what now looked like a massive sink hole.

Two flares flashed from Simon's suit as he fired counter measure missiles up into the sky, leaving trails of smoke as they shot upwards. Joe turned his attention down to the blackness below. He could see nothing, but his suits HUD displayed 21 red dots, all gathered at the bottom of the pit, none of them moving. He sent a thought downwards into the gaping hole.

"We would like to open a dialogue with you. We are not here to attack."

There was no answer, which he found frustrating. What was more frustrating was the absence of any mind that he could detect. It was as though there was nothing down there, although his suit's detectors said otherwise. The collapse had now stopped with the hole roughly 150 metres across.

"I'm not getting anything at all," he reported to the group.

At that moment, the 21 dots erupted upwards.

Without any warning, bipedal figures swarmed up the sides of the pit and split into four groups of four, each group headed at running speed towards each of the Alliance members. The remaining five were stationary at the centre of the bottom of the cavernous space. Five streams of white-hot fire streaked up to strike at Joe.

"Hold and fire!" Joe mentally shouted, as the five beams impacted on his suit's screens.

Below, on the ground, the five Alliance figures stopped, turned, and crouched, ready to fire at the approaching groups of humanoid figures. Four sets of dual missiles streaked into the sky from Mike, Sammy, Eline and Doortje, while the already launched pair from Simon acquired their targets and streaked down. One hit the group of four heading for Eline and the other hit the group heading for Sammy. Two massive explosions shook the ground as the two groups of aliens were engulfed in sheets of flame, dust, and superheated air.

From their kneeling positions, Mike, Simon and Doortje opened fire at their corresponding alien groups. Blue bolts of glowing energy shot from their weapon muzzles and impacted upon the aliens still running towards them. Three figures dropped and tumbled forwards, kicking up dirt clouds as they fell in heaps.

"*B1 mode is effective,*" Simon's thought was received by everyone. "*If you are not on B1, switch to it now and open fire.*"

All four team members obeyed as six more missiles powered down from the sky, smashing into the three remaining groups of alien figures who were racing forwards, oblivious of their casualties. Three more huge explosions rocked the ground kicking up large dust clouds and flame.

The flames did not last long since there was no oxygen in the atmosphere to sustain them, but the dust took several minutes to clear. Simon observed that the remaining five red dots on his HUD were retreating into a now apparent cave system.

"Remaining alien force retreating," he stated. "Any injuries?"

One by one, each of the Alliance members replied. No one was harmed. Then Mike asked, "Where's Joe?"

Using all his suit's scanning equipment, Simon could find no sign of Joe at all.

He had gone.

"*There!*" shouted Molly's thought. "*You see that small break? It's so small that you would never notice it.*"

She was referring to a tiny break in Joe's memory. They both moved back in time and examined the memory chain minutely. They saw Joe shout, "*Hold and fire!*" And then he was confronting a gang of five youths.

"*There is a definite break there, but I can't see any more than that,*" stated Joe.

"*Me neither. Something happened, and it looks like your memory was erased.*"

They were both silent for a while.

"*What could do that?*" asked Joe.

"It would have to be a highly competent operator," replied Molly. "And I don't need to tell you that none of us here could have done it."

She left the thought hanging between them as the implications sank in. This was very bad news. Joe's memories had been manipulated by a master operator and if it wasn't someone in the Alliance, then it could only be one other. The enemy.

"If only I could zoom in, or get more information from that blank area," mused Molly.

As the silence lengthened, Kate announced her presence.

"I can," she said.

Chapter 54 - Jim's Victory

Jim examined his new body. It was covered in burns. In some areas, completely black and charred. All of the fingers of his left hand were completely gone, melted in the heat. One of his legs was partially melted, exposing blackened metal plates and struts. His right foot was twisted too far to the left. If it were made of bone, it would have been broken. But even with all this damage, he felt no pain and it did nothing to detract from his feeling of triumph.

He had successfully driven the freaks from the planet! It was the first time he had been successful in a battle and the feeling was so sweet. It filled him with so much joy that he could not stop himself from singing and even swaying back and forth. His mini-mes, meanwhile, milled around looking for, and failing to find, targets.

Standing in the middle of the destruction, Jim swayed from side to side humming his favourite nursery rhyme. Rubble made up of concrete and steel girders lay all around. Small fires and smouldering debris filled the air with black noxious smoke.

"Hickory, dickery dock...." he sang to himself, as he kicked a scorched electrical panel and watched it sail into the air. *"The mouse ran up the clock...."* Turning, he limped to a blackened wall and leaned his massive form backwards onto it, crossing his arms. *"The clock struck one...."* he continued.

With no warning a thought pierced his brain like a scalpel, stopping his celebration in its tracks.

"Objective achieved. Damage minimal. You will continue."

Jim winced at the force of the thought. His consciousness shrank and he became a jibbering wreck for a few minutes. Eventually, he realised that the terrible pain was not going to reappear.

"Hello?" he asked. *"Are you still there?"*

The diamond hard thought replied, *"Affirmative."*

"I killed them all for you."

"Negative. 100% of the enemy escaped."

Jim was aghast. "You mean I didn't kill any of them?"

"Affirmative."

Jim pushed forward from the wall, turned and smashed his fist into it. His hand went straight through the reinforced concrete.

"How?" he screamed. "I fired and fired at them. My mini-me's chased them into this building and it blew up. They must all be dead."

"The enemy escaped," stated the emotionless thought.

"How?" asked Jim. "How did they escape? They were all in here."

"The enemy used a teleport. Their entire contingent teleported to their home base."

"A teleport? They have teleporting machines? Wow. I never managed to build one of those. How does it work?"

"*Irrelevant. We will affect minor repairs and transport you to the enemy base.*"

"*I don't need any repairs,*" seethed Jim, "*Send me now, I'll kill them all!*"

He was filled with rage. The freaks had escaped again! Every time he tried to kill them, they escaped. It was like trying to pick up a slippery eel from a bucket. His anger evaporated and he giggled at the thought.

He was still giggling when he disappeared along with all of the others, leaving the planet of Arcadia devoid of all life once more, the fires stuttering out as their fuel was exhausted.

Chapter 55 - Discovery

Joe and Molly were both surprised and shocked to hear Kate's thought, *"I can."*

"Kate!" exclaimed Joe.

"How are you here?" asked Molly. *"I didn't feel you."*

They could sense Kate smile. *"I think it's your fault, Molly,"* replied Kate.

"Mine?" asked Molly. *"What do you mean?"*

"I think that this Mark Five Assist is better than you thought."

Molly was shocked for a second time.

"What do you mean?" asked Joe.

"I can see and hear everything," replied Kate. *"It took me a while to figure out how to calm down the noise and focus on what I want to see and hear. It was like everyone was shouting at once."*

"I told you she was special," said Molly, as she sent out an exploratory probe towards Kate, only to find it blocked as before. This time it was like iron. A solid, impenetrable wall with no cracks or any signs of weakness. She had never felt a block like it before and it left her breathless.

"Kate, you've grown. This is amazing!"

"I can still feel parts of my mind unlocking. I feel like a flower in the warm sun spreading its petals wide. What does it mean?"

Joe replied before Molly, *"It means, Kate, that you are an amazing person with lots of hidden Psi talent. I knew you were the one! It also means that the Mark Five works Mol."*

"The one what?" asked Kate.

"It's too soon to say that about the Mark Five. It still needs more testing," said Molly.

Joe did not answer Kate's question, but to her new level of control, she found it easy to read his mind without him knowing. The power she had was intoxicating and she had to reel herself in before she saw too much. What she did see confirmed what she already knew. Joe loved her.

"Yes of course it does," replied Joe. "But I have a feeling that it will pass all of your tests with flying colours."

"Sure, but don't forget that not every mind is capable of handling a Mark Five. You can't just give it to anyone, it would burn them out," replied Molly.

"I realise that, but I have a couple of folks in mind already who I think could handle it."

"And one of those is yourself of course!"

"Well yes. You said yourself that my Psi score had increased."

"And I also said that I had no idea why," Molly reminded him.

Joe dismissed her concerns, "Whatever, it could give us the advantage that we need."

"Aren't you forgetting something?"

"Huh?"

"We have just proved that you, at least, have been manipulated. Your memories are not complete. I think that your Psi score is related to the same event. I also think that some form of manipulation is ongoing. That would explain some of my own lapses."

"True," mused Joe. "If only we could discover the who, why, and how."

"I can help," interrupted Kate.

Both Joe and Molly paused their conversation and mentally turned to Kate.

"How so?" asked Joe.

"I think that I can see what you can't," replied Kate.

"What makes you think you can do something that Mol and I can't? We've been using Psi for years."

Kate bristled. "And yet you've had your memory erased without you knowing it!" she said angrily. "If you ask me, you're not doing too well on your own!"

"*Don't worry about him,*" Molly indicated Joe. "*He's a tactless man,*" she said pointedly. "*Do you think that you can get something from that blank in Joe's memory?*"

"*Yes,*" replied Kate. "*I can't explain it, I just know it.*"

"*Well Joe,*" said Molly, "*I think that you should apologise and let the lady do her stuff, don't you?*"

"*I'm sorry, Kate. It's just that Mol and I have been working on this stuff for a long time and you are so new to it. I didn't mean to belittle your abilities.*"

Kate grumbled, "*Don't make it a habit. Let me see what I can do.*"

The three of them set to work. Kate in her room alone in her reclined chair, Molly, and Joe together in single beds lying side by side in another room.

Joe and Molly located the memory break and Kate zoomed in, with Joe and Molly looking on.

Using faculties that had just been awakened, she focussed on the almost imperceptible break in

Joe's memory, and expanded it, making it larger and larger, like zooming in on a small part of a photograph repeatedly. Soon the minute break was expanded into a huge area where each and every fraction of a second could be examined in detail

"*Wow!*" breathed Molly. "*That's brilliant Kate. Show me how you did it.*"

Obligingly, Kate zoomed back out and demonstrated how she isolated the memory break and how to focus in to examine every nano second.

"*This is great, I've learned a new skill, but I don't have your control to go down to the nano second level,*" noted Molly.

Kate did not reply. Instead, she pulled out all of the data from each nano second view and put it together to form a new memory that lasted 0.1 seconds. Once completed, all three viewed the content.

"*Oh my god!*" exclaimed Molly.

"*Holy shit!*" said Joe.

"*Oh fuck!*" said Kate.

"*What is that?*" asked Molly, referring to an image of pulsating, pink flesh that was held in a large bowl-shaped container.

"*Whatever it is, it's disgusting,*" replied Kate.

All three viewed the image together. They saw a dark room that was wet with running water and mist. It was too dark to see clearly, but they could just about discern a large bowl shape container atop a pedestal. It was difficult to see the size of the bowl, but viewing it against the water droplets, it must have been at least two metres across, with the pedestal being about one metre tall. Within the bowl lay a mass of rippling, pink flesh. As they watched, they saw a tentacle exude from the mass and slide over the bowl's rim, reaching down to the floor.

"*Is this the enemy?*" asked Joe.

"*It must be,*" replied Molly. "*Whoever or whatever they are, they are completely alien.*"

"Did you see that tentacle?" asked Joe. "No skeleton?"

"And all that water, they must come from a swamp or water world," replied Molly.

"Do you think that they are oxygen breathers?"

"Difficult to say. Looks like this is all we have. A pink blob with tentacles."

"It's more than we had before. At least we now know what the enemy looks like. We just have to figure out how to contact them or defeat them," continued Joe.

"You tried contacting them before, remember? That didn't go too well."

"That's true, but maybe now it would be different."

"Different? How?" asked Molly.

"Wel...." Joe started to reply when an exasperated Kate spoke up.

"Will you two shut up and think? This....," she indicated the restored memory, "thing... is clearly not the enemy."

Joe and Molly turned their attention to Kate. "What?" asked Joe.

Being in such close contact, Kate could read their emotions as easily as their thoughts. They were both surprised and puzzled. How could she have come to that conclusion, was the common thought between them.

"Look," replied Kate. "This thing, whatever it is, got you, Joe, into that room. How did it do that? And then it erased all memory of itself from your mind leaving no trace. You, Joe. The one who is supposed to know everything about this Psi stuff and the strongest of all your band of people. And not only that, but it also recently had some effect on you, Molly. You said so yourself, didn't you? Without you noticing as well?" She paused. "Well, if it can do all of that, then it could have killed us whenever it wanted. There would be no need for all these attacks. It could probably kill everyone here with a single thought!"

There was no further thought for a while as both digested what Kate had said.

It was Molly who broke the silence. *"Kate, once again, you are brilliant. I'm sure you're right."*

Joe added, *"My god, you're right. That is fantastic."*

"Maybe," replied Kate. *"But it leaves us with another problem: if this is not the enemy, what is it? What is it doing? And why?"*

There was silence once again.

"Just a minute, we need to bounce this off someone." Joe sent out a mental call, *"Steve? We need your help, please join us."*

Steve, who was eating lunch in the refectory, replied instantly, *"Of course, Joe. What's up?"* He continued eating his sandwich without pause.

Kate felt his prodigious mind join the group. It was different to Molly and Joe, she realised. She felt its expanse and weight of cognition as his thoughts smoothly aligned with hers.

"Greetings Kate, I see that you have grown."

She saw that he was talking to her alone - he was able to compartmentalise his thoughts. Looking into his mind, she saw compartment after compartment, logic engines, computational units and a massive neural network, all interfacing with his brain through his augmentation. She could see that this type of Psi enhancement was very different to her Assist, even the Mark Five. His augmentation gave him a much deeper connection and was physically much larger, enabling his mental faculties to be enhanced in areas that her Assist could not. And a key area for that augmentation were the logic and computational engines.

"Nice to meet you mind to mind, Steve," she replied. "I can see now why you consider your augmentation better than our Assists."

"You know it," replied Steve's thought. "You're wearing a Mark Five? I thought that they weren't ready?"

"They aren't, but apparently, I burnt out my Mark Four. Well, that's what Molly told me."

Steve's eyebrows raised as he finished his sandwich, *"Indeed. That's very interesting. I sense new faculties in you. What are they?"*

Kate mentally shrugged. *"Don't know yet, but I just helped Joe and Molly. Now we need your help."*

She could feel Steve considering and calculating, his logic circuits churning.

"How can I help?" he asked the group.

To Joe and Molly, there had been no pause in communication, and they were unaware of Steve and Kate's private talk.

Joe and Kate rushed through their findings, showing Steve the recovered memory and recounted Kate's conclusions.

Steve went quiet for a long while. Kate observed his logic functions calculating and evaluating. She wondered if the others had the same view, or was it just her?

Then he said, *"First of all, I agree with Kate's conclusions. These aliens are not our enemy."* He paused. *"We don't know what their motivation is, or what they are doing. We should also consider that they are likely to be continuing to monitor us - if that's what we can call it. They could even be listening in right now."*

"*Uh oh,*" thought Joe.

"*Exactly,*" replied Steve. "*There is one other thing that we could consider.*"

"*Which is?*" asked Molly.

"*If these aliens are not the enemy, but are capable of manipulating, or even perhaps guiding us, maybe they could be persuaded to help us?*"

"*That's a pretty big ask,*" answered Joe. "*We have no clue if they would entertain such an idea.*"

"*True,*" replied Steve. "*But think about it. They are already interested in us, otherwise why the interference? But they haven't made any aggressive moves against us. They seem to be watching while remaining hidden. What we do know is that they must be master operators. With them on our side, we would surely be able to drive the enemy back.*"

There was silence as everyone digested what Steve was saying.

"Well, kidnapping me was pretty aggressive!" thought Joe.

Molly interjected. "Wait! Steve has made a very interesting suggestion. These aliens are way above our level both technically and mentally. If we could make contact, it could make all the difference."

"Last time I tried to make contact, it didn't go well remember?" thought Joe bitterly.

"In any case, the question is moot," replied Steve. "We have no way of contacting them. We don't know where they are, nor do we have their mental patterns. It would be like trying to contact a particular fish in the whole of the ocean."

"Good point," replied Joe. "Oh, well, it was a good idea. I guess we'll have to rely on ourselves."

Kate spoke up, "I could try."

Three minds focussed their attention upon her.

"*I don't know if I can do it, but I could give it a go....*"

At that moment, an alarm sounded, shrieking in its intensity, and at the same time thoughts came crashing into the group.

"*We are under attack!*"

Chapter 56 - Jim Attacks Again

Fully renewed and repaired, Jim was back on Earth.

He was standing in a wood. Clustered around him were ten mini-mes. He looked around. The area looked vaguely familiar, but he couldn't place it. Observing his ten minions, his anger flared.

"Where are the rest of my mini-mes?" his thought shouted. *"I need them all. Ten isn't enough!"*

"You have been granted all the support that is required," replied the disembodied, diamond drill-hard thought. *"Perform your function."*

Jim did not argue. He was too fearful. Remembering the pain that he had suffered, he would do anything to avoid that.

He stomped off grumpily, his mini-mes following obediently. As he walked, he activated his body's scanning equipment to identify where the freaks were hiding. This time, they would not escape. This time, he would kill them all.

It did not take long for him to find the freaks' base.

He recognised it from his escape a long time ago. Well, it seemed a long time ago, maybe it wasn't. He wasn't sure. So much had happened since then.

Approaching the grand house with his ten mini-mes gathered around him, he had come across the tree where he had died. He stopped, looking down at the foot of the tree, pondering what had happened, but not understanding it.

While he stood still, he was unaware that his small force had been detected and that preparations were being made to repel the soon-to-come attack.

Presently, he pulled himself from his reverie, and looked up. Many of the mini-me's were wandering around aimlessly. Without direction, they were mindless automatons, standing or moving around without purpose. He would soon rectify that. He stood tall and resumed his walk towards the house.

Soon, his feet were crunching on the driveway gravel, and he felt elated. This time, there would be no escape. They had nowhere to teleport to. This time, he would kill them all and level their base. When he was finished, there would be nothing left.

As he continued his approach, he saw a flickering in the air. He knew what it was. It was a defensive screen. No matter. He would break through it soon enough. Raising his right arm, a barrel hissed out of his forearm and fired. The beam of force splashed against the screen and rebounded. Streamers of force radiated outwards as they were reflected away. The beams that were reflected upwards dissipated harmlessly into the atmosphere, but the other reflected beams hit nearby shrubbery which was instantly vapourised. The beams hitting the ground melted the surface into fused slag and blackened ash.

Lowering his arm, Jim saw that he had made no impression on the defensive screen. He was impressed, but not worried. While his new body had undergone repairs, his benefactor had shown him how to interface with and deploy the considerable arsenal of weapons built into his gigantic frame. He had another 62 different weapons to try yet. He was sure that one of them would get through.

Chapter 57 - Under Attack

Joe walked into the command centre of the Complex. It was close to the surface - just one floor below the house ground level and filled with Alliance members. It consisted of a circular arrangement of desks 10 metres across. In the centre, there were four chairs facing each other in a square. Sitting in the four chairs were two Augmented women and two Augmented men, their foreheads covered with the bulging metallic protuberances that made up their Psi-enhancing mechanism. Each one had a thin cable connected at the side which snaked downwards and into the floor.

Sitting at the desks, facing inwards towards the centre, were Simon and Alex and two female controllers. Simon looked worried, but Alex looked smug.

"*What's happening?*" Joe directed a thought at Simon.

"*Eleven enemy units here outside the Complex! How did they know the location of our base? Or even Earth, come to think of it.*"

"We will probably never know," replied Joe. "What are they up to?"

Alex answered, "They are failing to get through our new screens."

"For now," said Simon. "You haven't engaged the enemy like I have. They always have something up their sleeve."

"What about imagery?" asked Joe. "Can we see what's happening up there?"

Instead of answering, Simon swivelled a monitor around on his desk so that Joe could see it.

"It's the same combatant we encountered on Arcadia. I left a booby trap that should have destroyed it. But clearly not." His thought was bitter.

On the monitor, Joe could see a large humanoid figure, double the size of the other figures milling around outside their screens. As he watched, he saw it raise its left arm. The resolution was not great as the camera was on the wall of the house, some 50 metres away, and it was looking through a flickering screen, but he could just make out three barrels underneath its wrist. As he watched, he saw a burst of green fire belch from all three barrels. Whatever it was, it had some recoil to it because the figure was jerked backwards at the same time and green fire impacted the screens. The fire splashed out and covered the screen as though it were a liquid thrown at a window, but in this case the window was curved upwards and around to cover the house like an upside-down goldfish bowl. The fire spread left, right, up, and down across the curve of the screen at a rapid pace, coating it like a thin film of green milk.

"What is that?" asked Joe alarmed.

"It's some form of energy depletion force," yelled one of the controllers. "It's sapping the energy of the screen. Generator 4 just came online to cope with the load."

"I don't like it," thought Simon. "It's not dissipating."

"Relax," thought Alex. "Nothing can get through my new screens."

"I wouldn't be so sure," replied a worried Simon. "You're overconfident. The enemy has outwitted us at every turn, this could be no different."

"Generator 4 is at 75% capacity," the controller shouted out.

On the monitor, the green film was continuing to spread. It now covered the whole area of the defensive screen in the monitor's view.

"Can we switch to another view?" asked Joe.

Simon nodded and tapped his keyboard, changing the camera, to one that gave a wider view. They could see that the green film was still spreading. It was obvious that the purpose of the weapon was to cover the entire defensive screen, draining it of energy and thus collapsing it.

"Generator 5 just kicked in!"

Joe thought furiously. If they didn't do something quick, their screen would be gone, leaving them defenceless. Suddenly, he had an idea.

"*Reverse the polarity on the screen,*" he thought at the controllers.

"*Bu....,*" one started to reply.

"*Do it! Do it now, reverse it for 0.5 seconds only.*"

The controllers looked at each other. One shrugged and started tapping at her keyboard, setting up the command sequence.

"*Generator 5 at 70%,*" stated the other controller.

They all watched as the green film continued its spread. Second by second, it crept up and around. It wouldn't take long to cover the whole screen.

"*Generator 6 now online.*"

"*Ready,*" said the first controller.

"*Hit it!*" replied Joe.

The controller hit a key. Immediately, the green film stopped its advance and then shattered into millions of pieces that slid down the curve of the defensive screen as if they were shards of glass where they melted on the ground like ice in a hot sun.

"All generators now idling," the controller continued to report.

Joe, Simon, and Alex looked at each other, breathing a sigh of relief.

"That could have been bad, really bad," thought Simon. *"What next?"*

Joe didn't answer. He was staring at the monitor screen.

"Joe?" queried Simon.

"Can you zoom in on the big figure?" asked Joe.

Simon complied, tapping some keys on his keyboard. *"What's up?"*

Joe studied the figure on the screen. "There's something familiar about it. I just can't put my finger on why."

"You haven't seen it before," stated Simon. "I'm sure it's the same one we encountered on Arcadia."

Joe stared. The figure was standing still, hands on hips, its red eyes glowing. There was something about its stance that reminded him of someone. Then he had it, but it couldn't be! Incredibly, it reminded him of Jim!

Chapter 58 - Contact

Kate was still lying in her reclined medical chair in Molly's lab, but she was no longer alone. Molly and Steve had joined her. The two of them sat in ordinary chairs beside her, one on each side, both holding each of Kate's hands tightly. All three had their eyes closed and were in a deep mind link.

"I'm not sure where to start," thought Kate.

"Let's begin with the assumption that they are here, even now, watching and maybe even manipulating us as they have been all along," thought Steve.

"If that's the case, then they could stop us at any point," thought Molly.

"We're going to have to take that chance," replied Steve. *"We're under attack. So far, our screens are holding, but who knows for how long?"*

"It should be just a matter of finding the frequency band at which their minds operate. But that will be easier said than done," offered Molly.

"I'm not sure how to do that," responded Kate.

"Here let me show you," replied Molly. "You have our thoughts as a starting point. They are here at this frequency." Molly pointed this out inside Kate's mind. "All you have to do is keep going higher and higher, until hopefully you will make contact."

Kate understood. She could see what Molly meant.

"Okay I'll give it a go."

"I'll push from here," said Steve, his analytical mind whirling and computing all the while.

"I'll hang on for as long as I can," said Molly, "But you'll have to go much higher than I can reach."

Kate agreed. "Okay, here goes."

She opened her mind to let in the thoughts of those around her and started to tune into ever higher and higher frequencies. As she did, all of the external thoughts dropped off one by one, until only Steve and Molly were left.

Continuing, she marvelled at her own ability. Just a few hours ago this would have been impossible. It was the Mark Five Assist, she realised, as it tingled and grew warm around her ankle and wrist. Her integration with its circuits and receptors was still not yet complete, but its effect was undeniable. The sheer power and range that it delivered to her mind was breathtaking. It continued to supply more and more energy as she called for it, as she moved up and up into higher and higher frequency ranges.

Steve dropped off. She could still feel the weight of his mind shoring her up and grounding her. Molly was next to drop off.

"I can't take any more!" she said, her thoughts fading away, as Kate continued to wind up the frequency.

Now she was on her own. Here, in this upper range, the thought spaces, the frequencies, were empty, devoid of life. There was nothing. Nothing operated at these frequencies. Surely there was nothing that could, and she began to wonder if they had made a mistake. Maybe Joe's memory wasn't a memory after all. Maybe it was his imagination.

Even so, she continued, moving her thoughts ever higher, until she started to reach her own, prodigious limits.

And it was right at her upper limit that she began to sense something. Something not human. Something alien.

Carefully, and slowly, she reached out to make contact with that alien presence. She was surprised to get a response.

Instantly, a massive, overwhelming mentality flooded her mind, crushing her thoughts and awareness.

"*HOW?*" asked a voice.

She could not answer. The alien presence left no room for thought, let alone answering questions, its thoughts crashing into her like thunder.

"*AH, A DEVICE,*" continued the presence.

Kate was crushed into a small corner of her mind as the alien presence forced its way into her, its tendrils of exploration pushing and squeezing invading her entire being. She gritted her teeth against the pain as she felt its diamond hard probes exploring every recess, every niche, and every part of her. She even felt it travel down her spine, flooding every nerve with pain. In seconds it had completely filled her mind with its own.

"REMARKABLE," stated the alien.

The alien presence continued its searching and probing, its tendrils of thought piercing and viewing everything with complete disregard for her, its huge mentality assimilating everything. There was no time for Kate to try to communicate, the sheer speed and weight of its presence overwhelming her completely. She could do nothing. She was aghast at its dominance and immense power. This was like nothing she had ever experienced before, and she didn't know what to do. Through the pain she tried to push back against the invader to no avail. All she could do was watch.

"OTHERS," it stated as it discovered her mental links to Steve and Molly.

She felt a part of its mind detach from itself and surge downwards into Molly and Steve through her Assist. She cringed inwardly as she imagined what they would be going through.

"*PRIMITIVE,*" was its next statement.

Kate pushed and pushed at the vastness of it, trying to make room so that she could think and try to communicate. It was like pushing at a concrete wall, it was impossible. But she could not give up, everyone was depending on her. Tapping into her Assist, she felt it grow hot as she pushed with all her might. There was a slight movement giving her just enough room to marshal her thoughts so that she could try to converse with it.

"*Who are you?*" she asked.

She felt the weight of its scrutiny pressing heavily into her consciousness, as it moved its full attention back to her.

"*INTERESTING,*" it's thought deafening in its volume and intensity.

"Please," she said. "Please, not so loud. We would like to talk to you."

"INTERACTION NOT POSSIBLE," replied the unknown entity, with no reduction in volume.

"Please," Kate pleaded. "We need your help."

"ASSISTANCE NOT POSSIBLE," was the reply.

Kate tried to think. What could she say to this being that would make a difference? How could she find out if it really wasn't the enemy? And if it wasn't the enemy, how could she get it to help? She realised that she had not thought this through at all. What on earth could she say to connect with an intellect such as this? It was clearly so far ahead of them in terms of intelligence and capability. She felt like an ant trying to converse with a human. She couldn't think of anything, but she had to try.

"Please, I beg you. I don't believe that you are our enemy. Please don't let us all die."

She broke off. Was she making any difference? She had to keep trying.

"*For the first time in my life, I've made friends and I may have found someone....*" She hesitated, her feelings of panic, of failure and of love for her new friends flooding her thoughts. "*I may have found someone to love...*"

She stopped, was she making any sense? Why was she saying these things to this... this thing? She was probably doing a really bad job.

"EXPLAIN," asked the voice.

It projected her own emotions back at her in a huge deluge that momentarily stunned her. She struggled to recover from the onslaught and fought to understand what it was asking her.

"*You mean emotions?*" she asked.

"EMOTIONS?" it asked.

Did this being not have emotions? Could this be an opening, a way of making a connection?

"*Yes,*" she replied. "*Feelings, Like happiness, sadness, love, and hate. Don't you have them?*"

"*EXPLAIN.*"

Kate felt a small spark of hope. She had made contact, of sorts. It didn't seem to understand emotions. It was a start. Maybe if she could keep the connection going, she could build a relationship and then persuade it to help.

It was a tenuous idea, but it was all she had. She began to explain.

Chapter 59 - Gamble

The entire Complex shook with the next barrage from the enemy.

"*Screens still holding,*" a controller said.

Joe turned to Alex. "*Do you have a HAZPRO outfitted with the new screens?*" he thought at him urgently.

A surprised Alex replied, "*Well, one is nearly finished, I think. Why?*"

"*Could you get it ready in the next 10 minutes?*"

"*Well, I...*"

"*Can it be done?*"

"*What are you going to do?*" asked Simon.

"*Alex, check on it and get back to me,*" said Joe. "Simon, we can't go on like this. We have to do something. I have an idea."

Simon grimaced, "I hope you aren't thinking what I'm thinking."

Joe replied instantly, "I am."

"Joe, you can't!" Simon could not stop projecting his concern.

"Look," said Joe, "I think that thing out there is Jim. I can't explain it, but I'm pretty sure. Jim only wants one thing. Me. If I go out there alone, he will go after me, hopefully forgetting and leaving the rest of you alone."

There were audible gasps around the room.

"That's madness!" said Alex. "You'll be a sitting duck."

Joe smiled. "I thought you said that your screens were impenetrable?"

"Well, yes, I did.. But here in the Complex we have power to spare. In a suit, you'll have a limited energy supply. I don't know how long it would last."

As he spoke, the Complex shook again. On the monitors, they saw purple fire flashing onto their screens and setting the local wood ablaze.

"It's a gamble," admitted Joe, "but I think it's our only chance. We don't know if the screens will last. And even if they do, how long before they find a way in?"

He did not say it, but they all knew about the weaknesses of their defence. If just one of them was found by the enemy, then it would all be over.

"Also, you are all aware of what Kate is trying to do."

Everyone in the room was now paying full attention to Joe's words. They all collectively nodded.

"We need to buy her some time. We have to keep Jim occupied for as long as possible to give her the greatest chance."

There was silence as everyone considered what Joe had just said.

Finally, *"But it's suicide!"* from one of the controllers.

Joe smiled grimly. *"Maybe not. I have one or two ideas."* He directed his thoughts at Alex. *"So, Alex. Can you get the suit ready?'*

Alex nodded reluctantly. *"I've contacted my team, and they tell me they have one ready. It's the only one. It's not been tested though."*

"Okay" Joe replied. *"Then we have a go. Tell your team to equip it with one of the new weapon racks, and stuff it with everything they have. Tell them they have 10 minutes."*

He directed a thought at the controllers. *"I need a hardwire link to an external sender. Can you set one up?"*

They both looked at Joe with wide, frightened eyes. *"Yes, sir,"* replied one, who started tapping keys on her keyboard.

While the controller worked, Joe sent a mental thought out towards Kate. He intended to say something to her in case his plan didn't work, and he didn't return, but was thwarted. She did not answer.

He backed off. He could not interrupt what she was doing. He hoped fervently that she was having some success, because if she could not get help, he could not see this ending well. He felt sadness and regret. He should have told her how he felt about her. Now there was no time, and she might never know.

"Ready!" The thought pierced his reverie.

"Give me the link," commanded Joe, *"Alex, alert your team I'm on the way down."*

He turned to Alex and Simon as they each stood to face him. Pulling them into an embrace, he slapped their backs.

"Thanks for everything. See you on the other side."

Alex could think of nothing to say.

"Come back to us," said Simon.

He turned and marched out of the command centre and met Lee in the doorway.

"My friend, you are either very brave, or a complete idiot," came the thought from Lee.

The two of them grinned uncertainly at each other and hugged their goodbyes.

Joe disengaged from the hug and made his way towards the lift. As he did so, he sent out a thought through the link the controller had just set up for him.

"Jim? Is that you?"

Chapter 60 - Jim's Madness

Jim was starting to get frustrated.

He was cycling through his weapon systems, slowly and carefully, one by one. So far, none of them had been able to penetrate the freaks' screens.

He was not worried. He was sure that he would eventually break down their defences, and he still had plenty more weapons to try. But he was annoyed. He was desperate to break through and start pulverising their base. Having to keep trying different weapons until he found one that worked was boring.

Selecting weapon number 12, a section of his back opened, revealing a munitions array, one of which moved forwards and outwards until its large muzzle pointed upwards. Then a series of 10 green fireballs launched themselves into the sky, each one accompanied by a loud bang.

Jim watched as the fireballs arced upwards and then descended to impact upon the freaks' screens.

The concussion threw both himself and all of his mini-mes to the ground, as the entire surrounding area erupted in flame and a giant mushroom cloud rose slowly up into the air, with a layer of topsoil sucked up with the super-heated air.

Jim picked himself up. Wow! he thought. That was awesome! He was disappointed to see that the freaks' screen was still intact, with everything on the inside of it looking pristine. The area outside of the screen, however, was devastated. It resembled the surface of the moon, with craters, ash and slag now surrounding the area for several hundreds of metres.

The driveway was long gone, all the gravel melted into a fused slab of cratered stone. The wood across the road was on fire, the flames spreading rapidly, being driven by roaring winds sweeping in to replace the super-heated air rising into the atmosphere over the freak's screens.

As he looked around, Jim could hear sirens. No doubt the fire department and police were on the way. They must be wondering if World War Three had broken out, he thought to himself. He giggled as he imagined what they would be thinking when they saw the total destruction surrounding this house that hid the freak's base. They would not be able to get anywhere close. The fires and cratered ground would see to that. If they did not stay back, they would become casualties of this epic battle.

Jim didn't care. He turned his attention back to the domed screen. Time to select weapon number 14. As he did so, he detected a thought.

"Jim, Is that you?"

"Joe!" he seethed. *"I'm going to kill you and all of your freaks!"*

"Jim," came the reply. *"You don't mean that. Surely, we can talk this out?"*

"Never!" Jim screamed a thought at Joe. "You've always been the best. Well, you aren't now. I'm the best. Look at me!"

He flexed his biceps in a classic strength pose. He giggled as he did so.

"Yes, Jim, you are the best. You don't have to kill anyone to prove it."

"Don't try and trick me, Joe. I'll show you who's boss here,"

"You are the boss, Jim, I'll concede that. Just stop the attack and we can talk."

"No!" Jim screamed. "Not this time. No talking. I'm going to kill you all!!"

"There must be something we can do," continued Joe "What's the point in senseless killing?"

"There's nothing!" Jim was still screaming. "You are all going to die!"

There was a pause in the conversation.

"Okay, Jim," came Joe's thought. "Suppose I come out there. Will you leave everyone else alone and promise not to kill them?"

Jim considered. "You mean you will come out here and face me?"

"Yes, exactly that, but you must promise not to hurt anyone else."

Jim was excited. This was it! Face to face with his hated brother. A battle like the gunslingers in the old Western films. They would stand face to face, and he would be fastest on the draw and kill Joe.

"I promise," he replied, not really thinking about it.

"Okay Jim, I'm coming out."

Jim could hardly contain himself. He did a little jig as he waited.

Chapter 61 - Getting Ready

"*It is Jim, and he's completely lost it,*" Joe sent a quick thought to Lee and Simon. "*I can't reason with him. He's completely mad.*"

He removed the last of his clothing, throwing it to the floor. He pulled his naked form up using a handrail, and lowered his legs into the bottom half of the HAZPRO suit.

"*How can that be Jim?*" asked Lee. "*It's a monstrosity.*"

"*I don't know, but it's definitely him.*"

The mechanisms of the suit whirred softly as its inner shell closed around his legs, gripping them firmly with its soft, cushioning material.

"*Are you sure you want to do this?* asked Simon.

Joe winced as the suit continued to close its inner shell, reaching his groin, closing, and sealing tightly. He held up his arms and threaded them and his head and shoulders, into the upper half of the suit, as it was slowly lowered.

"I have to," he answered Simon. "This is between me and Jim. He promised that he wouldn't hurt anyone else if I went out."

"And you believed him? A madman!" snorted Lee.

The top half of the suit connected with the bottom half with a loud clunk. There was more whirring as mechanisms locked and sealed the two halves together. He was now hermetically sealed inside, it providing for all of his needs, including air, water and nutrients. Locked inside, he was in complete darkness. Until the suit powered up and interfaced with his Assist, he was blind to the outside world. His only connection with the outside was through his mental link with Simon and Lee.

"I've said it already, we have no choice."

Lee sighed. "You are probably right, but it doesn't mean I have to like it."

Joe felt air blowing on his face as the suit's air recycling system started. The inner, cushioning shell contracted around his torso and arms and the HUD flickered and came to life.

"Systems online," reported the suit, "Performing diagnostics."

"I don't like it either," replied Joe. "I tried to reach Kate."

"Has she made contact?" asked an excited Lee.

The suit's medical systems automatically connected monitors to various parts of his body, while inserting needles into his forearms and calves.

"I don't know. I couldn't contact her, or Steve, or Molly. I left them to it."

"So, we wait," thought Lee.

Joe felt the suit's inner shell contract over his head and around his face. Tubes slid out of recesses to present themselves near to his face so that he could draw on the water and nutrients it provided for him. He wouldn't be needing any. This fight would be over quickly one way or another.

"Simon, any thoughts on tactics?"

"Yes," replied Simon, *"Keep away from it. It's big, and it looks like it has a lot of power. I would avoid physical contact if you can."*

"All systems nominal," reported the suit.

Joe's Assist integrated itself with the suit and it came to life, acting as a second skin. He briefly wished that he had had the time to fit a Mark Five Assist but dismissed the thought. He didn't think that Molly had another ready anyway. The hoist that had lowered the top half of the suit disconnected and swung up to the ceiling. Three power cables and one air hose snapped and disconnected from the suit falling to the floor. Their open sockets sealed themselves with thick metal caps that slid across them.

Joe and the suit were one.

He stepped forward and turned around so that his back was facing the wall, which was covered in machinery and racks of equipment. Two robotic arms projected outwards holding a large munitions rack. With several loud clicks it locked into place onto his back. The suit accepted the new equipment and interfaced with it seamlessly. Many new icons appeared on Joe's HUD, each one indicating a different weapon or defence system.

He cycled through each one ensuring that they all worked as he stepped forward to face the teleport dais in the centre of the room.

"*Okay. This is it. If I don't make, it you know what to do.*"

Simon's thought replied, "*Withdraw to our secondary location, I know.*"

"Yes," answered Joe. "*And quickly, because if he can get through my screens, then it's only a matter of time before he gets through…..*"

"Good luck," thought Lee. "*Stay in contact, and if you need anything…*" He left the rest unsaid.

"No point sending anyone else out," replied Joe. "No one else has the new screens. I doubt any other HAZPRO would last 5 minutes. I'm on my own."

He stepped up onto the dais and projected a thought to the engineers and operators.

"Thanks for everything you've done, and well done for getting this suit ready."

He cycled to his defence screen and readied himself to enable all of the defence systems. He had to wait until he was outside before enabling them.

He drew a deep breath. He wished he could talk to Kate one more time. He should have told her how he felt about her, but it was too late now.

"Send me on my way, somewhere well away from the base."

Chapter 62 - Duel

Joe materialised outside of the Complex, in the middle of a field of barley. He immediately consulted his GPS system and located his position - he was 5 miles away from the Complex. Facing in the direction of the Complex, he could see smoke from fires and the mushroom cloud still rising into the upper atmosphere.

"Screens up. Auto reflect on. Launch counter measures," he commanded.

"Power envelope now at 100 minutes," reported the suit, as he felt the thump in his back as the two missiles launched skywards.

"Power on XO Assist, set HUD to auto," he continued issuing commands.

"Confirmed. Power envelope now 90 minutes."

He was not surprised to hear that the suit's power reserves were so low. The new screens were power-hungry. And once the battle started, it would get worse very quickly as the screens countered whatever was thrown at them.

This was not going to be a long encounter.

As if to reinforce his thoughts, a projectile rocketed down from above and smashed into the ground scarcely a metre away. The explosion was immense; he was thrown into the air, tumbling over and over as the suit fought to stabilise itself. His screens screamed and howled as they defended against shrapnel, debris, flames, and super-heated air. The suit did its usual amazing job of keeping him safe, the cushioning interior shell and its energy screens softening the blow from the explosion such that he hardly felt anything, except some nausea from flying through the air.

Not an energy weapon, he thought. The screens could easily handle it, but he had been caught off guard. He couldn't afford to let that happen again.

The suit righted itself and he floated down to the ground on jets of flame. The dust and smoke settled about him, leaving a vision of a 5 metre crater, with a blast radius of another 10 metres.

He stood outside the blast zone and took stock. His HUD dutifully displayed the enemy positions, and he was pleased to see them moving slowly towards him. Kate and everyone else were safe for the time being.

Selecting the first of the weapons from his weapons rack, he targeted the lead red dot on his HUD, assuming that this would be Jim. He commanded the suit to fire and watched an arc of blue flame pierce the sky. Breaking into a run, he commanded the counter measure missiles to deploy. As he observed their contrails swooping down through rear-facing cameras, he halted his run in a small dip in the field that he hoped would take him out of line of sight.

He felt the concussion of the missiles and energy weapon as they hit their targets. He didn't think that the counter measures would damage Jim, but he hoped to take out some of the other smaller enemies.

"You still there Jim?" He sent out a thought towards the enemy positions.

"*Joe.*" The thought came back dripping with vitriol. "*You can kill my mini-mes, but you can't kill me!*"

Joe was momentarily puzzled. Mini-mes? Then he realised that Jim must be talking about the smaller versions of himself. He consulted his HUD and saw that the number of red dots had reduced to 8. Good news, he thought. So far, so good. He needed to keep this engagement going for as long as possible, giving Kate as much time as he could. One way to do that might be to keep Jim talking.

"*I can try,*" he projected his thought at Jim. He didn't wait for a reply. "Launch counter measures," he commanded the suit again.

He felt the familiar two thumps in his back. As soon as they launched, he broke into a run again, moving out of the dip towards a distant line of trees that was in the opposite direction from Jim and his mini-mes.

Sure enough, he felt and heard a large explosion behind him as Jim targeted his position. Jim was locating his position from his missile launches. Okay round one to him, but it was not over yet. Targeting Jim again, he commanded the second set of counter measure missiles to deploy as he continued to run. Once again, he felt the concussion of the explosions as they hit. Two more red dots winked out in his HUD leaving 6.

Approaching the line of trees, he saw that they ran along the edge of the field. On the other side of them was a road, and along the road he saw vehicles, some of them stopped. Horrified, he understood what was happening. People travelling on the road had seen and heard the explosions and had stopped to see what was going on. Many of them were out of their cars and vans and were peering through the trees, not realising the danger they were in. They were probably surprised to see what they thought was a giant red robot running across the field.

He could not let innocent people die. He swerved, adjusting his run away from the stopped vehicles but he couldn't go back the way he had come. That would be suicide. He couldn't keep away from the road and increase the distance between himself and Jim at the same time. All he could do was do his best to stay away from the cluster of stopped vehicles.

Soon, he found himself running along the line of trees, parallel to the road. But then he realised his mistake. This was no good either, people could see him from their cars as he ran. He needed to get away from the road, fast. As if to confirm his conclusion, the ground in front of him heaved upwards as it was thrown into the air from a massive explosion. He could not stop in time and ran straight into the maelstrom of flame and debris.

This time, his suit struggled to protect him. His forward motion was suddenly halted as he was thrown high into the air, and back along the way he had come, blasted away from the explosion by the shockwave.

Alarms wailed and red icons flashed in his HUD as he sailed through the air. Jets automatically fired as the suit tried desperately to orient itself upright and halt his motion. He was jolted up and down, backwards, and forwards, the sudden changes in motion causing him to grunt as air was driven from his lungs. The suit failed to cushion his fall. He crashed down on top of a travelling van, which skidded to a halt as the driver slammed on the brakes. He had landed on the back half of the van, which was now completely crushed, ironically, breaking his fall as the aluminium of its cargo section collapsed under the weight and force of his fall.

He was momentarily disorientated, and it took a few vital seconds for him to realise what had happened. The suit silenced the alarms and ran diagnostics automatically. It also delivered a cocktail of drugs directly into his bloodstream, some to increase his alertness and some to numb any pain.

"*Joe!*" Simon's alarmed thought pierced his disorientation. "*Are you okay? You need to get up. Now!*"

"Yeah, I'm okay," he managed to reply, his mind rapidly clearing, thanks to the drugs.

He heaved himself upright into a sitting position, checking his surroundings. The driver of the van was running away. Good, he thought. Other vehicles were screeching to a halt in order to either avoid the stopped van, or the crater caused by the explosion which was half in the field and half in the road. Three cars had driven into a ditch running along the length of the road and were tipped over onto their sides. People were struggling to get out through door windows. Further down the road, behind the crater, a truck had jack-knifed, completely blocking the road. Flaming debris covered the tarmac, car bonnets and roofs, and many drivers and passengers had abandoned their vehicles and were running away

"*Get out of there,*" came Simon's thought. "*Jim is closing in on your position.*"

Consulting his HUD, Joe saw the 6 remaining enemy dots moving towards him. This was not good, he knew. He pushed himself to stand upright, and jumped down from the van, ignoring any onlookers. He started running again. This time, he crossed the road, leaping over the hedgerow into another field, choosing a direction completely opposite from the rapidly approaching Jim.

As he ran, he cycled through his display options to assess the suit's condition. Fortunately, the damage was not too bad. The suit automatically switched to secondary circuits for any primary circuit that was damaged or inoperable. However, most concerning were his power reserves - they were down to 30%, meaning that not only could he not take another hit like that, but also, he could not maintain this rate of energy consumption for long. The battle would be over in the next 10 minutes, one way or another.

He selected the next weapon from the weapon rack and instructed it to fire and to keep firing. He felt rapid thumps from his back as he tried to put as much distance between himself and the public. He hoped fervently that no one had been injured and that there would be no further casualties as Jim and his mini-mes followed him across the road. Jim would not think about the public; he would smash through them crossing the road with complete disregard for any lives lost.

Joe selected his rear camera view and saw purple wheel-like objects flashing and pinwheeling away into the distance towards Jim, each one accompanied by a thump from his back.

"Why are you running away, Joe?" came Jim's thought. *"Afraid to stand up to me?"*

"I'll stop and face you soon enough, Jim."

He leaped over another hedge into another field, this one just grass. He fully intended to stop as soon as he could get Jim away from innocent people. The thumping on his back ended as the last of the purple pinwheels was fired.

"*Stop and face me now, you coward,*" continued Jim. "*I....*" His thought suddenly cut off briefly and continued with a scream as Jim inadvertently continued to project his thoughts. "*Shit!...*"

Whatever those purple pinwheels were, they were causing Jim some trouble, thought Joe grimly. Nearing the next hedge, he slowed to a stop and selected his next weapon. He was sure that he had not stopped Jim, but he hoped he had slowed him down a little or even caused some damage. He turned and fired. This time, there was no jolt at his back. Instead, a blue gout of flame, spitting and fizzing, flaring bright, roared skywards.

This is where he would make his last stand. This is where he would live or die.

"*Any news from Kate?*" he sent a thought to Simon, including Lee in the link.

"Nothing," came back the reply. "How are you doing?"

"Causing Jim, a bit of trouble, but I may not be able to defeat him. I'll buy you as much time as I can. Keep checking on Kate."

"We will," replied Lee. "I just wish there was something we could do to help you."

"Unless you have another suit outfitted with the new screens, there is nothing."

"The engineers and technicians are working on it, but the next one won't be ready for at least 2 hours."

Joe noted that all the red enemy lights had disappeared from his HUD, except one. That would be Jim. He did notice that Jim was moving slower than he had been. He hoped that was a good sign.

"Two hours will be too late. I have less than 10 minutes."

He felt both Simon's and Lee's shock.

"*You there Jim?*" he sent a thought to Jim.

"*Yes, you bastard! You wiped out all of my minimes, but I'm still here, and I'm coming to get you!*" an angry Jim replied.

"*I'll be waiting,*" replied Joe.

"*This is it,*" he sent to Simon and Lee. "*I'm making my last stand here. I'll do what I can. Look after Kate for me if I don't make it.*"

"*We will do whatever it takes,*" replied a frustrated Lee. "*I wish it didn't have to end like this.*"

"*Remember what I said,*" said Simon. "*Keep away from him as much as you can.*"

"*Easier said than done,*" came Joe's response, "*Not much power left to do any more running.*"

"*Try weapon number 8,*" came a thought from Alex, "*It's one of my specials. But wait till he is in range. It's a one shot, so make it count.*"

"*Thanks for the advice. I'll do just that. I'm signing off now. He's here.*"

He watched Jim crash through the hedge at the far side of the field where he was waiting. A small glimmer of hope kindled inside of him as he saw Jim was limping. Maybe there was a chance after all.

"*Hello Jim,*" he sent a thought.

"*I've got you now, Joe. Are you ready to die?*"

The two of them faced each other, each one standing still at their respective end of the field. One, a massive, muscled, matte white automaton containing what was left of Jim. The other, a two metre tall, red robotic figure, housing and protecting Joe.

"*You know we don't have to do this.*" Joe tried again to reason with Jim.

"*Shut the fuck up!*" shouted Jim's thought. "*You've always been better than me, but not anymore. Today I'm the best, and I'm going to kill you!*"

He saw Jim raise his arm. Here goes, Joe thought, as a beam of pure white light flashed across the distance between them. Impacting upon his screens, it rebounded and flashed all around him, turning grass, bushes, and the hedge behind him instantly into flame. His screens dissipated the attack easily. Taking Alex's advice, he selected weapon number 8 and targeted Jim. He remained still, hoping to convince Jim that his beam was having an effect, and fired.

As soon as he fired the weapon, he felt a huge thump in his back as a massive, blue fireball launched into the air. It did not go very high, and it moved slowly, too slowly. Jim saw it, and tried to dodge to the right, but as the ball slowly descended, it unerringly changed direction to follow his increasingly desperate attempts at avoidance, moving rapidly right and then left. But Jim's movement was hampered by a clearly damaged leg, and he could not move fast enough to get away from it as it landed and completely enveloped his form in its radiance.

Joe looked on in awe and sadness, watching Jim flapping his arms and jumping around inside a blue sphere of light, until it exploded.

The explosion was huge. Even though Joe was at the other end of the field, some 150 metres away, it knocked him off his feet, and he flew backwards. The suit had no time to correct his fall, so he fell onto his back. His breath was knocked out of him in one big whoosh.

Joe felt the suit whirring as it took over his movement and sat him up. This, he knew, was not a good sign. It meant that the suit was damaged and that it was doing what it could to put him in a position to carry on fighting.

As if to confirm his thinking the suit reported. "Power reserves at 10%, weapon systems offline."

A small pistol deployed from an access port in his right wrist and fitted itself into his hand, while a wicked-looking knife slid out of its recess in his left forearm, projecting past his left hand. Close combat weapons. Probably not much use against something like Jim.

Where was Jim? Joe looked around, he couldn't see him anywhere. A massive cloud of dust and smoke obscured his vision.

"Switch to IR," he instructed the suit, which dutifully showed an infra-red display of the area on his HUD.

It did not take long to locate Jim. There was only one infra-red signature in the surrounding area. It was a series of interconnected bright red dots which Joe assumed were sources of heat such as servos and generators, the largest of which, glowed in the centre and was probably the main power source. But what was concerning was the fact that it was moving slowly towards him.

There was nothing he could do. He tried to rise to his feet, but the lower leg mechanisms were too damaged and no longer worked. Thankfully, they were still intact so his own legs inside were probably okay. He couldn't tell because the suit would have pumped him full of drugs to mask any pain. All he could move was his arms and head.

Before he could contact Simon or Lee or anyone else back at the Complex, Jim was upon him, a fist crashing into his screens around his head. There was still enough power left to keep his screens up and provide some protection, but they wouldn't last long. He was rocked to the side with the force of the blow. Throwing out an arm, he steadied himself but, in the process, he let go of the pistol, which dropped onto the grass.

Now that he was up close, Joe could see that Jim had suffered some damage too. Both of his legs were gone, wires and twisted metal struts protruding from the stumps. He must have dragged himself using just his arms, one of which ended at the elbow, where he could see more wires and metal exposed.

"*Stop, Jim!*" he projected an urgent thought.

"*Never!*" was the screamed reply, as he smashed his fist into Joe again and again.

Bringing up his left arm, Joe slammed his knife into Jim's side. It did not seem to have any effect, as Jim kept up his rate of attack.

Under the relentless onslaught, his screens would fail soon. Joe pulled his left arm back and slammed the knife home again. Still, Jim, continued his attack. Intending to keep up his own attack, Joe tried to pull his left arm back again only to discover that the blade was stuck. It must have hooked itself on something inside of Jim's body. An alarm sang in his ears as the suit warned him that his power reserves were gone.

It was over. Jim had won. The realisation that he was going to die made him reflect upon what he had done with his life. His discovery of Psionics, meeting Molly and the two of them developing the Assist. And once he was fitted, and it was fully working, how he had heard the callings of all those people with latent talent, how he had found each one of them and how he had welcomed all of them into the fold.

And finally, he thought of Kate. Beautiful, amazing Kate, who had found him and rescued him. He wished that he had told her how he felt about her, but now he wouldn't get the chance. He was full of sadness at the thought, but strangely, he was not afraid. He had done his best. He had given Kate as much time as he could. There wasn't anything else he could do for her. He was ready to die.

The alarm stopped, his screens flickered off and he was engulfed in darkness as the suit's power reserves were finally exhausted. There was now nothing stopping Jim from crushing him, as though he was a tin can.

The first hit clanged and smashed his head against the internal cushioning. He gritted his teeth and sent out a final thought, *"Tell Kate I love her!"*

He was surprised to get no response. My Assist must be broken as well, he thought to himself. The second hit dented the side of his helmet. He could feel it pushing into the side of his head. The third dented the front, cracking the visor, letting in some light. All he could see were shadows and Jim's torso as it moved back and forth with the effort of hitting him. Another hit and the crack widened. He could see Jim's red, glowing eyes.

Suddenly, the attack stopped. Through the crack in his visor, he could see that Jim was staring up into the air. What was going on?

"NO!" screamed Jim. "Let me kill him!"

He saw a red glow and then nothing. Jim was gone. What is going on? he thought to himself.

"Guys," he sent out a thought again. *"What's happening?"*

He immediately connected with an elated Lee. *"She did it! She got them to help us. I don't believe it!"*

Joe smiled to himself. Kate had come through once again. What a truly amazing woman. She must have made contact and the aliens had intervened. They must have teleported Jim away. Just in time, he thought. That was close.

"*Kate,*" he sent out a thought to her, but he received no response.

"*How is Kate?*" he asked Lee.

There was a delay before Lee replied, "*We're sending out a team straight away to pick you up.*" His thoughts were guarded.

"*What's wrong? Is Kate, okay?*"

"*Just get here as fast as you can.*"

A sense of foreboding came over him. "*Get the recovery team here quick.*"

All he could do was wait, trapped inside his suit.

Chapter 63 - Aftermath

Eline and Doortje stood in the corner of the medical room, their arms around each other and their heads on each other's shoulders. Both were quietly weeping.

Lee stood beside the only door, looking on as Sally attended her patient, who occupied the only bed in the room.

Kate's encounter with the aliens had clearly taken its toll. She lay still on the bed, eyes closed, breathing softly. She was covered with a blanket that had been pulled down to expose her arms, and up to expose her feet. Sally sat on a stool and was gently examining the damage to Kate's left ankle. She had already examined her right wrist.

The bracelet part of Kate's Assist had turned a mottled black and red colour, where it had melted and burned through her skin, embedding itself deep into her wrist. The skin around the wound was red and swollen with the edges next to the bracelet blackened and curling upwards. The rings on each finger had suffered a similar fate. Many of the connecting chains were melted into gobs of shiny metal, that no longer connected to the others, while her little finger had been severed completely by a melted ring which hung loose from what remained of its chain.

The room was quiet, except for the twins, who were doing their best to stem the flow of tears. They both looked up as Sally lay a large white bandage gently across Kate's foot and stood, straightening her back. She walked over to the right where cupboards lined the wall underneath a worktop. She picked up an instrument tray. Walking back to Kate's left side, she placed the tray on the bedside cabinet and removed cotton wool and medicinal alcohol from it. Kate's arms were already fully exposed, since she was still wearing her white T-shirt. Sally swabbed the back of Kate's wrist and expertly slid a cannula into a vein. She secured it with tape and then attached a drip from the stand at the head of the bed.

Sally looked up from her task and stared at Lee, who nodded, opened the door, and stepped outside. While she lay another bandage over the top of Kate's right wrist, Lee waited outside for Joe.

Lee did not have to wait long. Joe ran round a corner, almost falling as he changed direction to move towards the medical room door. He skidded to a stop in front of Lee.

"How is she?" he sent a mental question.

Lee held out his hands and gripped Joe on his shoulders. *"Just quiet down, Joe. Don't go bursting in there like a bull in a China shop."*

Joe faced Lee, pulling Lee's arms from his shoulders. *"How is she?"* he asked again.

Lee looked down at the floor, *"It's bad."* He could not conceal his sorrow from his thoughts as he replied.

Joe nodded and pushed Lee aside. Opening the door slowly, he stepped inside, closing it behind him.

Sally stood in front of him. *"No telepathy,"* she told him, *"She's too weak. I don't want her to exert herself more that she must."*

Looking over Sally's shoulder, Joe asked, *"How bad?"*

Sally looked directly into his eyes, "*I won't lie to you, she doesn't have long. I've given her something for the pain, there is nothing else I can do.*"

Joe was shocked. "What? That can't be. There must be something you can do?"

Sally merely moved out of the way, allowing Joe to see Kate.

"Kate," he whispered out loud. He walked over to Kate's right side of the bed and looked down at her peaceful face. "Kate," he whispered again.

Kate's eyes fluttered open. Looking up at him, she gave a wan smile. "Joe," she croaked.

Joe went to take her hand but saw the bandage resting over it. He lifted it carefully. Seeing the damage, he could not stop himself from drawing a sharp intake of breath.

"Oh Kate, I'm so sorry."

"Joe," she whispered. "I did it."

"Yes, you did," he replied, tears forming in his eyes. "You saved us all."

Her thin smile broadened. "They made some demands." Her voice was quiet and weak. "I agreed to them all."

"That's okay. I'm sure you did the right thing."

"Joe?"

"Yes, I'm here."

"Am I going to lose myself again?"

Joe's breath caught in his throat and tears ran down his cheeks. "No Kate, you will always be you now."

Across the room, Eline and Doortje sobbed and a white-faced Sally approached the bed standing on the opposite side to Joe.

"That's good, I liked being me," whispered Kate.

Joe looked across the bed into Sally's eyes. "There must be something you can do?" he pleaded.

"She needs a new Mark Five," she replied. "We don't have one."

"Molly..." started Joe, but Sally's shaking head stopped him.

"She's in a coma. She should be okay. But she can't help us right now."

The realisation of the situation hit Joe in the stomach like a pile driver.

"What happened to your face?" asked Kate in her weak voice.

Joe reached down to stroke her cheek, "Just a bruise and a few cuts," he replied. "It's nothing."

Kate appeared to be satisfied with his explanation as her eyes closed.

Joe looked back at Sally, tears streaming down his face. "Is there no Mark Five anywhere?"

Sally shook her head, her own eyes filling with tears.

"What about a Mark Four? We could use that until Molly recovers and then replace it with a Mark Five."

Sally looked down at Kate. "The Mark Four would just fuse again. Her brain has changed now. It's a Mark Five or nothing."

Joe struggled to contain his sobs. "She can't die, she just can't."

Kate opened her eyes. "Joe," she whispered again.

"I'm still here," he replied.

"Joe, I think I love you."

Joe broke down, sobbing, his breath catching in his throat. "I love you too," he replied between sobs. He bent down and kissed her full on the lips.

Kate's wan smile returned. "That was nice," she said as Joe laid his cheek against hers.

"There's something important I need to tell you all," she whispered.

"What is it?" asked Sally, who was also sobbing now.

"I can't remember, my mind is closing. All those spaces that were open are going...." Her voice was barely audible. "I think I'm going to go to sleep now."

"No, please don't go!" sobbed Joe. "Don't leave me."

"It's okay, Joe," she murmured quietly. "They told me that no one dies."

"Who did?" asked Sally, struggling to control herself.

"The Non'anan," was Kate's quiet reply. "They're watching us."

A sobbing Joe threw his arm across Kate's chest. He had lost it completely and was unable to speak.

Kate's breathing became slower and slower. Her last words were, "Oh wow!" and then she said no more as her breathing stopped.

"No!" Joe whispered between sobs.

He lay across Kate, his sobs wracking his body as he cried. Sally put her hand out to Joe's shoulder trying to comfort him as her own sobs became uncontrollable. In the corner, Eline and Doortje wailed, holding tightly onto each other.

Sometime later, Joe opened the door to the medical room and stepped outside. Closing the door behind him he turned his red rimmed eyes to Lee.

"It's over," he said.

Chapter 64 - The Enemy

In a room lit by a single, bare bulb hanging from the ceiling, a naked woman rolled off a man. She lay on her back next to him for a little while, and then she sat up and moved backwards to lean against the bed head. Reaching over to the bedside table, she picked up a packet of cigarettes and a lighter. Lighting up, she pulled her legs up to sit cross-legged, dropping the packet and lighter beside her.

She pulled on her lit cigarette and blew out a cloud of smoke, looking down at the naked man, who lay still, eyes closed, still breathing heavily. She looked away from him and surveyed the room. It was shabby, like a cheap hotel room, furnished with a single chair, a single bed, with two bedside tables and single wardrobe. On the wall opposite the bed was a door, while on her right was a small window with no curtains. She put the cigarette to her mouth and breathed in deeply, holding the smoke in her lungs for a couple of seconds before blowing out another cloud of smoke.

Looking through the single, small window, she saw that it was dark outside, but she could see lights from nearby buildings as well as hear the faint murmurings of traffic. Resting her hand holding the cigarette on her knee, she studied the device on her wrist. It was made of black metal, wrapping completely around her wrist, and looked crudely built. Which in fact it was. It was not made to look pretty, it was made to perform a function.

She studied the spikes emanating from the device that pierced her skin and the red welts surrounding each one. She followed the path of red lines radiating up her arm from one particularly inflamed wound. Without looking, she knew that her left ankle would look the same.

Her body was rejecting the devices. Medication delayed her body's response, but it was only a matter of time before they would have to be removed surgically. If they were not, the infection would eventually kill her. This had happened four times already. Each time, new and more powerful devices had been fitted. And each time, the same problem; rejection and infection. Still, she would not be without them. Her Intra-

Dimensional Assist allowed her to move between parallel worlds.

Scientists, philosophers, and cosmologists have long theorised that our universe was just one of a number of infinite universes existing simultaneously next to each other. The man lying next to her discovered how to travel between them.

Looking down at him, still lying with his eyes closed, his breathing more normal, she supposed that he was a genius of sorts. Five years ago, he had invented the Assist. Three years later, he had expanded its capabilities to give them access to parallel worlds. One year after that, they had met, and six months after that, they had discovered the mind meld. A fusion of their two minds. He provided the range and scope, and she provided the raw power. Together, melded as one being, they had travelled to many parallel worlds and had occupied many of them. Only one was proving to be a problem.

Transferring the cigarette to her left hand, she reached over to the bedside table again, and picked up a small packet. Placing the cigarette in her mouth, she used both hands to open the packet to extract two red pills. Throwing the packet to the floor, she reached over to the bedside table once more to pick up a bottle of water. Placing the burning cigarette on the sheets in front of her, she carelessly threw the pills into her mouth and swallowed them down with a swig of water that overflowed from her mouth, running down her chin and dripping onto her breasts. Placing the bottle back where she had found it, she picked up the cigarette. It left a brown singe mark on the ruffled sheets.

Another pull on the cigarette saw it finished. Picking up the packet, she lit another using the final embers of the finished one.

"Well, that was a fucking disaster!" she blurted out angrily.

The man lying beside her opened his eyes. "Really? I thought it was pretty good." He was smiling.

She looked down at him, blowing smoke into his face. "Not the sex, you fucking moron! Using Jim! It was a complete unutterable disaster!"

"I know what you meant, you stupid bitch!"

"Then stop being an arse about it."

"When you stop being a bitch. Which will never happen."

There was a flicker of a smile on her lips as she took another drag on her cigarette. "You got that right."

"Pass me one," instructed the man, still lying flat on his back.

The girl picked up the packet and lighter and threw them at him. Both landed on his chest, the lighter rolling off onto the bed beside him.

Extracting a cigarette from the packet, he lit up, and blew smoke up at the ceiling. "It nearly worked."

The girl blew out her own smoke, grabbing the packet from the man to light another. "Nearly is not good enough," she said bitterly. "And now, thanks to those repulsive pink blobs, we are fucked." She flicked the butt into the air, watching it land near the door, not caring if it started a fire.

They were both silent for a while.

"Just what the fuck were they anyway?" she asked breaking the silence.

"It appears," replied the man, "that there is a very old and very advanced race somewhere in that particular world."

"I fucking hate them, whoever they are."

"Indeed. We should be thankful that they are not in our own world."

"I suppose so." She changed subjects. "And just when is that bitch Molly going to sort this out?" She held up her right arm, showing off the red welts.

The man held up his own right arm which was equally covered in red lines travelling upwards. He studied it briefly.

"I've told her she has 5 more days to come up with a way of stopping the infection, or I will rip her heart out."

The girl nodded. "About time, you've been too soft with her."

Blowing more smoke towards the ceiling, he replied, "You know that without her we wouldn't have these Intra-Dimensional Assists, or the parallel world transports, or our weapons programme."

"That may be, but I don't like her."

The man smiled. "Jealous, my love?"

"Fuck off!" she scoffed.

They were silent again.

After a while, the girl spoke up again. "At least our campaigns in the other worlds are going well."

The man took a final drag on his cigarette and emulated the girl by flicking the butt away into the room. "They don't seem to be as developed in the others, so it's been easy to crush them. But this one...."

"Yes, this one. Only ten worlds away and yet very similar. Do you think that's why it's being such a problem? Because it has alternate you, me, and Molly in it?"

"Must be." He put his hands behind his head. "You know, I might have an idea about how we could turn this around."

"Bollocks! You heard what those pink aliens said - No interference or they would act."

"Yes, but what if I had a way of infiltrating that world without the pink shits knowing, or finding out?"

The girl turned towards him, her jet-black hair cascading over her shoulders. "Really?" She considered and a wicked smile curled her lips. "If you can do that, I'll let you fuck me again!" She leaned over and traced her fingertips over his chest.

The man smiled broadly. "You'd let me fuck you anyway."

"True. But this time I'll make it good for you."

"Mmmm." He appeared to ponder. "Okay. Try this. Suppose we use Jim again..."

"Jim was useless, and he's dead anyway," she interrupted.

"Hear me out. We have Jim's memory patterns recorded. So, we rebuild him and reload his memories, but we wipe out all of his hatred for alternate Joe. We build his body so that it's undetectable from the real thing, human in every way."

"Go on." She was getting interested in his proposal.

"We then transport him back to his world using a roundabout route, say through several alternates until he arrives at the problematic one."

She nodded.

"So, Jim arrives and he no longer hates alternate Joe. He wants to make things better and join his organisation. Alternate Joe, being the sentimental sap that he is, let's him in. He rejoices that he is reunited with his twin and is totally taken in. Then, once inside… Kaboom!"

"He's a living bomb!" she breathed, "My god, that's genius."

"You know it."

She reached back to her bedside table and picked up the water bottle. "When can we start?"

He shrugged. "Now?"

With a wicked smile, she unscrewed the top from the water bottle and emptied it over her breasts. "Joe?"

"Yes, Kate?"

"Come here and lick this off first."

Epilogue

6 months later

In the middle of the night, in a dark back street in the city of Oxford, something was happening. A gentle wind wafted down its length, stirring scraps of discarded paper, crisp packets, and paper cups in and around rubbish bins and dark doorways.

A fox, with its muzzle deep inside a black bag of rubbish, suddenly pulled its head out from the bag, its ears pricked up, listening for something. It looked first up, and then down the street, its yellow eyes piercing the darkness. Its ears suddenly flattened against its skull, and it scampered off into the night.

Initially, nothing appeared to be out of the ordinary, but then an area of blackness appeared two metres above street level. The wind picked up, swirling, and blowing rubbish skywards in mini tornadoes. A low hum filled the air and, in the distance, dogs began to bark.

The blackness expanded slowly until it looked like a hovering black disk. It hung there with no signs of support for a little while the wind dying down until suddenly, a figure appeared. It flew out of the disk and crashed to the floor with a sickening crunch and a cry of pain.

The figure rolled onto its back, the black disk disappeared with a loud crack and the wind died.

The figure, dressed completely in black, moaned and struggled to rise. Eventually it got onto all fours, whereupon it crawled to the side of the street and fell against a wall.

Voices could be heard in the distance.

"What was that?" A male voice.

"Dunno." Another male voice.

"Let's go see." A different male voice

Soon footsteps, could be heard and then three youths sauntered around a corner into the street, all three of them dressed in tracksuits, with hoods covering their faces.

"Nothin' here," said one.

"What's that?" asked another, pointing at the crumpled figure.

They pushed and shoved at each other as they walked over. One reached down and pulled at the figure's black clothes.

"Hey, it's a girl!" he shouted, as the figure was pulled back and its face was revealed.

The gang of three looked at each other and then laughed raucously.

The girl moaned and her eyes flickered open, her jet-black hair cascading over her face. "Who are you?" she asked.

The three youths laughed again. "What are you doin' here darlin?" one asked.

"Got any money?" asked another.

Fear flickered across her eyes. "I need help," she replied.

One of the gang clutched his groin. "I got some help for you right here." He grinned lasciviously.

The girl held out her hand. The gang laughed and moved closer. They didn't notice the rings and chains on her fingers. There was a blue flash and all three were thrown backwards, crashing to the floor, rolling into the bins. She let her hand drop, wincing at the pain in her side and watched the gang recover themselves.

"Better get lost or there's more where that came from," she told them.

One by one, they staggered to their feet. They looked at the girl and then at each other. As one, they came to a decision and walked silently away, one of them looked back over his shoulder and shouted, "Fuck you!"

The girl breathed a sigh of relief. Then, with a grimace of pain, she used the wall to push herself to her feet. Once upright, she surveyed her surroundings.

"Here we go again," she breathed.

Looking down at her right wrist she noticed the chain connecting to the ring on her little finger was hanging loose. It must have broken in the fall. With her left hand, she pressed the end of the chain to the ring and watched it turn liquid, quickly joining itself back together.

"Good girl Bella," she murmured.

She took a shaky step. When she didn't fall, she took another. Soon she was shuffling along the street.

She turned a corner and stopped, contemplating the long walk ahead of her. 'I must appear normal,' she thought to herself.

"I'm coming, Joe," she whispered.

Printed in Great Britain
by Amazon